GUNFIGHT AT CAMP CLARKE BRIDGE

THE MAN WITH THE LEMAT
BOOK THREE

ZACHARY LANE

LEMAT BOOKS

CHAPTER ONE

"Ahhhhh!"

The scream woke Jesse Jones. "Martha!" he shouted as he ran to his wife's bedside.

"It's time, Jesse!" Martha said. "Get Doc. Hurry, the baby's coming."

Jesse raced to the front door. "Adam! Get Doc. It's time!"

Potter mounted and was soon thundering toward Sidney.

Jesse Jones hurried to his wife. Martha took his hand and with each contraction her fingernails broke the skin of his palm.

"Promise me something," Jones said with a smile. "Next time you have a baby, cut your fingernails first?"

"Oh, Jesse," she said. "I'm so sorry."

He kissed her forehead. "You are forgiven," he said. "I love you."

It took a while before he heard pounding hooves and Doc's surrey squeaking to a halt outside.

Other hoof beats followed.

Did Potter wake the whole town? Jones wondered.

Doc burst through the front door.

"Back here in the bedroom," Jones shouted.

"I know where she is," Doc shouted on his way to Martha. "Well, don't just stand there!Boil some water and get some clean linen."

Jones exited the room almost running over Adeline Abel in the process.

"I'm here, Martha," Adeline Abel shouted as she ignored him and slammed the bedroom door behind her.

Jones found Adam Potter and Parson Abel had seated themselves at the table as he raced to ladle water into a tea kettle and put it on the pot-bellied stove to boil.

Martha screamed again sending Jesse into a panic. "The linens," he said. "Where did we put the linens?"

"Calm down, Jesse," said Parson Abel. "Sit down. You're running around like a chicken with its head cut off."

"Doc said boil some water and find the linens," Jesse pleaded.

"I know," Parson Abel calmly replied. "Our family doctor told me the same thing when our first child was born. I was running around like you are now. He said I was suffering from new dad's syndrome. New dads always panic, he said, so he told me to fetch some boiling water to give me something to do."

"You mean he doesn't really need the boiling water?" Jones asked.

"Oh, he needs the water, alright, but what he doesn't need is you in the room when he's delivering a baby," Parson Abel replied. "It's an excuse to get you out of his way."

"You should see yerself," said Potter. "I've seen you with bullets whizzing by yer ears and you never panicked like this."

"How about using some of that hot water to make us some coffee," said Abel.

"I'm glad I'm not married," Potter announced.

His words were followed by silence throughout the house. That silence was broken by the shrill sound of a baby's first cry.

"It's a boy, Jesse," Adeline shouted. "You have a son!"

Sunday August 8, 1875 showed up gray and gloomy, but by midmorning the clouds melted away under a warm summer sun.

Parson Abel stood waist deep in the water of Lodgepole Creek. "Today," he began, "we gather as witnesses to what God is about to do. Years ago in the Jordan River, in waters not unlike these, John the Baptizer stood and pointed to Jesus and said, 'Behold the Lamb of God who takes away the sins of the world.' John baptized Jesus and in so doing purified the waters of baptism from that time forward. Later, Jesus said in the twenty-eighth chapter of Matthew's Gospel: 'Go, therefore, and make disciples of all nations baptizing them in the name of the Father, and of the Son, and of the Holy Spirit.'"

"You're a bit long-winded today," Doc said loud enough for Parson Abel to hear.

"I heard that, Doc," he responded.

"I meant you to," Doc replied.

The congregation laughed.

Parson Abel ignored the last comment and the laughter. "I'll ask the Elders to help Jesse and Martha bring their son to the waters of holy baptism," he said.

Two men stepped down the bank and into the water. Two others helped Jesse and Martha.

Tears of joy ran down Martha's cheeks as she cradled her newborn son wrapped in an Indian blanket while one of the men helped her into the water.

The couple stood side-by-side with Parson Abel who addressed them and the crowd gathered nearby.

"How is this child to be named?" Abel asked the couple.

"Jesse Jones, Junior," Martha replied.

"Jesse Jones, Junior," Parson Abel pronounced as he poured water over the child's head. "I baptize you in the Name of the Father, and of the Son and of the Holy Spirit." After a short pause he continued: "There is significance in what has just happened here in these waters. Writing to the church in Rome, in the sixth chapter, St. Paul teaches us that in baptism our old sinful self drowns in the baptismal water, and a new creation comes forth just as Christ once came forth from the tomb. Today Jesse Jones, Junior has died to his sins and has risen from that death to a new life in Christ Jesus His Savior. May God be glorified."

"Amens," erupted throughout the crowd.

Doc Hardesty offered his office as a place for Jesse, Martha and their newly baptized son to change into dry clothing before their arrival at the social hall was met by applause.

"We don't applaud ourselves for what we have done, but to give thanks for what God has done," said Parson Abel.

Doc stood next to Parson Abel. "I hope you weren't too offended that I gave you such a hard time," he said.

"Actually, I would have been more offended had you not said something," said Abel. "When you don't say something sarcastic I naturally conclude that you don't care anymore."

"Well, in that case," Doc said, "I don't think you have to conclude that at all, do you?"

"I don't," said Parson Abel. "And to this day I have kept our little secret, haven't I? I've never I called you by your real name, have I Aloysius?"

"Not so loud," Doc pleaded. "Someone might hear you."

Kodiak Crabtree sat upright in the saddle surveying the valley below him. Some two miles to the north a small town had taken root. A meandering creek gave it its southern border and there were buildings on both sides of the railroad tracks. To his left a large circular building made of wood served as a round-house. Here locomotives could be turned around and headed back to where they came from.

Kodiak removed his hat and scratched his head. Trail dust clung to him like sweat on a hot day. He tried brushing it off, but failed. To his right sat Slim Montrose; to Kodiak's left, Stetson Burnett.

Montrose was rail thin and six-feet, three-inches tall by Kodiak's estimation, and weighed no more than one-hundred fifty pounds. He wore a moustache along with a scruffy goatee with barely enough chin whiskers to fill it out. Montrose fancied himself a slimmer version of Buffalo Bill Cody. He had a lightning fast draw. Kodiak had witnessed this first hand when someone had the audacity to call Slim "string bean." The man was dead before he cleared leather.

Burnett was the larger, with a thick beard and an equally thick southern accent.

"There she is, boys," Kodiak announced. "That's Sidney, Nebraska down yonder."

"Ain't much to look at, is she?" Slim said. "What day is it? I'm afraid I lost track."

"Gotta be Monday," Burnett said. Don't ya remember hearing church bells yesterday?"

Slim nodded.

"Nope, she ain't, much of a town," Burnett added after very little thought. "My pappy would call that a *poke and plum town*. By the time ya poke yer head into the town, ya find yer plum out of it."

The men shared a laugh.

"Ya know," Kodiak said at last. "I sure wish I'd met yer pappy. He's got the best sense of humor I ever did see."

"I'll tell ya what," Burnett said. "I do miss him. Ya all know, when 'ol Beauregard fired on Fort Sumter, my pappy gathered up his rifle and joined the Confederacy quicker than a squirrel can shinny up a tree. Never seen him again neither. Don't know fer sure, but I reckon he's dead."

"More 'n likely," Slim said. "Lost my pa and two of my brothers fightin' them Yankees. Got Yankee lead in me too. Nearly lost my right leg.

"What about you, Kodiak?" Stetson asked.

"I don't want to talk about the war," Kodiak said. "I seen all the fightin' and dyin' I wanna see. All I'm interested in right now is getting these cattle into the stockyard in Sidney, gettin' paid, gettin' a bath, and gettin' drunk.

"What about the affections of a nice soft woman?" asked Slim Montrose.

"Yeah, I'd like that, too," Kodiak replied.

"We're about five miles ahead of the herd," said Slim. "What's say we ride into town and arrange for the sale?"

Kodiak Crabtree stood up in his stirrups and plunged his right hand into his pants pocket. He retrieved a piece of paper and read the note scribbled on it. He sat himself back down. "Says here that once we hit town we're supposed to head on over to the Swan Holmes Bank. The owner of the bank is charged with paying for the herd on behalf of the Coad Brothers Ranch."

"Well, ya'll, I think it's high time the three of us rode into town and introduced ourselves to the owner of the bank," Burnett said. "The sooner we get paid, the sooner we get a bath, get drunk, and find a woman."

THE SWAN HOLMES BANK was the only stone structure in town, except for the courthouse; all the others were wood. Kodiak noticed that the year *1874* was etched in stone near the A-line of the roof.

"Look at them steps, will ya?" Kodiak said. He pointed to three steps leading upward into the bank where engravers had left their mark. The first step had *THESE STEPS,* the second *LEAD TO,* and the third *SUCCESS* chiseled into them.

Kodiak dismounted and tied off his horse. Slim Montrose and Stetson Burnett followed his lead.

"Never seen a bank like this west of the Missouri River, except for Omaha," Kodiak said.

"Either this bank is that important or the one who runs it thinks it is," Montrose added.

"Yeah," said Burnett.

The three men stood taking it all in. They pressed their faces against the windows. Through the glass they saw a polished oak floor. At the far end of the room three well-dressed teller stood in booths. On opposite ends of these booths were two armed guards.

"Good thing we're not bank robbers," Slim announced with a chuckle.

The front door of the bank opened and out stepped a man dressed in suit and tie. "May I help you, gentlemen?" he said.

"Yeah, I believe you can," Kodiak said drawing himself from the window. "We've got a herd of cattle up from Texas to deliver to the Coad Brothers ranch. We come here to get paid."

"Mr. Holmes is expecting you," the man said. "Please step inside and I will let him know that you have arrived."

The doorman walked to a corner of the bank where a huge man sat behind a desk; a thick handlebar moustache graced his upper lips. The man gestured to them.

"Gentlemen," he said. "Welcome to Sidney. I hope that you had a pleasant journey from Texas. Pardon me if I don't stand to greet you, but as you can see my wife Beatrice is a master of my favorite recipes." He laughed a hearty laugh. "The name's Swan Holmes and I own this bank. May I ask who I have the pleasure to be doing business with?"

Kodiak took the lead with introductions. "My name is Kodiak Crabtree. This here is Slim Montrose. And this is Stetson Burnett."

"Delighted, gentlemen," Holmes said. "The Coad brothers will be pleased that you have arrived safely."

"We came for our money," Kodiak said. "The herd'll be along in a couple of hours."

"You will be pleased to know that I do have your money," Holmes said. "But giving it to you now will never do. No, it just wouldn't be right. You see the Coad brothers have asked me to inspect their investment before paying you. They have agreed to put you and all of your men up in the Moore Hotel at their expense. They have rented several pens at the stockyards to hold their cattle. When your men arrive with the herd and you have them safely in the pens at the stockyard, you let me know and I'll have my carriage brought around. I will inspect this delivery and get you all paid. Is that fair enough?"

"Yeah, it's alright by us," said Kodiak.

"Good," Holmes responded. "Then, I'll bid you a polite adieu until your shipment arrives."

The doorman escorted the three cowboys to the door and shut it after them.

CHAPTER TWO

That afternoon Jesse Jones watched through the window of Swede's Mercantile while wagon after wagon arrived in town. Jimbo Livingston, that mountain of a man, drove the lead wagon, parked it in front of Swede's, and hopped to the ground to tie off his team of horses.

"Wagon train's here," Jesse shouted.

His shout sent Adam Potter scurrying into the back room. "How many wagons?" Potter asked.

"Can't tell for sure," said Jones. "Jimbo will tell me when he comes in."

"I'm thinkin' that if there is only half as many wagons as last time, we need to send them around to the alley," Potter replied. "Otherwise they'll block access to the other stores in town."

Jones turned to his wife. "When Jimbo comes in I'll have him send someone to get Adeline to give you a hand in the front end of the store. I asked Jimbo to send someone ahead of the wagons to let us know they were coming. He must have forgotten."

Jesse met Jimbo at the front door.

"I'm sorry Jesse," Jimbo said. "I know I've forgotten something, but I just can't remember what. I've been thinkin' about it all the way in from Camp Clarke. Do you remember what you told me?"

"Yeah," Jones said, "I remember. I told you that when Henry T. Clarke sends you in to Sidney for supplies that you send a rider ahead to let me know."

"That's it," Jimbo said. "I just knew you'd remember." Jimbo stared at Jones for a moment. Jones saw the realization of Jimbo's mistake set in. "I didn't do that, did I?"

"No, you didn't," Jones said. "Now, I'm caught short-handed to load your supplies. Would you send someone from your wagon train up to Parson Abel's and ask if Adeline can come and give us a hand?"

"Anything you say, Jesse," Jimbo said. He stepped outside and sent one of his men to get Adeline Abel. With that job accomplished he returned to Jesse.

"How many wagons does he have?" Potter asked a second time.

"I got ten," Jimbo answered.

"Ten?" Potter said. "That's five more wagons than you had last time."

"Yeah, and I'm sure that's gonna increase, too. Mr. Clarke wants to finish his bridge over the North Platte River early next year," said Jimbo.

"We can't keep up with that," Martha Jones said.

"Not without help anyway," said Jones.

Sheriff Isaiah Blanton came through the front door of Swede's.

"Jimbo," Blanton said, "The mayor sent me. I gotta ask you to move your wagons off the street. You're blocking access to a lot of businesses."

"I know that, Sheriff," Jimbo fired back. "But what am I supposed to do? Mr. Clarke sent me into town to pick up supplies."

"Isaiah, would it be alright for him to park his wagons in the alley?" Martha asked.

"I'd say that would be alright," Sheriff Blanton replied. "Just as long as he doesn't block any of the streets those alleys cross."

"Think you can do that, Jimbo?" Blanton said.

"Yes, sir, Sheriff," Jimbo said. "I'll do that right away."

"I know that Mayor Truax appreciates it, and all the business your wagons are parked in front of will as well," Blanton said.

Jimbo Livingston left to take care of the business of moving all the wagons into the alley behind Swede's and the blocks adjacent to it. Sheriff Blanton accompanied him.

"What are we going to do, Jesse?" said Martha.

"Can I put my two cents worth in?" asked Potter.

"Of course," Jones responded.

"I think we need a warehouse. Our backroom isn't big enough to accommodate the supplies needed to build Clarke's bridge," said Potter.

Jones looked at Martha. "I'll go see Swan Holmes tomorrow," he said.

In the restaurant of the Moore Hotel, Kodiak drank coffee with Slim Montrose and Stetson Burnett when they were approached by a one armed man.

"You the three men who brought the Coad brothers' cattle into town?" the stranger asked.

"Who wants to know?" Kodiak replied.

"I'm sorry," the stranger said. "I should have introduced myself." He extended his left hand to shake Kodiak's hand. Kodiak found himself in a strange position. He'd never shaken hands with a left hand before, but adjusted and shook the man's hand with his left hand.

"The name's Bill DuFreeze. I manage several properties in town. I've just come from the stockyards and inspecting your cattle."

"I'm Kodiak Crabtree," he said. "The trail boss. Slim Montrose and Stetson Burnett helped me ride herd on the men. You can't bring two thousand head of longhorns north without first having hard workin' men like these two."

Bill DuFreeze pulled up a fourth chair at the table where the three men sat. "You and your men have done a fine job. All the animals look healthy and none-the-worse for the trip. I've been authorized to see to it that you and your men are paid."

"So, just who are you workin' for?" Kodiak asked. "I thought that Mr. Holmes was paying us on behalf of the Coad brothers."

"Gentlemen, I assure you that everything is on the up-and-up. In fact, I'm authorized to give you each three months wages instead of the two you were expecting." DuFreeze stood. "Now, if you will follow me back to the stockyards I will see that you and your men are paid in full for all your hard work." DuFreeze walked to the door and Kodiak motioned for his men to follow.

Kodiak noticed that DuFreeze never turned around the entire walk to the stockyards. In the stockyards, the sound of two thousand head of cattle lowing, and eight thousand hooves stomping and rumps banging against wooden fences drowned out any conversation whatsoever.

DuFreeze entered a small shack at the far end of the stockyard. Kodiak and his men followed. Inside, they found a small man behind a desk.

"Casey," DuFreeze said. "These men are here to pick up the money owed to them for driving the Coad brothers' cattle in from Texas."

"Yes, sir," Casey said. "How many men do you have with you?"

"Me as trail boss, Montrose and Burnett are my point men. Then I have two swingmen, two flankers, three drag riders, a wrangler and a cook. How many is that?" Curry counted out loud.

The little man behind the desk replied, "That's you, ten others and the cook for a total of twelve." He thought for a moment and replied, "That's five hundred six dollars."

"Y'all hear that?" Burnett said. "He did all that in his head."

"Sir, I do this for a living," the man said staring over his glasses at Burnett.

"Now, double it," DuFreeze said.

"Double it?" the little man's eyes shot to where DuFreeze stood.

"Double it!" DuFreeze said.

"But, that's over a thousand dollars," the man said.

"Double it!" DuFreeze replied.

The man at the desk withdrew a strongbox from a desk drawer and counted out loud and ended with the total. "That's one thousand twelve dollars." He handed the wad of money to DuFreeze.

DuFreeze walked over to Kodiak. "Mr. Crabtree," he said. "Would you please thank your men for all their hard work? It was a pleasure doing business with you." He handed Kodiak the money.

Kodiak held the money in his hand and stared down at it.

"This was way more money than we anticipated. If we can ever do anything for you again, let me know."

"Oh, I will," DuFreeze said with a pleasant smile.

KODIAK BELIEVED there was truth in saying there is nothing worse than a cowboy with money. He had seen it first-hand. Putting money in the hands of cowboys was like pouring water into their hands. The result was the same; soon their hands would be empty. Yet, the money was owed them, they had earned it by riding herd over two thousand head of cantankerous cattle. Through hot, parched Texas days where well-known water holes were dry, to the sudden storms and heavy rains in Kansas, his men had earned their pay. So, he paid them what they had earned and rat-holed the rest.

At the end of each ride Kodiak knew his men would want four things; a bath, clean clothes, a bottle of whiskey, and a beauty. He was the same way, but there was something about DuFreeze that puzzled him, so personally he opted for only the first two things, breaking his normal pattern.

Why would any man who knew the going rate for drovers pay them double the amount they earned? he wondered without an answer.

Kodiak had a hard time getting waited on in Swede's, but at last a nice looking woman named Martha made sure he found a new pair of trousers, a new shirt and a new pair of boots. He wanted a new set of drawers, but could not find it in him to ask a woman to help him with that. He traipsed back to the Moore Hotel and the promise of a hot bath and found Montrose and Burnett waiting for him in the lobby. Both were still in the trappings they rode into town in.

"Something's botherin' us," Montrose began. "We want to

know why you only paid everyone their normal rate and kept the rest of the money for yourself? Us included."

"Let's go back into the restaurant," Kodiak said. "Out here in the lobby the walls have ears." The two men tailed after him. The restaurant was packed, but they found a place in the corner where they could talk.

A waitress appeared at their table. "What'll it be, gentlemen?" she asked. "You were in here this afternoon drinking coffee, but I'm afraid I can't let you do that tonight. This is a busy place."

"Bring us each a steak dinner and give me the bill," Kodiak announced.

"Now, about your question," he said after the waitress left them. "I decided to hang onto this extra money and hand it out after we've returned to Texas. By then they'll be flat busted and in need of the money." Kodiak looked around the table. "Or do you two have other ideas."

There was a silence at the table before Burnett and Montrose vied to be the one to address Kodiak first. Burnett won.

"Since y'all seem to know what's on our minds, let me tell ya what Montrose and I've been thinking," Burnett said. "We've been thinking that this one-armed DuFreeze fella is up to more than he's letting on. I mean why would he give us so much money?"

"I agree," Montrose jumped into the conversation. "He's got better plans for us. I'm not sure what they are, but I wouldn't mind hangin' around for a few days to find out. Let's send the others back to Texas and hang around Sidney for a while."

"What about the extra money?" Kodiak asked.

Again Burnett and Montrose looked at each other before Burnett answered.

"We say let's keep this money to ourselves. We're the only ones who know about it," Burnett said.

"Alright," Kodiak said. "From now on this is our little secret."

Jesse Jones sat at Sheriff Blanton's office playing out a hand of solitaire. He had supervised the loading of the supply wagons destined for Camp Clarke and sent Martha and Jesse Junior home for the evening. Tonight he pinned on a deputy sheriff's badge and stayed behind to assist Sheriff Blanton. The sheriff anticipated a rough night in Sidney when muleskinners, drovers, and fortune hunters collected at the local watering holes. Custer's Black Hills Expedition in July and August of 1874 to find a suitable site for a new fort had confirmed the existence of gold in the hills.

That discovery, Henry T. Clarke said, put Sidney on the map as the closest railhead to the Black Hills, Jesse remembered. That was the why behind the building of the Sidney Black Hills Trail and the need for the Camp Clarke Bridge.

For his part, Blanton was in another part of his office where he trimmed a kerosene lantern and stretched out on his cot for a cat nap. He had often told Jesse that he'd discovered the power of naps; catching a few winks as often as he could because no night ever went without interruption:Especially now that Sidney was suffering growing pains.

Jesse put the finishing touches on his first solitaire win of the night when a heavy fist pounded on the jailhouse door.

"Sheriff Blanton, you'd better come to the Last Chance and see this," a deep voice announced.

"Is that you, Jimbo?" Jesse asked.

"It is," the voice answered. "Is Sheriff Blanton in there with you?"

"I heard you, Jimbo," Blanton said. "We'll be right behind you. Jesse, why don't you pop on over to Swede's and see if Potter wants to tag along?"

"Got it," Jesse said. He slipped out the back way, made his way along an alley and arrived at Swede's. In the distance Jesse heard the faint popping of small arms fire. He unlocked the front door of Swede's and yelled. "Ready for some action, Potter? Sounds like we got a situation at the Last Chance."

In minutes, Jones and Potter walked together and caught up with Sheriff Blanton at the Last Chance Saloon. The sound of gun fire was much louder now. Jesse Jones peered over the swinging door to size-up the situation before any of the three set a foot inside.

"There are a couple drovers using shot glasses for target practice," Jones reported. "They're lining the glasses on top of the piano."

Two shots rang out.

"Nice goin', Chuck," a voice shouted. "Ya killed one glass and wounded another."

Laughter broke out.

"Set 'em up again," another man yelled. "It's my turn." The man broke free of a saloon girl's embrace, but bent down to give her a kiss. "Got a ten dollar gold piece riding on this shot, so how about a kiss fer good luck?"

"What do you think, Jesse?" Blanton asked.

"Everyone's back is turned to us," Jesse said. "Be careful. If we spook them, someone might throw down on us."

"That's a chance we're gonna have to take, otherwise someone might get shot," Blanton said. Jones and Potter nodded in agreement.

Blanton stepped through the door. Jones stood on his right and Potter on his left.

"Hold it!" Sheriff Blanton yelled. "This is Sheriff Blanton and I want everyone to put your hands up." The commotion stopped instantly and all but one man put their hands up, the man with the ten dollar bet.

"I got one more draw, Sheriff," he said. "I got ten dollars ridin' on it."

"Do as I say," Blanton replied.

The man turned and in a single motion drew his gun and fired.

It was the last thing he ever did.

CHAPTER THREE

J esse Jones tried to open the door of Holmes State Bank and found it locked. He looked at his watch. It was nine a.m. *That's odd,* he thought. *The bank opens at nine.* He pressed his face against the glass of the door and saw a man on the other side of the door move to unlock it and let him in.

"May I help you?" the man said.

"I'm Jesse Jones and I've come to see Mr. Holmes," Jesse said.

"I recognized you right away, sir," the man replied. "Do you have an appointment with Mr. Holmes?"

"No," Jones said. "I didn't know I needed one."

"You do now we've implemented new security measures. Can't be too careful you know. Would you like me to see when Mr. Holmes might have time to see you, Mr. Jones?"

"That would be fine," Jones replied.

"And may I tell Mr. Holmes the nature of your business with our bank?"

"Tell Mr. Holmes that I would like to talk with him about a loan to build a warehouse."

"Very good, Mr. Jones. I'll ask Mr. Holmes when you might come back to see him. Do stay right where you are."

"New security measures?"

"New security measures." The man nodded. He turned his back on Jones and tottered off in the direction of what Jones surmised was Swan Holmes' office.

Jones saw new security every where he looked. The armed guards now stationed on either side of the teller counters. The tellers themselves were enclosed in what Jones believed to be cages with bars in front of them to limit their access to any customer. A man holding a shotgun stood in front of the door behind which the man who let him into the bank had disappeared.

The man was not gone long.

"Mr. Holmes will see you now, Mr. Jones," he said when he returned. "Would you follow me, please?" The man led him through the doorway where he had disappeared before, down a long corridor to another door where yet another guard with a shotgun stood watch. The man knocked at the door.

"Is that you, Jenkins?" a voice inside the room asked.

"Yes, Mr. Holmes," the man replied.

"You may bring Mr. Jones in," the voice announced.

"Yes, sir, Mr. Holmes," Jenkins said. He turned the doorknob and ushered Jesse Jones into the room.

It was a spacious room with wood paneling and what Jones believed were rather expensive works of art. Holmes' desk and high back chair in which the bulbous Swan Holmes sat were crafted from mahogany.

"Do have a chair, Mr. Jones," Swan Holmes announced with a flourish. "You will pardon the appearance of my office, I only moved in here today."

"You have put in quite the security system, Mr. Holmes. I don't remember any of this."

"I don't need to tell you that this bank does a lot of business and we anticipate that the gold rush into Dakota Territory will mean even more assets coming into this bank. More assets mean that we're a greater target for desperados like the James Gang. Tighter security is warranted I assure you."

Jesse Jones seated himself in front of Swan Holmes.

"Now, what is it that I can do for you, Mr. Jones? Jenkins said something about you wanting to borrow money to build a warehouse?" Swan Holmes said.

"Yes, my business is growing with the construction of the Camp Clarke Bridge. I have no room to store the amount of supplies Henry T. Clarke is asking me to order. Swede's just isn't big enough."

"Well, well, isn't this a coincidence," Holmes exclaimed. "I've got half a warehouse available near the tracks. A man named DuFreeze has the other half. Yes, sir, I think I can make your trip to Swan Holmes Bank a worthwhile proposition."

Jesse returned to Swede's Mercantile with the key to the warehouse.

"Hey, Potter," Jesse called out. "How would like to take a little walk with me?"

"Where to?" Potter asked. Jesse held up the key. "What do you have there?"

"It's a key to a warehouse along the tracks. Swan Holmes gave it to me. If we can get Adeline to watch the store, we can have a look at it," Jones said. "I sent Martha back to the house this morning. She said she had work to do. She took Jesse Junior along with her."

It was not long before Adeline took over for Potter, and the two men walked over to the Moore Hotel and gathered Jimbo

Livingston to join them in the warehouse inspection. Swan Holmes' key let them in.

"Well, what do you think?" Jones asked after their initial walk through.

"I like it," Jimbo said. "Now, I won't have to tie up the streets with wagons. I can bring them here where they will be out of the way while they wait to be loaded."

"What I like," Potter said, "is that there is a loading dock at both ends of the building. We can off-load freight from trains at one end while we are on-loading freight onto wagons on the other end. Who did you say rents the other half of this building?"

"A man by the name of Bill DuFreeze," said Jones.

"I don't think I've met him," said Potter.

"I have," Jimbo said. "He owns the lumber yard. The guy has only one arm. The story goes that he lost it while riding with Bloody Bill Anderson during the war. Some even call him One Arm Bill DuFreeze. I don't think anyone calls him that to his face. I heard he's got a mean streak in him."

"Does everyone agree that what he sells is different enough from what we sell that we don't have a conflict?" Jones said.

"I'd say," said Potter.

"Hello, inside," someone called from the doorway. He was far enough away they could not make out who stood there.

"Over here," Jones said. "What is it you want?"

Whoever was framed in the door way began a slow walk to where Jones, Potter and Livingston stood. He was joined by two other men.

"I'm looking for Jesse Jones and Adam Potter," the man said as he walked closer.

"We're both here," Jones said. "What do you need?"

"The name is Kodiak Crabtree," he said. "But, you can call me Kodiak. Everyone else does. And the men with me are Slim

Montrose and Stetson Burnett." The gap between the men closed and they stood face-to-face. "I understand that one of you two killed one of my men last night. I'm the trail boss that brought in the herd for the Coad brothers."

Jesse's senses went on high alert. He wasn't looking for a fight, but if this man Kodiak wanted one, he'd come to the right place.

"Now, I wasn't there last night when you killed him and I don't rightly care if you had a good reason or not. I aim to stand up for my men, so I'm servin' notice like I just did with a sheriff a few minutes ago. Whenever you least expect it, we're gonna be there and we're gonna kill ya. All of ya." Kodiak looked Jimbo over. "And who are you?"

"Jimbo Livingston."

"Well, if I was you I wouldn't be hangin' around these two men or you just might find yerself dead as well," Kodiak said.

"Look, mister," Jimbo said. He took two steps forward and stepped between Jones and Potter. "I'll be friends with who I please."

Montrose and Burnett shifted their stances. Jones thought they were about to slap leather, but Kodiak stopped them.

"Now isn't the time, boys," Kodiak said.

Jesse replayed two scenes over and over in his mind as his rode home late that afternoon. The first scene was the shooting of the drover in the Last Chance. He wondered if there was anything he, Blanton or Potter could have done differently to spare the man's life. Jesse couldn't think of anything. It all happened so fast.

All over a stinkin' ten dollar bet, Jones heard himself say. The scene played out in his mind's eye.

Everyone's back is turned to us, I said. Be careful. If we spook them someone might throw down on us.

That's a chance we're gonna have to take otherwise someone might get shot, Blanton said. Potter and I nodded in agreement.

Blanton stepped through the door. I stood on his right and Potter on his left. Sheriff Blanton yelled Hold it! This is Sheriff Blanton and I want everyone to put your hands up. The commotion stopped instantly and all but one man put his hands up; it was the man with the ten dollar bet.

I got one more draw, Sheriff, he said. I got ten dollars ridin' on it.

Do as I say, Blanton replied.

The man turned and in a single motion drew his gun and fired.

The three of us fired as one and all three rounds struck the man. He died instantly. He never twitched when he fell.

There isn't anything we could have done differently.

The second scene that played out in Jesse's mind was in the warehouse a couple of hours ago. He remembered how Jimbo Livingston put his life on the line and stepped between him and Potter.

That's a far cry from the Jimbo Livingston who worked for Cincinnati Culver back in the day; someone who would have just as easy shot ya as looked at ya, Jones thought.

"Kodiak is dead serious," Jones muttered under his breath. "I think the only reason he didn't let his men draw on us was that he wants to bushwhack us. That way he won't lose any of his men." *How can I explain my fears to Martha? It ain't just me anymore. I got a wife and family* he told himself as he rode into his front yard.

Martha came to the door. "Supper's about ready," she said. Her smile melted away the difficulty of his day.

"I'll be right in after I put the horse away and wash the dust off," Jesse said. Jesse unsaddled his horse, stowed his gear in the barn, and washed the dust off in the water trough before stepping inside. There the smell of fried chicken delighted his senses. "So, what's the occasion?" he asked.

"Can't a gal just delight in having her husband home for dinner?" she answered. Martha bent down and lifted little Jesse Junior into the highchair Jesse had handcrafted for him.

"We found a warehouse today." Jesse sat at the table.

"Oh, Jesse, that is good news."

"It's a warehouse that the bank owns and Swan Holmes will lease it to us," Jones continued. "We can move in right away, so we'll want to make sure we get an order off to Omaha as soon as possible. I plan to ride out to Camp Clarke in a day or two to find out what they'll need so we can ship to them as soon as it arrives."

Martha passed the platter of chicken to Jesse who helped himself. Martha looked directly into Jesse's eyes. "Jesse," she said. "There's something you're not telling me. What is it? And don't ask me how I know, but I know something's bothering you. Adeline would say that it's *woman's intuition.*"

Kodak Crabtree heard a knock on his hotel room door. "Ya, what do you want?" he said. He fumbled for a match to light the kerosene lantern on the bedside table.

"Gotta message from a one-armed man downstairs," replied the young man's voice outside the door. "He told me to give it to you and wait for your reply."

Kodiak sat up in bed and eyed his pocket watch. "It's three o'clock in the morning," Kodiak growled. "Tell the man to go away and come back in the morning. I only just got into bed an hour ago and I ain't in no mood fer chit-chattin'."

"He ain't gonna like me comin' back to him empty hand-ed," the boy replied. "He wants a reply."

"Tell him I gave you my reply," Kodiak said. "My reply is for him is to take his one good arm and go away and come back in the morning." In anger he blew out the lantern and plopped his head back down on his pillow. He listened. The young man's footsteps walked away from his door and soon fell silent.

Kodiak was almost asleep again when he heard heavier footsteps on the wooden floor outside his room. They stopped there. Kodiak waited. He cocked his head to detect any other sounds from the hallway.

BLAM! His door flew open and the one-armed man stood in the doorway. "Nobody tells me to go away and come back in the morning. I paid you generously the other day and now I own you." The one-armed man shut the door behind him.

Kodiak fumbled for another match and lit the lantern. The glow gave the room an unearthly feel. "What do you mean barging in here like this?" Kodiak asked.

"I mean to talk to you, that's what I mean," the man said. "And I don't cotton to being called a one-armed man. The name's DuFreeze. Bill DuFreeze. I lost my arm ridin' with Bloody Bill Anderson, so I sure ain't gonna take no tripe off a little pip-squeak like you. Do I make myself clear, Mr. Crabtree?"

There was no anger in DuFreeze's voice. DuFreeze was calm yet firm, but Kodiak knew that he meant business.

"I got an assignment for you and those two men of yours. An assignment that will make the extra money I gave you seem like chump change," DuFreeze announced while pulling up a chair and sitting next to Kodiak's bed. "In the morning I'm gonna lead a cattle drive of about one-thousand head to the Coad brother's place twenty miles north of town. There's a little watering hole about eight miles out. What I want you and your men to do is to lie in wait for us there, and stampede the cattle after the camp is asleep tomorrow night. Do you think you can handle that?"

"Someone's gonna have to stop that stampede if you're gonna rustle 'em," Kodiak replied.

"All of that is none of yer concern," Du Freeze announced. "Get the cattle to stampede to the east and let me handle the rest. And I don't rightly care if J.F. Coad loses a couple of men in the process, if you get what I mean."

"I get it," Kodiak replied. "But I planned to settle a score with the Sheriff and with Potter and Jones tomorrow. Me and the boys got other plans."

DuFreeze grabbed Kodiak by the collar with his one good arm and lifted him from the bed. "As of this minute yer plans are changed. Do yer other killin' stuff on yer own time. Right now you are working for me. Tomorrow morning is butts in saddles time for the three of you."

CHAPTER FOUR

Jesse was pleased when Adeline Abel took it upon herself to invite Swan Holmes to dinner that evening. He thought it the perfect opportunity to get to know Swan Holmes better and to talk with him about the paperwork that would make the warehouse available.

Adeline set a splendid table for eight using the tableware her family brought over from the old country. Parson Abel sat at one end of the table. To his right Adeline sat. On her right sat Jesse Jones, and his wife Martha. Swan Holmes sat directly across from Parson Abel. On his right sat his wife Beatrice, Adam Potter and Doc Hardesty.

"My compliments to the cook," Swan Holmes said as he laid aside his fork. "This meal was second only to what my wife would have provided me this evening." He patted his rotund belly. "And as you can easily see I have not missed very many meals. I have this rather peculiar habit, you see. For some reason every time my right elbow bends my mouth flies open." The volume of his laugh shook the table.

"We are all absolutely overjoyed that you and your lovely

wife could come to dinner on such short notice," Parson Abel said.

"It's just a shame that your wife could not join us this evening, Doc," Swan Holmes added.

"It is," Doc agreed, "but she has always felt uncomfortable in large group settings."

"Unlike Doc who thrives on gatherings of this size, especially when food is involved," Parson Abel said.

"You know that is completely unfair," Doc responded.

"Unfair, but true," Abel said. Holmes laughed at that remark.

Adeline jumped in to change the subject. "Mr. Holmes we know so very little about you and your wife, would you mind telling us about yourself?"

"Both my wife and I are originally from Ohio. My father found himself on the wrong side of the Civil War, so he moved all of us to southeast Missouri where he made a rather nice living as a gunrunner. Not something I'm proud of, but as the Good Book says, "God helps those who help themselves.""

"So, what brought you to Sidney?" Adeline asked.

"Great question," Swan Holmes replied. "After my father died toward the end of the war, I took my inheritance and moved to Council Bluffs where I was fortunate enough to make acquaintance with Edward Creighton before he passed away in seventy-four. That gave me all the business sense and financial wherewithal to open a bank in Sidney."

"That's quite a story," said Martha.

"Yes, Beatrice and I are very pleased to have settled here. With all the talk of cattle ranching and gold in the Black Hills, we plan to make a lot of money here before retiring to California." Holmes patted his wife's hand.

"Now," he said. "That brings us to the reason I accepted

your invitation to dinner tonight." Holmes slid his hand into his vest pocket and withdrew a piece of paper. "This is the agreement whereby you will lease the warehouse property I have. I want you to spend a day or two reading over this document before you sign it. In fact, it might be best if you rode to where Henry Clarke is building his bridge over the Platte and getting a signed agreement from him to purchase supplies through you." He handed the document to Martha. "Here you go, my dear, have your husband look this over. Then share it with Parson Abel and Doc and Mr. Potter here. When you are satisfied that you can fulfill the terms of this lease agreement sign it and return it to the bank." Holmes lifted up the wine glass in front of him. "Here's to a long and prosperous relationship."

KODIAK and his men were ready. They had secreted themselves among the sandhills north of Sidney and waited for the cattle drive to camp near the watering hole as 'One-armed' Bill DuFreeze had told them. Kodiak had appointed Slim Montrose to keep an eye on the camp and let him know when everyone had bedded down for the night.

"It's all quiet down there," Slim reported in a voice barely above a whisper.

"Good," Kodiak said. He looked at his watch. It was ten fifteen. "We'll give them until midnight. By that time the outriders will have settled down and should be half asleep in the saddle."

Kodiak and Montrose spent a nervous hour and a half while Burnett slept under a starlit night.

"I don't know how he can sleep like that," Montrose said. "I'm a nervous wreck and Burnett sleeps like a baby."

Kodiak smiled. "Maybe he doesn't have enough brains in his head to realize the danger ahead," he said.

"I heard that," Burnett said. He tossed off his blanket. "Is it time to go to work?"

"Yeah," Kodiak replied. "Montrose, go take one more look before we mount up."

Montrose scampered to the top of a sandhill and looked down at the camp. All remained quiet. In the moonlight he could see the four outriders mounted, but obviously asleep. Montrose waved an all clear.

The three men checked their revolvers and saddled their horses in silence. They walked their horses until they were positioned between two sand hills with the camp in front of them.

"When I fire I want you two to get behind them doggies and drive them to the east like DuFreeze told us. I'll work to keep the men in the camp pinned down," Kodiak said. He unsheathed his Winchester and drew a bead on the outrider at the rear of this herd.

Kodiak's rifle spit lead and the outrider dropped dead from his horse.

"Yeeeeehaaa," Burnett shouted. He and Montrose came in behind the herd. Their six guns fired into the night.

"Yaaaaaa!" Montrose yelled.

The frightened cattle lunged forward.

The camp awakened and men were on their feet taking aim at the two men driving the herd.

Kodiak cocked and fired. One drover spun around with a bullet in his back and crumbled to the ground. Kodiak aimed again. He recognized DuFreeze among the men and was careful not to make him a direct target.

Kodiak fired as close to DuFreeze as he could without hitting him.

The cattle gained speed. The stampede was underway.

Kodiak watched as DuFreeze answered his shot with a shot of his own.

DuFreeze sent a shot so near Kodiak heard it whistle by. Kodiak took this shot as acknowledgment of a job well done. He rode hard to catch up with Montrose and Burnett stampeding the herd.

By his own estimate they raced east for four miles before Burnett got in front of the cattle and slowed them down. Suddenly, the three men were joined by nine other men all dressed in black with black bandanas masking their faces.

One of the masked men rode up next to Kodiak. "We'll take it from here," he said. "Gather your men and ride back into town."

"Who are you guys?" Kodiak asked.

"That is none of your business. Your business was to get the cattle to us and you've done that. Now skedaddle," the man said. "You are no longer needed here. When you're needed again, DuFreeze will contact you. Until then stay in the hotel and keep your mouth shut."

Montrose and Burnett pulled up their horses near Kodiak.

"This is the end of the line boys," Kodiak said. "We're to ride back into Sidney and stay put until DuFreeze tells us what to do next."

THE FOLLOWING MORNING, Jesse Jones woke early and prepared for the day. He would accompany Jimbo Livingston on the return trip carrying supplies to Camp Clarke. Jesse dressed by candlelight in the living room of his cabin. When he had finished he returned to the bedroom and kissed Martha on the forehead.

"I'll be back in a week," Jesse told her.

"Shhhh," Martha replied. "Or you'll wake little Jesse." Jesse smiled down on her. "And Jesse, be careful. Come back to us."

"I will." He kissed her a second time and made his way to the door.

Jesse saddled his horse and rode into Sidney where Jimbo had assembled a wagon train along the street beginning with his wagon parked in front of Swede's Mercantile. Each wagon was pulled by four mules, two in the lead and two following, making the wagon train itself nearly four blocks long.

"Ready?" Jimbo asked of Jesse when rode up on his left.

"Yep," Jesse said.

Jimbo raised his massive right arm and extended it forward.

"Wagons ho," he yelled and the wagon train surged ahead.

The wagon train reached a juncture three miles north of Sidney before the sun made its warm presence felt.

Jimbo noticed three riders heading toward them about three-quarters of a mile away.

"Got riders coming our way," Jimbo said all the while pointing out the men to Jesse. "They look familiar to me," he said as they neared the wagon train. "Aren't these the three men from the warehouse?"

"Yes, they are," Jones said. "What are they doing out here at this time in the morning?" Jesse's mind took him back to an incident like this at Courthouse Rock years ago. He didn't like the memory. If something should happen to him who would take care of his family.

"Hopefully, they're not out here to pick a fight," Jimbo said.

Jesse watched Kodiak and his two men ride by on their right. The men stared at Jimbo and Jones but never stopped riding.

The remainder of the trip to Camp Clarke was uneventful

except for a half dozen head of longhorns seen grazing in the distance.

"What are they doing out here?" Jones asked.

"See 'em all the time," Jimbo replied. "No one has fences out here so cattle roam free. There'll be a fall roundup soon when cowboys will gather the cattle together and any not branded will be."

That evening the wagon train finished the two day, forty-five mile jaunt to Camp Clarke. Jimbo Livingston stepped down off the lead wagon and reported to Henry T. Clarke.

"Unhitch your wagons," Clarke told him. "I'll get you some help unloading tomorrow morning. Good to see you, Jesse," he said. "Why don't you freshen up a bit and meet me in my tent. Mine's the third one on your left."

The cool water collected from the North Platte River revitalized Jesse after a dusty day in the saddle. When he finished, Jesse walked down the makeshift street to Henry T. Clarke's tent and knocked on a tent post.

"Come in," Henry T. Clarke said. "What brings you to Camp Clarke?"

"Paper work," Jones said. "With the business you're sending my way I've decided to rent warehouse space. I just need you to sign off on a form Swan Holmes at the bank gave me."

Jesse handed Henry T. Clarke the form and he gave it a quick read.

"I think everything is in order and Mr. Holmes does not seem to be overcharging you for the warehouse space," Henry T. Clarke said. He removed a pen from its holder on his desk, dipped it in ink and signed with a flourish. Henry T. Clarke blew on the ink to speed along its drying before handing the form back to Jesse. "I want you to stick around tomorrow," he said. "I'd like to show you the bridge pilings we have in place.

Our new bridge will measure over two thousand feet long when we've finished."

IN SIDNEY that same evening Kodiak was eating dinner in the Moore Hotel. He was raising a bite of steak to his mouth when DuFreeze walked in and wove his way through the other dining room patrons to pull up a chair.

"You and your boys did a nice job last night," DuFreeze announced.

"May I get you something to eat, Mr. DuFreeze," the waiter interrupted.

"I'll have what my friend here is having," DuFreeze said.

"Right away, Mr. DuFreeze," said the waiter. He trotted off to the kitchen.

DuFreeze reached into his coat pocket and withdrew a large envelope and placed it on the table. "Here's a little somethin' for your trouble last night."

Kodiak reached for the envelope, but DuFreeze's hand prevented him from taking it. "I got another job for you and your men tonight. Head north of town about ten o'clock and you'll be met by one of my men. You'll recognize him by his dark bandana pulled up over his face. He'll tell you want you gotta do."

"Why are you doing this?" Kodiak asked.

"What do you mean?" DuFreeze said.

"You're chasing me and my men all over the place. What's going on?" said Kodiak.

DuFreeze smiled.

"I'm training up you and your men to lead a gang on your own. We got plans for you. Big plans," said DuFreeze.

"You said *we*. Who is *we*? I wanna know who I'm working for," said Kodiak.

"Let's just say that I've got a silent partner," DuFreeze answered.

"Am I to assume that it isn't one of the Coad brothers?" Kodiak said.

"I can't tell you anymore than I already told you," DuFreeze said. "You're just gonna have to trust me. What I can tell you is that if you work out the way I think you will, you and your men stand to make a great deal more money than you've ever made in your entire life," DuFreeze said.

Kodiak did what he was told to do. He gathered Slim Montrose and Stetson Burnett and the three of them arrived at a point north of town where they were met by three men dressed in black with black bandanas over the nose and mouth. Black hats were pulled down so their identities were completely hidden.

"Follow us," one of the men said. He never waited for a response, but turned his horse north and rode hard. Kodiak and his men followed. It was not long before they raced off the main road and headed east. Kodiak saw a campfire in the distance and they did not stop until they found themselves inside a huge corral with the blazing fire in the middle of it.

One of the men handed Kodiak and his men each a black bandana.

"Put these on," he said.

The moon that night lit up the ground and Kodiak could see what several others of the dark riders were doing. They were rebranding the cattle. The brand Kodiak and his men had used in Texas; the FF Bar was branded over to recreate the BB Bar brand on the rumps of their rustled cattle.

"Don't just sit there," the man holding the branding iron yelled. "We got a lot of cattle to brand. Two of ya get another fire going and one of ya grab a branding iron. We ain't got all night."

Montrose and Burnett lit a fire on the ground and black masked men started delivering doggies for rebranding.

I never did like the smell of burning flesh, Kodiak thought to himself as his branding iron seared <u>BB</u> over the old brand.

"Be careful with your branding," a man standing near Kodiak warned him. "These brands must pass inspection by the U.S. Army. We're drivin' north to the Red Cloud Agency in a day or two."

CHAPTER FIVE

B rody Belt poured a cup of coffee and looked out the
window of the home he shared with his wife Cynthia.
For him the workday was already two hours old. He'd risen at
five a.m., dressed and gone about his morning chores which
daily included milking his two cows, and feeding and watering
his livestock. He turned and watched Cynthia scurry about in
the house, setting the table for the breakfast she was
preparing. Her appearance delighted him. She was beautiful.
He had told her so in response to her complaint that her hair
was a mess.

"You know, sweetheart," he began as he entered the
kitchen. "I noticed something when I was in the barn this
morning."

Cynthia looked up from her work. "What did you notice?"

"I noticed that cows don't give milk, you have to take it
from them," Brody said with a chuckle. Cynthia joined him
with a chuckle of her own.

"Living out here is so hard at times," she said. "If we didn't
have a sense of humor I don't know how we'd survive."

"That's for sure," Brody responded. "And if we didn't have each other there would be no hope at all."

"I love you, too," Cynthia said. "Parson Abel always says that no matter the situation there is always hope."

She walked over and joined Brody at the window and gave him a hug.

"Sometimes that hope gets a bit tattered, doesn't it?" Brody said. "So tattered that it looks like a worn out boot."

They kissed.

"After breakfast I think I'll straighten the picket fence. I noticed part of the fence got laid over during the night," Brody said.

"Wonder how that happened?" Cynthia asked.

"Must have been a wind gust or something," Body replied.

After breakfast Brody Belt grabbed some tools from the barn and walked over to where the fence was laid over.

Strange. I never noticed this before. Not only was our picket fence knocked over last night but there are hoof prints all around the yard.

Then he saw it. Not far from the south side of the house stood a Texas Longhorn.

"What are you doing here?" Brody asked not really expecting an answer. Brody calmly walked back to the barn, saddled his horse and walked it close enough to the steer that he could get a rope around its neck.

"Cynthia," Brody shouted. "Come out here and see what I found in our yard."

Cynthia came around the corner of the house and saw the Longhorn Brody had lassoed.

"What's he doing here?" she asked.

"That's the same question I asked a moment ago," said Brody. "I think this is the culprit that knocked our fence down overnight. Can you get close enough to read the brand?"

Cynthia walked around the flank of the animal and got close enough to read the brand without spooking it.

"It's got the DOUBLE F BAR brand," she said. "Doesn't that brand belong to the Coad brothers' ranch north of Sidney?"

"It sure does," Brody said. "They've got a huge spread over there and they graze a lot of cattle. From what I've been told they let their livestock roam free until branding time. It looks like this fella wandered off."

"What are we going to do?" Cynthia asked.

"I'm gonna put him in the pen with our cattle until I finish up a few chores. Then I'll make my way over to the Coad Ranch and return him," Brody said. "I think the sooner I ride out there the better. The one thing I don't want to happen is for someone to accuse me of cattle rustlin.' I've heard of men gettin' hung for that offense."

ADAM POTTER STOOD on the platform waiting for the noon train to arrive. He had work to do. Lots of it. His mind raced to the task at hand. The railroad would uncouple a boxcar and send it down a side rail to the warehouse Swan Holmes had given them a temporary lease on. Potter had already hired a group of men from the Last Chance to help him unload the freight. They were to begin unloading at one thirty. That didn't give Potter much time to have everything ready. What he hoped to avoid was having workers standing on the dock and not having anything to unload. He saw that as an unnecessary expense and one to be avoided if at all possible. Potter heard the faint sound of a distant train whistle and turned his eyes up the tracks to the east where a wispy cloud of smoke caught his attention.

The station manager stood on the platform next to Potter.

He was looking to the east as well, craning his neck to see. When the manager stood erect again, Potter saw a smile creep across his lips just below his moustache.

"Eleven fifty-seven," he noted. He turned to Adam. "Not bad. Not bad at all. Got us a new engineer at the controls today and it looks like he's running right on time." He snapped his pocket watch shut and returned it to his vest pocket. "Makes a man feel proud. I recommended him for the job."

Potter returned his smile.

True to the station manager's estimate the locomotive puffed into the station on time. Potter saw the station manager give the engineer a thumbs up. High above him the engineer looked down with a prideful look on his soot covered face.

"Nice job, Robert!" the manager yelled. "Nice job!"

"Someone run and find Doc! Hurry!" the screams of the conductor brought the congratulatory celebration to an end. The man darted from the passenger car and into the startled crowd waiting to board. Someone broke free from the crowd and raced into town screaming, "DOC! DOC!" at the top of his lungs.

Adam Potter followed the station manager as he raced to the conductor.

"What is it, Arthur?" the manager asked.

"Got a sick woman on board," Arthur replied. "She took sick after we left North Platte. Says her insides are on fire. She's awful pale."

The conductor grabbed the step rail and swung himself back on-board with the station manager hot on his tail.

For reasons unknown to him, Adam Potter followed.

"Over here!" an older woman yelled. She stood half a car-length away.

Passengers lining the aisle preparing to depart parted to make way for the three men.

A young woman with coal black hair sat scrunched against the wall of the train car. Her face was as pale as white linen and so contorted it was difficult to make out her features. Potter guessed her age at twenty-five, but it was impossible to know for sure.

"Get out of my way!" Doc yelled. "I'm a doctor! Get out of the way!"

Doc slid across the wooden seat and put his left hand on the young woman's forehead. "She burning up," he said. "How long has she been like this?" Doc looked up, begging for an answer to his question.

"Since North Platte," the older woman announced. "I'm her mother."

"She can't very well stay on this train," said Doc. "Someone get me a stretcher and let's get her up to my office." Doc stood up. "I need everyone in this train car to sit down and wait. No one gets off this train until this young lady is in my office!"

As all the passengers returned to their seats.

BRODY BELT DROVE the steer to the northwest. He had a lot of ground to cover before reaching the Coad ranch. The best he could hope for was that he'd find a couple of cowpunchers riding the range this afternoon. If he was even luckier, he thought, they might be cowpunchers from the Coad ranch out looking for strays.

An hour or so into his ride, three horsemen appeared on Brody's right. By Brody's estimates they were about a half mile away. The sandhill they rode on gave them a good view of Brody and the steer in front of him. One of the riders stood tall in his saddle and Brody could see the sunlight glint off a shiny object.

Binoculars, Belt thought to himself. *These could be just the fellas I'm looking for.*

Brody watched as the three men spurred their horses and headed straight for him. They covered the distance to Brody in a matter of minutes.

"Well, will ya look at this," one of the men said. "This here sodbuster's got one of Mr. Coad's steers."

"Sure does," a man with a gravelly voice replied.

Brody did not know any of the men who now surrounded him. What he did notice was that each of the men wore the same black bandana around their necks.

"I found this little fella on my farm this morning and I'm just returning him," Brody replied. "Are you men from the Coad ranch?"

"We are," the first man said. "We've been out looking for strays since early this morning. We were driving cattle yesterday when some rustlers took us by surprise. Killed a couple of our men. Now we find you out here this afternoon."

"I had nothing to do with killing any of your men," Brody replied.

"Spence," the man said. "Go take a look at the brand on that steer, would ya? I wanna make sure it's one of Mr. Coad's steers before we hang him."

"Wait a minute!" Brody choked out. "I didn't have anything to do rustlin' any cattle."

Two of the men surrounding Brody drew their revolvers and pointed them at him while the third dismounted and walked over to the steer. He circled around to the right flank of the animal.

"Yep!" said Spence. "This is one of Mr. Coad's steers alright. It's got the DOUBLE F BAR brand, Flapjack."

"Well, mister," Flapjack said. "Would ya mind tellin' me what you are doing with one of Mr. Coad's steers?"

"Like I told ya," Brody said. "He wandered onto my farm this morning. I'm returning him. Honest I am."

Flapjack looked around. "Boys, I ain't seein' any trees nearby. So we can't hang him. What do you think we should do with him?"

Spence grinned. "I vote to shoot him right here."

"Wait a minute," Brody begged. "This has gone far enough. I haven't done anything."

"What do you think, Ace?" Flapjack asked.

Ace pushed his hat back and scratched his head for a moment. "I'm for shootin' him right here, just as Spence said," Ace announced.

"Well, mister," Flapjack said. "It ain't lookin' so good for you. Two of us wanna shoot ya, and I want to hang ya. Either way it looks like yer gonna be dead."

"But, I haven't done anything," Brody pleaded.

"The three of us say that you have. You've been judged by a jury of your peers and found guilty," Flapjack said. "And by the authority given to me as a cowboy, I sentence you to death by shootin.' Ace, I'm giving you the honor."

Ace jumped down from his horse and grabbed Brody and pulled him from his saddle.

"Hold it!" a voice cried out behind them. "Let the man go and do it now."

"Yes, sir, Mr. Dufreeze," Ace said.

KODIAK RECEIVED the message to help move cattle at noon. He left the Moore Hotel in the company of Slim Montrose and Stetson Burnett. Following One Arm Bill DuFreeze's message delivered earlier in the day, they rode twelve miles north of

Sidney before taking a cross-country trail near the corral where they had recently helped brand cattle.

Other men, all dismounted, were gathered there, each wearing a signature black bandana as a scarf around their necks. This time there was no campfire; in fact every bit of evidence identifying it as the branding spot had been removed. It seemed to Kodiak that even the holes where the fence posts once stood were filled in. Kodiak, Montrose and Burnett saw a group of cowboys nearby and walked over. Kodiak overheard their conversation.

"We sure pulled one over on that sodbuster this afternoon," one of the men remarked.

"Yeah, Flapjack," a second one said. "Dadgummit, if it hadn't been for DuFreeze showin' up we could of had us a time. The look on that guy's face was priceless when you said we was gonna shoot him."

"Ace, you nailed it," the man named Flapjack replied. "Hey, I want ya to know that I was serious about hangin' him. What do you say, Spence?"

"Either way," the third man replied. "I'd just as soon killed him as looked at him."

DuFreeze rode up.

"Didn't mean to ruin your conversation, but when you get a hankerin' will you please mount up?" DuFreeze said sarcastically.

"Go away, we'll be done in a minute," Ace replied looking up at DuFreeze. "We're talking about that sodbuster we scared out of his wits this afternoon." Ace turned his back on DuFreeze.

Like lightening DuFreeze drew his six-shooter and fired one round that missed Ace's foot by inches.

The cattle bellowed nervously.

"Hey!" Ace screamed. "What was that for?"

DuFreeze raised his arm to the point where Ace was looking down the long barrel of DuFreeze's Navy Colt. "The next round goes right through that flat forehead of yours if you ain't got yer butt in the saddle by the time I count three."

"But, we ain't done," Ace interjected.

"One!" said DuFreeze.

"Give me a moment to gather my bedroll," said Ace.

"Two!" said DuFreeze.

Kodiak had never seen a man move so fast in all his life. With his right hand Ace grabbed his bedroll and put it behind his saddle. At the same time his left hand grabbed his saddle horn, he stuck his left leg in the stirrup and swung his right leg over the saddle.

"Three!" said DuFreeze.

Ace smiled at DuFreeze. Kodiak could see several teeth missing from that smile.

"Don't ever tempt me like that again," DuFreeze said. "When I say mount up you put yer butt where it belongs."

"Yes, sir, Mr. DuFreeze, sir," Ace offered with a mock salute.

"Don't be stupid, Ace," Flapjack said. "Yer gonna get yourself killed one day all because the guy at the other end of yer antics doesn't got a sense of humor."

DuFreeze rode by Kodiak and his men. "Good to see that you could make it," he said. "Better mount up. I won't tell you again." This time his voice was gentle. He reached in his pocket and removed a piece of paper which he flipped to Kodiak. He rode on a bit further before turning to face to whole cadre of men.

"Everyone take your positions around the herd. I'm putting Kodiak in charge," DuFreeze said. "I'm assuming you can read a map, Mr. Crabtree?" Kodiak nodded. "You'll sell these cattle to the Red Cloud Agency near the Dakota border. Bring the money back to me. I'll meet you on this spot two weeks from today. Now, move out."

CHAPTER SIX

Jesse guided his horse off the trail to bed down for the night. He had planned to return to Sidney in the early morning, but the loneliness of riding the trail by himself caused him to stop for the night. He found a scrub brush behind a sandhill and tied his horse to it. Jones was off the main trail far enough that any passersby would not notice him and disturb his sleep. The weather was such that his bedroll was sufficient to rest under without lighting a campfire. It was a clear night with innumerable stars twinkling overhead as he lay with his head propped up against his saddle with a blanket over him.

What time is it anyway? he wondered. Jones removed his watch and pressed the button on top. The medal cover popped open and by the moonlight he read eleven thirty. *I'll get up with the sun and ride the rest of the way,* he thought. *Martha will be surprised to see me a whole day ahead of schedule.* Jesse sighed a contented sigh. With his thoughts turned toward home he fell asleep under the stars.

The thundering sound of hoofs, cattle mooing, and men

yelling woke him with a start. He quickly tossed off his blanket and scurried up the side of the sandhill that hid him from the trail. Before his eyes cowboys drove a herd of cattle miles long up the trail in the direction of Camp Clarke. He noticed that each of these cowboys wore a black bandana around their necks. Jesse recognized a couple of the cowboys as the three men who had confronted him in Swan's warehouse.

What were their names again? Oh, yeah, now I remember Kodiak Crabtree was one. Let's see. The other two were named Montrose and Burnett, he recalled. *What are they doing out here driving cattle at night?* He flipped open his pocket watch as the last rider rode by. It was two thirty. Jesse climbed back down the hill and returned to his makeshift bed.

Jesse was up before the sun made its appearance and splashed its light on a sleepy world. He saddled his horse, tied down his bedroll and mounted. His haversack yielded three pieces of beef jerky. Today he called that jerky breakfast. Taking the reins in his left hand, he fed himself with his right while trotting his horse on the trail toward home.

A two hour ride brought Jesse Jones to the north side of Sidney where he rode past Boot Hill and glanced over his left shoulder in time to see the cross marking his first wife's grave. Memories of the past and his new wife and son swept over him like a prairie wind. He couldn't change his past, but he had to protect his future.

Riding further into town he rode up to the Moore Hotel where he knew Parson Abel and Doc Hardesty could be found egging each other on over eggs and bacon.

"Well, looky here," Doc said to Parson Abel. "Jones has made it home early."

"Doc. Parson Abel," Jones said in greeting.

"Sit down, Jesse," Parson Abel said. "We were just talking about you."

"No, we weren't," Doc said. "We were talking about the weather and hadn't gotten to you yet. But now that you're here we can talk behind your back in front of your face."

"Never mind this old codger, Jesse," Parson Abel said. "It's good to have you back in town."

"I saw the craziest thing early this morning," Jones began. "I'd pulled off the trail to get some sleep, but about two o'clock the sound of a cattle drive woke me. I scrambled to the top of a sandhill and sure enough, there was a cattle drive underway up the trail toward Camp Clarke."

"At two in the morning?" Doc asked.

"Yep," Jones replied. "I couldn't believe it either. I recognized three of the men as the ones from Swan Holmes' warehouse."

THROUGH THE LARGE window on the front side of the Moore Hotel, Jesse Jones saw Brody Belt ride into town. At first Brody seemed to recognize Jones' horse in front of the hotel but he rode on. Moments later he returned, tied off his horse and stepped inside. He walked up to the table where Jones sat with Parson Abel and Doc.

"Is Sheriff Blanton around?" Brody asked. He sat down at the only chair remaining at Jones' table.

"Haven't seen him yet this morning," Doc answered. "I think he's still out making his morning rounds."

"So what brings you into town so early?" Abel said.

"Had a little run in with some of J.F. Coad's men yesterday and Cynthia thought I should ride into town and tell the sheriff about it," said Belt.

A waitress stood between Jones and Brody.

"What'll you boys have?" she asked.

"I'll have what Doc has," Jones replied.

Brody surveyed the table. "That sounds fine to me."

"Two cackle fruits and kill the cow," the waitress yelled toward the kitchen.

"Two cackle fruits and kill the cow," the cook echoed back.

"They sure got a language all their own," Doc said when the waitress walked away.

"Kinda like the medical profession," Parson Abel said without looking up from his breakfast.

"Not the same at all," Doc replied.

"Oh, is that so?" Abel replied. "Then you're forgetting that you gave me something you called *horse pills* last week when I complained of a headache."

"That's entirely different," Doc answered.

It was obvious to Jones that Abel had gotten the better of this conversation because he took two bites of his eggs without saying another word. Jones decided to keep his opinion on the matter to himself and changed the subject.

"So what happened?" Jones asked.

"What?" Brody replied. Obviously he was still following the conversation between Parson Abel and Doc.

"So what happened yesterday?" Jones repeated.

"I found a longhorn steer on my place yesterday. He'd knocked over our picket fence. Anyway, after I did my morning chores I put a rope around him and Cynthia noticed the DOUBLE F BAR brand on him," Brody said.

"That's the Coad brothers' brand alright," said Doc.

"That afternoon I drove the steer in the direction of the Coad ranch," Brody continued his story. "I got about three-quarters of the way there when I was surrounded by three men. If I heard their names correctly they went by Flapjack, Spence and Ace. I assumed they were from the Coad ranch and were out looking for strays. Anyway they accused me of rustling and they were about to shoot me on the spot when a one-armed man named DuFreeze rode up and told them to let me go."

"That is a little strange," Parson Abel said. "I'd always heard that the men who work for J.F. Coad are more civilized than that. They'd never shoot anyone who was returning cattle. He runs a clean operation."

"I've heard that too," Brody replied. "But that's not the oddest part. The oddest part was that each of the three men who threatened to kill me wore black bandanas. I don't know if that means anything or not. I just thought it odd."

"That is odd," Jones said. "On my way back from Camp Clarke last night, I pulled off the trail to get some sleep. About two this morning I was startled awake by the sound of a cattle drive. The sliver of a moon last night showed me the riders were all wearing black bandanas."

"Now that's something odd alright," Doc replied with a nod.

"Doc you have a propensity for understatement?" Parson Abel said.

"A what?" Doc asked.

Adam Potter missed his breakfast appointment this morning. He had drawn the short straw and instead of a warm breakfast, he was responsible for opening Swede's Mercantile. That meant he came down the stairs from his apartment at Swede's a little after six a.m. to sweep the wooden floors of the dirt collected the day before. He also straightened out some of the retail displays knocked over in the hustle of yesterday's bustling business.

All the while he hustled about the store his mind kept

coming back to the beautiful young lady who he'd helped from the train. She was still upstairs in Doc's office in the room adjacent to his. No doubt her mother was rooming up the street in the Moore Hotel. Potter had seen her strolling that way late yesterday afternoon.

This morning while dressing Potter had heard someone rap on Doc's door. He heard Doc open the door and let someone in through the outside entrance to his office. But he could not make out whom that someone was. Potter's best guess was that Adeline Abel had relieved Doc so he could join the others for breakfast. He thought about traipsing upstairs to check in on the young lady and then thought better of it. There was work to do before the store opened. Besides, Doc would return from breakfast before long and Adeline would come down the stairs to join him in the store. That would be a better time, Potter assured himself.

Adam Potter opened the store promptly at seven o'clock. Townsfolk had long been at work by then. Many had awakened to the sound of reveille at Fort Sidney. Old Mrs. Peabody was the first one in the store as usual. *Since her husband died coming into the store is a social outing,* Potter remembered Adeline telling him. *He left her with very little money to make ends meet.*

"Good morning, Mrs. Peabody," Potter said.

"Good morning to you, young man," Mrs. Peabody said. She gummed the words out because she had no teeth. "Is Adeline available to wait on me?"

Potter shook his head. "She should be along any minute."

"I don't mind tellin' ya, young fella, that I prefer a woman waiting on me. There's just things women have in common with other women," Mrs. Peabody said. "Meanin' no offense."

"None taken," Potter replied. "You have a good look around and I'm sure Adeline will be here any moment."

The door to the upstairs living quarters opened and Adeline came down the stairs.

"I thought I heard you down here, Mrs. Peabody," Adeline said.

"This young man is cordial and all," Mrs. Peabody responded, "but I told him right out that I wanted a woman to wait on me."

"If you ladies will excuse me, I'll go upstairs and say good morning to Doc," Potter said. He made his way to the stairs.

"That young lady you brought in the other day is doing much better," Adeline said. "That is, in case you are interested."

Potter knocked twice on Doc's office door and then let himself in. Doc sat behind his desk reading the morning newspaper.

"How is she, Doc?" Potter asked.

"She's fine," Doc replied. "Must have had a case of food poisoning. Once she cleaned all that stuff out of her system she's feeling much better. Would you care to look in on her?"

"Could I?" Potter asked.

"Let me poke my nose in and see if she's up to having visitors," Doc said. He knocked on the door to his examination room. "Miss Archer, do you feel like having visitors? One of the men who helped you off the train yesterday is here to see you."

JESSE WALKED the three blocks to the warehouse building and unlocked it. He raised the huge door facing the railroad tracks. Before long a locomotive backed a single boxcar down the siding and brought it to a halt in front of the warehouse door. After a few minutes the half-dozen men Potter had hired joined Jones on the platform separating the boxcar from the warehouse.

"Gentlemen," Jones began. "We won't wait for Potter to get started. The railroad needs this boxcar by the end of the day, so let's get started unloading."

Jones jumped aboard the boxcar and began unloading the contents onto the platform. Three other men joined him inside the car while the others used wheeled carts to move the freight inside.

"Sorry, I got distracted," Potter said. "I dropped in on the young lady we removed from the train yesterday."

"What young lady?" Jones asked.

"Doc never told you?" said Potter.

"No," said Jones.

"There was a young lady who fell ill on the train yesterday. I helped get her over to Doc's office. She's much better this morning," said Potter.

"Glad to hear that," came Jones' reply.

"Doc said he'd likely dismiss her today," Potter continued. "Doc thinks she had food poisoning. Her mother is staying at the Moore Hotel. Sounds like they'll be staying for a few more days."

"It also sounds like you know a lot about this young woman," Jones said.

Potter tried to explain but all that came out was "Uhhhhh."

"It's alright," Jones said. "I hate to tell you this, but I think that the women would say that you are a bit *twitter pated.*"

"I don't even know what that means," said Potter.

"Twitter pated," Jones said, "means that you are *touched in the heart.*"

Out of nowhere Doc joined in the conversation. "It's another way of saying that you are head-over-heels for someone."

"Or simpler still that you are in love with someone," Parson Abel added.

"When did you two come in?" Jones asked.

"Just a few minutes ago," Parson Abel said.

"Yeah, right when you said Potter here was *twitter pated,*" said Doc. "Potter, you've got to remember that I am a doctor and I'm used to diagnosing all sorts of diseases. Let me have a good look at you." Doc drew himself close to Potter and looked deeply into his eyes. After a brief pause his announced: "My diagnoses is that you have a fatal disease. You are indeed *twitter pated* over the young woman named Elizabeth Archer."

"Is that why you came here? I mean did you two deliberately come all the way over here to tell me this or did you come to give us a hand unloading?"

"Neither one," Parson Abel announced. "First we had no idea you'd be diagnosed with *twitter pater*, and second we didn't come here to lend a hand' That's work for much younger hands. We came here to ask Jones if he got Henry T. Clarke's signature to do business with us."

"I did," Jones said producing the signed document. "Henry T. Clarke's signature is right there at the bottom." Jesse took out his watch and noted the time. "It's three-fifteen. The bank closed fifteen minutes ago. I'll have to wait to see Swan Holmes in the morning. This has been one of those crazy days filled with distractions. The fact is I got into town early today hoping to be home in time for lunch and I got sucked into doing a lot of other things."

"Why don't you ride on home now, Jesse," Parson Abel said.

"Are you two going to stay and help?" Jones asked.

"Nope," said Doc. "What we're really good at is supervising."

CHAPTER SEVEN

Jesse woke in his own bed for the first time in several days. It was a bed so small both he and Martha slept on their sides to keep from hanging over the edges. Although quite small this bed represented a much more secure life than he had ever achieved sleeping under the canopy of night.

He was alone in their bed when he woke. Lying there, he heard Martha clamoring in the kitchen and her loving interactions with their son. Her muffled words and Jesse Junior's cooing had a calming effect on him. Having his family around him always soothed away Jesse's anxieties over business dealings, unexpected late night cattle drives, and threats against his life.

Jesse rolled onto his back, smiled and listened. Martha was preparing his morning coffee. He heard her take off a metal grate on the stove top and stoke the stove with wood. Then came the sound of pouring water.

She's filling the coffee pot. He reached for his britches at the foot of the bed and slipped them on. They were chilly against his skin. His sockless feet recoiled at the coolness of the Lodge-pole pine flooring. *In typical Nebraska fashion we've gone from summer to autumn in a single night,* he thought. Pulling on his chambray shirt and carrying his socks and boots, Jesse stepped into the living room.

"Good morning, sunshine," Martha said. "Did you sleep well?"

"Never better," Jones said. He slid a chair away from the table and finished dressing. He watched Martha remove the cheesecloth containing coffee grounds from the pot and dump them in a bucket near the stove. She would soon add egg shells to the bucket as she emptied the contents of each egg into the cast iron skillet.

"After breakfast would you take out the bucket and dump it on the garden, Jesse?" she asked. "Egg shells and coffee grounds make great mulch for the garden over the winter." She paused a moment before continuing. "How was your trip to Camp Clarke? Were you able to get Henry T. Clarke's signature?

"I was," Jesse said. "He's agreed to do a lot of business with us through Swede's Mercantile. I'm thinking about heading into Sidney this morning to see if I can put the finishing touches on the warehouse rental." He grabbed Martha around the waist and lifted her high enough he did not have to bend down to kiss her.

"Oh, Jesse, that's wonderful," she said. He returned her to the floor.

Jesse Junior cooed and smiled. They turned to him and returned his smile.

"You make me so happy," Martha said. "I always feel so secure in your arms."

"I was thinking the same thing as I was lying in bed a few minutes ago," said Jesse. "Parson Abel always says that a wife *completes* her husband. That certainly is the case with you."

"All I can say to that," Martha said, "is I love you."

"I love you, too," Jesse said.

"Do you and little Jesse want to ride into town with me after breakfast?" he said.

"I can always do a little shopping. It would also be a good idea for me to relieve Adeline for a spell at the store."

"After I meet with Swan Holmes I'd like to meet with everyone and go over the supplies Henry T. Clarke will need up north at the bridge site. You know, he was telling me that the bridge he's building will be two-thousand feet long. They're putting the piling in now and will complete the bridge in the spring."

"That's huge," she said.

"It is," Jesse agreed. "Oh and to let you know that I was paying attention to you earlier, *yes* I will dump the bucket on the garden after breakfast."

JESSE FOUND GETTING in to see Swan Holmes was far less difficult this time around. He saw that the armed guards remained where they were positioned before, but his greeting at the door was more cordial.

"Welcome, Mr. Jones," Jenkins said. "Mr. Holmes heard of your return yesterday and has been expecting you. He told me to bring you back to his office the minute you arrived."

"Thank you, Jenkins," Jesse replied. "Would you lead the way?"

"Please follow me, sir," Jenkins said. He took Jones behind the door where the man with the shotgun stood. They walked the long corridor together until they arrived at a second door guarded by the second man holding a shotgun. Jenkins knocked.

"Is that you, Jenkins?" Swan Holmes asked from inside the room.

"It is, sir. And I have Mr. Jones with me," said Jenkins.

"Good. Good. That's very good," Swan Holmes said. "Don't just stand out there, Jenkins, show Mr. Jones in."

Jenkins opened the door and after Jones stepped into the room so did he.

"Is there anything else, Mr. Holmes?" Jenkins asked.

"Not at this time, Jenkins," Swan Holmes said. "And you needn't stay in the corridor. By now I'm sure Mr. Jones knows his own way out."

"Thank you, sir," Jenkins said. He closed the door behind him.

"Well, well," Swan Holmes announced. "So, you have made the trip north to visit with Henry T. Clarke. And how is Mr. Clarke these days?"

"He sends you his greetings," Jesse replied. Holmes motioned Jesse to sit in the chair directly in front of his desk. Jesse complied.

"I hear tell that this bridge of Mr. Clarke's will require a lot of supplies to build." Swan Holmes rubbed his chin in thought. "Did I hear that his bridge will be one-thousand feet long as it traverses the North Platte River?"

"Two-thousand is the figure Clarke is tossing around now," Jones remarked.

Swan Holmes scratched the figure down on a notebook in front of him. "My, my. That's somewhere between a quarter-mile and a half-mile long," he said. "Am I to assume then that Mr. Clarke signed our little contract?"

"Yes, sir, he did," Jesse said. He reached into his shirt pocket and laid the signed paper in front of Swan Holmes.

Holmes gathered the document in his pudgy hands and

brought it to his eyes to read. In a moment a pleasant smile crossed his lips. "Everything seems to be in order," he said. "Your trip north was well worth your time. You know what the Good Book says, 'God helps those who help themselves.' Yes, sir, Mr. Jones, you have certainly helped yourself."

Swan Holmes reached into his desk and drew out another document. "Now all the bank requires is that you sign this rental document and the warehouse is yours for as long as you want it." He placed the document in front of Jesse and handed him a pen. "Sign here," he said while pointing at the signature line at the bottom of the page.

Jesse Jones took pen in hand and signed his name.

Holmes clapped his hands. "Wonderful," he said. "Just wonderful. With the help of Swan State Bank you are about to become one of the wealthiest men in Sidney. Why, I wouldn't be a bit surprised if you came to me in a day or two asking for a loan to build a house in town."

"I don't think so, Mr. Holmes. My wife is very fond of our cabin along Lodgepole Creek," Jones said. "It's quiet there and with none of the hassles of city life. There's something about standing outside at night and seeing all the stars. Parson Abel says that it's a reminder of how small man is in comparison to the God who created all things."

KODIAK COULD EASILY MANAGE his own men and all of the others DuFreeze had given him, except Flapjack, Spence and Ace. The bad part was he had to tolerate the three because they were all assigned the chuck wagon. Spence drove the wagon. Flapjack was cook with Ace as his assistant.

"Beware of Flapjack," one of the riders had cautioned

Kodiak. "One of our trail bosses told Flapjack his cooking was so bad that dogs wouldn't eat it. Next thing ya know, the trail boss had the back door trots for three days. Flapjack could be seen laughing with Spence and Ace about how he got even with the trail boss for all the bad things he said about his cooking."

Kodiak decided that no matter how bad the food tasted he would not criticize Flapjack or his men.

The cattle drive to the Red Cloud Agency was not easy. The sandhills of western Nebraska prevent anyone from making a bee-line from one place to the next. Kodiak relied on the map DuFreeze tossed him to pick his way through the terrain. On they pressed, veering to the northwest by keeping the Oregon Trail on their left. Kodiak noted the endless parade of covered wagons making their trek further west. DuFreeze's map brought the herd past Courthouse and Jail Rocks which rise four hundred feet above the Platte River Valley.

Further up the trail Kodiak was impressed with the work being done at Camp Clarke. Steam driven pile drivers pounded the wooden piles deep into the river bed and adjacent land.

"How long will this bridge be?" Montrose yelled.

"Long enough to cross the river," a construction worker shouted back.

Jimbo Livingston heard the conversation from his vantage point among the supply wagons. He noted the cattle bore the double-B brand.

The third night out Kodiak ordered Montrose and Burnett to halt the herd within sight of Chimney Rock with its spire stretched toward heaven. They were not camped long before Kodiak heard the report of a pistol. Upon inquiry he found one of the drovers had shot a rattlesnake that had startled his horse, nearly throwing him.

Flapjack reined in the mules pulling the chuck wagon. Ace

gathered wood for the campfire. Kodiak watched him zigzag through the underbrush of the North Platte River to find firewood dry enough to burn. Spence turned that firewood into a bonfire and three coffeepots soon produced enough coffee for the outfit. At the chuck wagon Flapjack off-loaded the supplies needed for dinner including a stewpot which he'd soon fill with beans, bacon and onions.

After supper the men divided up into three small camps. Kodiak, Montrose and Burnett made up one of them. Flapjack, Spence and Ace made up another. The third camp had three other men, while the remaining men were positioned on the flank and rear of the herd as they bedded down for the night.

"How much further?" Montrose asked. He took a drag on his cigarette.

Kodiak removed the map from his pocket. "Another two or three days," he said. "The map shows our next stop is near Scotts Bluff. From there we turn north and we'll stop for the night about forty miles out." Kodiak scanned the map. "Not exactly sure where that stop will be. DuFreeze hasn't marked it very well. At the end of the third day we should be at the Red Cloud Agency."

"Sure ain't much to look at out here," Montrose uttered.

"Sage brush and sandhills that's all we've seen for miles," said Burnett.

"You left out the rear end of doggies," Montrose added.

"Like I said there ain't much to look at out here," Burnett said with a flourish.

"And the way it looks it' all we're gonna see for the next hundred miles—sagebrush, sandhills and the rear end of doggies," Kodiak concluded.

THREE DAYS later Kodiak brought Montrose and Burnett to his side.

"According to the map we are about five miles away from the Red Cloud Agency," Kodiak said. "I'm going to ride on ahead and make arrangements to sell the cattle. I want you two to stay here and ride herd over the men. Keep the livestock bunched together and ready to move out when I return."

Burnett withdrew his revolver and spun the chamber; checking each cylinder in the process. "I don't trust that Ace fella any further than I can throw him," he said. "And I can't throw him very far."

"Just be careful not to start anything," Kodiak said. "I don't want to have to report back to DuFreeze that we killed one of his men."

"I won't, but I might wing him a little," Burnett said.

Kodiak rode north along a single lane trail referred to on the map. As it topped a hill he looked out over a vast plain dotted with hundreds of tepees. In the distance stood several buildings and further still several more. Kodiak reasoned that the first set of buildings was the Red Cloud Agency and the second set, the much larger, that of Fort Robinson. Both sets of buildings were rimmed to the north by high buttes as Nebraska transitioned into Dakota Territory.

When Kodiak neared the first set of buildings his reasoning was confirmed. Over one of the buildings was a sign that read *Red Cloud Agency.* He directed his horse in that direction while the residents of the teepees surrounded him and clamored for his attention.

What do they want? Kodiak asked himself. Some of those surrounding him made gestures to their mouths. *Are they starving?*

There were many conversations going on at once around Kodiak. Angry voices seemingly haggling over blankets and beads on his right. On his left pleading women and children with outstretched hands pressed around him.

Kodiak dismounted at the hitchin' rail in front of the building marked *Red Cloud Agency* and stepped inside. There was a continuous chatter inside the building as well as outside.

"What can I do fer ya, mister?" a man asked from behind the counter. The man turned to his left and spit out tobacco juice that clanked in the bottom of a spittoon out of Kodiak's sight.

"I got a herd of cattle about five miles back," Kodiak said.

"How many?" the man asked. He wiped the remaining tobacco juice from his lips with his shirt sleeve.

"About fifteen hundred head," Kodiak said.

A Native American woman grabbed Kodiak's shirt vying for his attention. The man behind the counter shouted at her in her own language and pointed toward the door. The woman released him and left the building.

"So, do you own this livestock?" the man asked. "I can't be too careful, you know sometimes men rustle cattle and try to pass them off as their own."

"A one-armed man named Bill DuFreeze owns them," Kodiak said.

The man reached under the counter and pulled out of list of what Kodiak surmised were registered brands in the area. "What's the brand on yer cattle?" the man asked.

The question caught Kodiak by surprise, but he was careful not to show it. DuFreeze never mentioned anything about needing to know his brand.

"And the brand?" the man asked a second time.

Kodiak thought for a moment. Then he remembered the new brand the men burned over the old. "Uhhh," he began. "It's the Double-B Bar brand." Kodiak prayed under his breath he had guessed correctly.

The man stared at Kodiak for a moment as if reading Kodiak's apprehension. He looked down at his list and then back into Kodiak's face.

There was a moment of silence.

"Well, mister," the man said at last. "That's a legitimate brand alright. Bring 'em in and I'll see to it ya get paid."

CHAPTER EIGHT

While Kodiak was transacting his business at the Red Cloud Agency, Jesse Jones was treating his wife to lunch in the Moore Hotel. Jesse Junior cooed at her feet, playing. Jesse loved to watch the interaction between his wife and his son. He delighted in seeing Martha smile and talk to Jesse Junior. She never cooed back but spoke to Jesse Junior.

'He isn't going to understand words if we don't talk to him like everyone else,' Martha would say. 'You'll see. He'll be speaking before you know it.'

A waitress arrived to take their order.

"Our special today is biscuits and gravy," she said as if her words were newly memorized. "Or you can order off the menu. And make sure you save room for pie."

Jesse noticed Parson Abel coming in and motioned for him to join them.

"Adeline will be along in a minute," said Parson Abel. "Potter said he'd watch over things at the store until we're done eating. Have you ordered yet?"

Martha looked up. "Your timing is perfect. We were just about to do that."

Parson Abel recognized the waitress. "You're new here, aren't you?" he asked.

"Yes, sir," the waitress said. "Came in by train a couple of days ago."

"You must be the young woman Adam Potter helped up to Doc's office," Abel said.

"I am," she said.

"I believe Adam said that your name is Elizabeth," Abel said. "Is that right?"

"Yes. Elizabeth Archer," she said.

"Well, Miss Archer, my name is Parson Abel. I pastor the little church up the street from here," he said. "My wife will be here in a few minutes, but I know she'd like me to invite you and your mother to dinner tonight. We can talk more then. You let us know if that will work for you."

"Thank you," Elizabeth responded.

"So, what's the special today?" Parson Abel said.

"Our special today is biscuits and gravy," she said. "Or you can order off the menu. And make sure you save room for pie."

"My wife and I will have the special." Parson Abel looked up and motioned Adeline to join them. "I hope you don't mind, my dear; but I've taken the liberty to order the biscuits and gravy special for lunch and to invite this young lady and her mother to dinner tonight." Parson Abel stood and made the introductions. "Elizabeth Archer, this is my wife Adeline. Adeline, this is Elizabeth Archer. She and her mother are new to Sidney."

Adeline extended her right hand. "Pleased to meet you, Miss Archer. We'd be honored to have you and your mother as our guests for dinner tonight."

Jesse noticed that Elizabeth was unsure about what to do

next but extended her right hand and took Adeline's. "Pleased to meet you," she said.

Elizabeth looked to Jesse. "And you, sir, what will you and the misses have for lunch?"

"The special is fine," he said. Jesse looked at Martha who nodded her approval to biscuits and gravy as well.

Jesse stood. "Before you go back to the kitchen, allow me to introduce myself and my wife. I'm Jesse Jones and this is my wife Martha. We own Swede's Mercantile along with Parson Abel and his wife, Doc Hardesty and his wife, and Adam Potter whom you have already met."

"Nice to meet all of you," Elizabeth said. She scurried off to the kitchen.

"She seems nice enough," Jones said. "A bit on the shy side. But, I guess that's understandable. She's only been in town a couple of days."

"Allow me to change the subject before I forget," Parson Abel said. "Did you get all the paperwork to the bank this morning?"

"Yes," Jones replied.

"Let's talk about that tonight over dinner. There's something about Swan Holmes that's a red flag for me," Parson Abel said.

ONE-ARM BILL DUFREEZE had a new assignment. He found himself sitting high in the saddle in the afternoon sun surveying the land south and east of where the cattle he'd rustled received their Double-B Bar brand. His new assignment was a simple one; find out who's living on this land and buy it up.

If we're running rustled cattle nearby, we don't want anyone interfering, his boss had told him. *And if you can't buy the land, find a way that we can get it. Whatever it takes, I want these land owners off the land and I want it done now.*

"It's at times like this that I wish I had the *gentle persuasion* of Flapjack, Spence and Ace with me," he said to himself. "But if I run into any problems the three of them will be back in a few days." A wry smile crossed Bill DuFreeze's lips.

DuFreeze turned his horse south and rode for about a half an hour before he found himself at the top of a ridge with open prairie in front of him. He took out a pair of field glasses to take a closer look. Someone had built a beautiful home. There was a barn nearby on the southeast corner of the property and what appeared to DuFreeze to be a root cellar in the northeast corner. He saw a man in the front yard with a posthole digger replacing fence posts for a white picket fence.

"I know that man," DuFreeze mumbled to himself. "It's the sodbuster, Flapjack and his men were going to shoot, the man who was returning the steer to Mr. Coad."

Bill DuFreeze encouraged his horse to a trot and rode down to where the man was hard at work. The man recognized DuFreeze as he neared because he waved.

"What are you doing out this way?" the man asked. He rested himself against his posthole digger and wiped the sweat from his brow with his handkerchief.

"My boss sent me on an errand," DuFreeze remarked. "The name's DuFreeze. Bill DuFreeze."

"I'm Brody Belt," the man said. "Can I help you down from your horse? I noticed that you have only one arm."

"No thanks, Mr. Belt," DuFreeze said. "I kinda got used to not having my right arm after all these years." Bill DuFreeze grabbed the saddle horn and swung down from the right side of his horse. "Lost it during the war. The sawbones who treated me said I'd get an infection and never survive to the end of the war. I lived to prove him wrong."

"I'm certainly glad you came along the other day," Brody Belt said. "Those men would have killed me for sure if you hadn't been ridin' up when you did."

"Yeah those three men are bad ones alright." Bill DuFreeze looked around. "This is quite the place you have here, Mr. Belt," he said.

"Built it all myself. Except the barn, of course," Brody said. "Had a lot of help on the barn. A few men I know in Sidney came out for a barn raisin'. It was quite a sight."

Cynthia Belt came out the front door with a basket of laundry to hang out to dry.

"Cynthia, come on over here for a minute," said Brody. "I'd like to you meet someone."

She put down the laundry basket and joined the men in the front yard.

"Cynthia, this is Mr. DuFreeze. Remember I told you about the three men who tried to kill me but another man saved me. Well, this is that other man," Brody said.

"Pleased to meet you, Mr. DuFreeze," Cynthia said.

"You know, I was just telling your husband that you have quite a place here," said DuFreeze. "I'm just wondering..." He paused for a moment. "I'm wondering if you'd be interested in selling it."

DuFreeze rode to the northeast with a trail of dust behind him. He'd been rejected in his endeavor to buy out the Belts. At one point the conversation got so heated he thought Brody was going to make a play for his gun. Good thing he didn't because DuFreeze knew few could match his speed.

In my younger days that young sodbuster would be taking a dirt nap, he thought. *And I'd have had that pretty young thing of his, too. Doggone if I ain't feelin' civilized.*

DuFreeze had in mind a better way to get Belt's land and it had to do with setting the wrong man against Belt. Brody Belt and his puny farm would be no match for the most powerful man in the territory—J.F. Coad.

The story, as DuFreeze recalled it, was that J.F. and his brother Mark came west and took over the old stage station at Scotts Bluff. It was a profitable business that allowed the Coad brothers to finance a huge cattle operation. The two brothers wound up with all the grazing land south of Camp Clarke all the way to Sidney.

If J.F. Coad were to find out someone was stealing cattle that belonged to him, there would be you-know-what to pay. Besides, this would prevent anyone from pointing an accusing finger at him for the missing cattle.

Once DuFreeze crossed the main road leading into Sidney he was on Coad property. Still it would take him an additional hour before the massive Coad brothers' ranch came into view. There we no fences except for a corral where the horses were kept. J.F. hated fences that kept cattle contained and he hated the men who put them up. Fences represented a loss of freedom for this immigrant from Ireland.

On DuFreeze's right stood the bunkhouse for the twenty men J.F. Coad employed. Up the lane a bit further stood the massive ranch house built almost entirely of Lodgepole pine. Inside the home, plank siding added to the rustic demeanor. Many times DuFreeze accompanied J.F. into his study where J.F. displayed the heads of animals he had shot; buffalo, antelope, bear, moose. DuFreeze recalled how ladies recoiled at the sight, over which he and J.F. shared a laugh.

Bill DuFreeze watched as a hired hand darted from the

wraparound porch and into the house. *Alerting J.F. of my arrival no doubt.* His thoughts were confirmed moments later when a man dressed in a starched collared shirt and suit appeared on the porch. DuFreeze secured his horse to the hitching rail in front of the house. The man came closer. The man stood half a head taller than DuFreeze, with short silver hair, meticulously groomed moustache, and steel grey eyes.

"Well, how did you make out at the Red Cloud Agency?" J.F. Coad asked. "You took a lot more time than usual to get back. Where are the other men? Did you have a problem?"

"Yes, sir, we did," DuFreeze began. "We were driving the cattle north out of Sidney when we were ambushed. Me and the boys have been chasing after the rustlers the last few days. Flapjack, Spence and Ace are still on it."

"How could this have happened?" J.F. Coad asked in anger.

"We were in bivouac and a group of men stampeded the cattle. They had a rear guard that kept us pinned down. We followed them north, but every time we got close that rear guard went into action," DuFreeze announced.

"I won't tolerate this!" J.F. said. "I want you to take more men with you in the morning and get to the bottom of this. Involve Sheriff Blanton in Sidney and do everything possible to bring these rustlers to justice!" J.F. Coad went back inside.

Well, Mr. I'd-Never-Sell Brody Belt. It looks like J.F. Coad has declared war on you. One Arm Bill DuFreeze chuckled to himself.

ADELINE ABEL SHUTTLED about the dining room making last minute preparations for the arrival of her guests. Parson Abel watched her from the doorway as she set the silverware and napkins at each place setting and looked down at her handiwork. She caught a glimpse of him out of the corner of her eye and turned.

"We're having a lot of guests tonight. I love having a full table," Adeline said. She turned back to the table. "Let me make sure that I've counted correctly. There'll be Jesse, Martha and Jesse Junior. That's three. You and I make five. Doc makes six. Adam is seven. Elizabeth Archer makes eight. What did she say was her mother's name? I've forgotten."

"I believe she said it was Edith," Parson Abel said.

"That's right. Edith. Let's see now. With Edith Archer that makes nine. Martha will hold little Jesse, so we only need eight place settings," Adeline said. She counted out loud: One, two, three, four, five, six, seven, eight. Good." She turned again to her husband. "Have I miscounted anywhere?"

Parson Abel walked to his wife and hugged her. "You are a wonder," he said. "I invite people to dinner and six hours later here you are about to make it happen."

"That's the life of a parson's wife," Adeline said with a smile. "I had no idea what I was getting into when I married you, but I wouldn't trade this adventure with you for anything."

They kissed.

Their guests arrived a short time later and 'ooohed' and 'aaahed' over the beautiful table Adeline had set. When introductions were completed everyone found their place card at the table and was seated.

"Before we begin our fellowship time around the table let us thank God for His blessings," Parson Abel announced. The full company bowed their heads.

"Heavenly Father," Parson Abel began, "we humbly ask you to bless our time together this evening. Bless this food my wife has prepared on such short notice." Everyone chuckled. "Lord, bless this food to the nourishment of our bodies for You have already nourished our souls through Christ Jesus our Lord. Amen."

As food was passed conversations began, including Parson Abel's conversation as he sat next to Edith Archer. "We are so glad you could join us this evening," he said.

"We are thankful for the invitation. If my daughter hadn't fallen ill, we wouldn't have been here at all." Edith looked to her left and noticed the close conversation Elizabeth and Adam Potter were having before returning to her attention to Parson Abel. "She's found a wonderful young man in the process," Edith said.

"She has. Adam Potter is a wonderful man. May I be so bold as to ask where you are headed?" he asked.

"We are on our way to Cheyenne to stay with my sister. When my husband died, she invited us to stay with her and her husband. So, we packed up and left Springfield, Illinois," she said.

Parson Abel felt a tap on his right shoulder.

"Parson, may I interrupt you for a moment?" Jesse Jones said.

"Mrs. Archer, will you excuse me?" Parson Abel said.

"Of course," she answered.

Parson Abel turned to Jesse. "What's on your mind?" he asked.

"This afternoon you said something about *red flags* in our relationship with Swan Holmes," Jesse said.

"I did," Parson Abel said. "I haven't been able to put my finger on it yet, but I'm concerned about a man who uses the phrase *the Good Book says that God helps those who help themselves.* The Good Book doesn't say that."

CHAPTER NINE

DuFreeze rode into Sidney. He had a tale to tell Sheriff Blanton; an unpleasant tale of a sodbuster who had turned to crime. Down the main street he rode smiling to himself for the ingenious plan he had devised on such short notice.

He tied his horse in of front a building with bars on the front window and the name *Isaiah Blanton, Sheriff* on a plaque next to the door. He knocked and was invited inside.

Sheriff Blanton sat behind his desk going through a pile of wanted posters trying to familiarize himself with names and faces of men who might wander into town.

"What can I do for you, Mr. DuFreeze?" Blanton asked.

"I didn't know we had been introduced," DuFreeze said.

"We haven't," Sheriff Blanton announced.

"Then how do you know who I am?"

"I make it my business to know people who come into town," Blanton said. "You don't know me, but I've seen you around enough to ask questions."

"So that means you already know that I'm Mr. Coad's foreman," DuFreeze said.

"Yep," Blanton answered. "So what brings you into Sidney today, Mr. DuFreeze?"

"I've come to report the theft of about fifteen hundred head of Mr. Coad's cattle."

Blanton withdrew a note pad from his desk and began taking notes. "And just when did this happen?"

DuFreeze grabbed a chair and sat down across from the Sheriff. "About a week ago."

"A week ago?"

DuFreeze noted that his answer startled the sheriff. "Yeah, a week ago. Been tracking them myself but they headed across country. Looks like they may be drivin' the herd toward North Platte. Anyway, I've got a couple of my men trailing them."

"Then what do you need me for?"

"Well, we had a strange incident the other day. There was this sandy haired sodbuster east of town that a couple of my men cornered. He was driving a steer bearing the Double F Bar brand. That's Mr. Coad's brand. We figured he was part of the gang and was given a head in exchange for his help. Now, I made my men let him go, but his story is suspicious."

"And what exactly is his story?" Blanton asked.

"He said that this steer wandered onto his property and that he found it in the morning after the steer knocked down a part of his picket fence."

"That sounds like the Belt place east of town," said Blanton.

"That's who he said he was—Brody Belt," DuFreeze said.

"I can't believe that Brody Belt would rustle cattle, Mr. DuFreeze."

"Look I can't say one way or the other whether or not he'd rustle cattle, but I can tell you that I saw the whole thing with my own eyes. Mr. Belt was drivin' a longhorn with J.F. Coad's brand on his hide. And I know one thing fer certain. Mr. Coad ain't gonna like it if I report back to him that I told you this story and you did nothin' about it."

"I never said I wasn't gonna do anything about it. I just said I can't believe Brody Belt would resort to rustling cattle. He isn't the type," said Blanton.

"Just what type is it that steals another man's cattle, Sheriff? I've seen a lot of things in my life and I've gotten to the point I don't trust anyone." DuFreeze noted.

"Brady Belt *is not* a desperate man, Mr. DuFreeze," said Sheriff Blanton.

"You try tellin' that to J.F. Coad," DuFreeze said. He arose from his chair. "After all, the Good Book says that God helps those that help themselves."

KODIAK CRABTREE and his gang met DuFreeze at the spot DuFreeze had designated. It was a dark night with low-level clouds wandering in front of the moon.

"Did everything go alright?" DuFreeze asked.

"Couldn't have been better," Kodiak answered. "The men worked hard and we got the cattle to the Red Cloud Agency without a hitch." Kodiak stepped down from his horse and took a cinched bag from his saddlebag. The contents within the bag jingled. Kodiak handed the bag to DuFreeze who had dismounted as well.

DuFreeze opened the bag and stared at the contents within. "Yes, sir, you boys did a right good job." Kodiak could tell that DuFreeze delighted in the gold coins because he kept staring at them. "Well now the Good Book is right when it says that God helps those that help themselves. Boys, it looks like we helped ourselves to a heapin' helpin' of good fortune. And this is only the beginning. You got another thousand head or so to rustle right out from under the watchful eye of J.F Coad's right hand man. Believe me when I tell you that I ain't a gonna stop ya. In fact, I'm gonna share the profits with ya."

The men joined DuFreeze in a laugh.

"Right now, I'm gonna pay all of ya for the work ya done. I'll let ya know when you'll ride for me again. In yer absence I even came up with a name for ya. Since ya'll do your best work at night, I'm callin' ya *the night riders*," DuFreeze said. "Kodiak and Flapjack, I want you and your men to stay behind after I send the others back to Sidney. I got somethin' special for you to do for me."

DuFreeze paid off the men and sent his *night riders* back to town.

"Climb down from yer horses, boys, and gather around," said DuFreeze to Kodiak, Flapjack and their men. "Got another job for you, Flapjack."

"I'm all ears, boss," Flapjack said. "What do you have in mind? Me, Spence and Ace are at your service. Ain't we, boys?" Spence and Ace nodded in agreement.

"Ya'll remember the sodbuster that I told you not to kill a while back?" DuFreeze began.

"Ya, we remember," Flapjack said. "He had a steer that belonged to Mr. Coad."

"Yes, that's the one," DuFreeze announced. "You're gonna have a little fun with that sodbuster. How would you like to see him swing by the neck until dead and all legal like, too?"

"How can we do that?" Ace said. "There ain't no way that *we* can legally hang a man, 'cept if we caught him rustlin' cattle.

"I mean a *legal* hangin' done by the law," DuFreeze said. "Then all ya gotta do is stand there next to the gallows and see a man hang without fear that you're next in line to have yer necks stretched."

"What's the fun in that?" Ace asked. "I wanna feel the rope in my hand and watch him squirm when I slip it over his head and tighten it around his Adam's apple."

"I know ya do, Ace," Flapjack interrupted. "But I fer one don't want ya to be hanged for doin' it. Now, listen to Mr. DuFreeze on how we can get a guy hung the legal way."

"Here's what I want the three of you to do, Flapjack. I want you to ride into Sidney tonight and each of ya steal a longhorn from the corral they're in. Got that?" said DuFreeze.

"So far, so good," Spence said.

DuFreeze took a of piece a paper from his shirt pocket. "I drew up a map for you to follow. I want you to take the cattle to the farm I've circled on this map. Put them in his corral and then hide in the hills around his place and don't let him or his misses leave. Now get going."

Flapjack, Spence and Ace mounted and rode toward Sidney.

"Why did you send those men to do this job and not us?" Kodiak asked.

DuFreeze turned to him. "Because they're expendable."

BRODY BELT GRABBED a hot pad and poured a cup of coffee. He had a heavy day of chores in front of him so he had climb out of bed before his wife Cynthia. He noticed the steam rising from his cup so he blew over it in an attempt to cool it off before taking his first sip. He walked sock-footed to the front door and stepped outside. The front porch provided a place to stretch and let the country air fill his lungs. He sipped his coffee and enjoyed a brief respite ahead of the day he'd risen so early to face. Reaching the eastern edge of his porch he felt the sun warm his face. In the corral near his barn he noticed what appeared to him to be several sets of massive horns.

"Longhorns," he said aloud. "How on earth did longhorns get mixed in with my cattle?"

Brody Belt hustled inside to put his boots on.

"Cynthia," he shouted. "Better rise and shine. We've got some of Mr. Coad's longhorns in our corral this morning."

"We've got what?" came Cynthia's reply from the bedroom.

"We've got longhorns in our corral," Brody answered.

"How did they get in there?" she asked.

"I don't know. I'm putting my boots on to go outside and take a look." His boots slid on easier than usual and Brody soon found himself at the corral staring at three head of Texas Longhorns mixed in with his other livestock. He unlatched the wooden gate and walked toward the longhorns which seemed contented to graze on what little grass remained in the corral. On the right flank of each longhorn Brody noticed the Double F Bar brand; the brand belonging to J.F. Coad.

"Hold it right there, Mister!" a man shouted.

Brody looked to the ridgeline southeast of his corral. A man stood there with rifle in hand.

"Who are you and what do you want?" Brody yelled back.

"We want you to stay put," the voice answered. "We caught you red handed with Mr. Coad's longhorns. This time there ain't no body gonna set you free until Sheriff Blanton gets out here. Then yer gonna hang for the low-down cattle thief that you are."

We? Brody thought to himself. *That means there's more than one man on the ridge. I can't stand out here where I'm a sitting duck.* He turned to retrace his steps.

A rifle discharged and the bullet dug a hole near his left foot.

"I told you to stay put!" the voice yelled. "Next time I won't miss."

I've got to chance it, Brody said to himself. *I'm a dead man if I don't.*

Cynthia stood on the porch in front of him, his Winchester in her hands. She chambered a round and fired along the ridge where the gun smoke had appeared. That was all Brody Belt needed to make his escape. He darted for the house. Cynthia fired a second round to keep the men on the ridge pinned down. Together they ran back inside their home. A bullet fired from the ridge smashed the glass out of their kitchen window.

"We're not safe in here," he said. "Grab little William and we'll go out the back window and into the cellar. It's the only chance we'll have." The couple raced through the house. Bullets thudded through the walls and smashed fragile objects. Brody escaped through the bedroom window at the rear of the house and helped Cynthia and his son escape. They heard gunfire from the ridge but it was all aimed at the house and not them. They reached the storm cellar, opened the door and locked themselves inside.

Jesse Jones and Sheriff Blanton rode at a gallop to keep up with Ace.

"Hurry up, will ya!" Ace shouted. "We got that filthy cattle thief and his wife holed up in their house." On Ace rode. Every few minutes he turned to motion the riders behind him to hurry.

When they reached the hill southeast of Brody Belt's homestead, the three men dismounted and scrambled to where Flapjack and Spence were firing their rifles at the house. Jones noticed that there was no return fire.

"Here they is, Flapjack," Ace said. "I brung the sheriff and his deputy like ya told me."

"What's going on here?" Jones asked.

"We were out lookin' for Mr. Coad's stolen cattle and we came across them three longhorns in the corral over yonder. When I seen that they had Mr. Coad's brand on 'em I sent Ace after you," Flapjack said.

"You can stop firing," Sheriff Blanton said. "There ain't no one in the house."

"There is too," Spence said. He stood to confront Sheriff Blanton. "We seen 'em run in there. He ain't gettin' away this time."

With the suddenness of a rattler Flapjack stood up and pushed Spence. "You hush up!"

"I ain't a-gonna hush up," Spence said. "We didn't shoot him before but we're gonna now."

Spence got off another shot at the house before Flapjack landed a fist to his face and knocked him down.

Jesse took out a white handkerchief and tied it to the end of his rifle. "I'm going down there. Keep me covered." Before anyone could say otherwise, Jones made his way down the embankment and toward the house.

"Brody, this is Jesse Jones. I want to talk to you," he yelled. There was no answer from the house. Jones walked uninterrupted all the way to the front door. He knocked. No answer. With a shove he forced the door open. A few minutes later he emerged. "There's no one in here!" Jones yelled.

"There's gotta be!" Spence yelled back. "You let 'em get away, you'll answer to Bill DuFreeze!"

"That's right!" Ace chimed in. "You'll answer to Bill DuFreeze. He ain't gonna like it one little bit!"

Jesse rounded the corner of the house and made his way to the storm cellar where he remembered Brody had hidden with

Doc in a previous encounter with hired killers. Jesse knocked. "Brody, are you in here?"

"Is that you Jesse?" the reply came from within.

"Yeah, it's me. Is Cynthia in there with you?"

"Yeah," Brody replied. "We got bushwhacked this morning."

"You're safe now. You can come out."

Jesse heard the cellar door unlock and watched as the door slowly opened and Brody Belt poked his head out.

"Sheriff Blanton is keeping his eye on the men who shot up your place," Jesse said. "But they've accusing you of stealing those longhorns in your corral. That's a serious charge."

Brody walked out followed by Cynthia holding their son William.

"Mornin', Cynthia," Jesse said.

"Mornin', Jesse," she replied.

"I'm afraid that I gotta arrest you, Brody," Jones said.

"But I haven't done anything," he replied.

"I know that, and Sheriff Blanton knows that, but those men say that you stole some of Mr. Coad's cattle," said Jesse. "We've got no choice but to put you in jail until we can sort this whole thing out."

"I'm innocent," Brody protested.

"I'm sorry, Brody, but the law is the law," said Jones.

CHAPTER TEN

The ride back into Sidney was uneventful. Sheriff Blanton rode point. Behind him came the Belts in their wagon; Brody holding the reins with Cynthia and son William on the seat beside him. Flapjack, Spence and Ace followed the wagon with Jesse Jones bringing up the rear so he could keep an eye on the three of them.

"I don't want any funny business," Jesse had told them. "Anything on your part that rouses my suspicions and I'll drop you dead in your tracks. This is a set up from the get-go, the only thing is I can't prove it."

"We heard stories about the gun you carry," Flapjack said. "Is it true that you can fire eight shots before reloadin?"

"Yep, that's what they say alright," Ace added.

"Let's say that you not try my patience," Jesse fired back.

As the entourage paraded down the main street of Sidney, eyes turned to watch it go by.

"What's goin' on, Sheriff?" one of the bystanders asked.

"Go about your business," Sheriff Blanton replied. "Everything's under control."

With the horses tethered, Sheriff Blanton led Brody Belt and his family into his office.

"Alright boys," Jesse said to Flapjack and his men, "Take your horses over to the livery stable and wait for me at the Moore Hotel."

"Ain't ya gonna listen to our side of the story?" Spence said.

"I kinda got an earful from Ace on my way back to the Belt place," Jesse said. "Now, we need to hear Brody's side of the story."

"Ya can't trust him to tell the truth," Flapjack jumped in. "He's a cattle thief and a liar."

"He's also my brother-in-law," Jesse said.

"So, that's how it is, huh?" said Ace.

"Yep. That's how it is," said Jesse. "Now get outta here before I change my mind and run the three of ya in and let Brody go."

Flapjack, Spence and Ace did as they were told.

Jesse joined everyone inside Sheriff Blanton's office.

"So, you're telling me that you found the three longhorns in your corral this morning?" Sheriff Blanton was asking as Jones entered. Belt was seated at the table in Blanton's office with Blanton standing over him. Cynthia was holding William and standing to Brody's right.

"Yep!" Brody answered. "I told Cynthia what I saw, slipped on my boots and went outside. That's when those men started yelling that I was a cattle thief and firing at the house. We slipped out the back window and locked ourselves in the cellar."

"Cynthia?" Blanton asked.

"That's how it was, Sheriff."

"I think something's wrong with this whole situation. Why would anyone want you arrested?" Jesse asked.

Brody thought for a moment. "The only thing I can think of

that's been unusual lately is that man that came to our place a few days back," he said. He looked up at Cynthia.

"That's right," she said. "The man said he wondered if we'd be interested in selling our place and when we said *no* he got really angry."

"Did he give you his name?" Sheriff Blanton asked.

"What I remember is that he only had one arm," Cynthia said. "His right arm was gone."

Brody Belt rubbed his forehead. "Let me think a minute," he said. "That's it! The man's name was DuFreeze. Bill DuFreeze. He said his boss had sent him on an errand."

"I wonder what the connection is between this Bill DuFreeze fella and the three men who shot at you today," Sheriff Blanton said.

"And I know a way to find out about that connection," Jesse announced. "A chain is only as strong as its weakest link. And I don't think there is a weaker link in this chain than Ace."

Jesse entered the Moore Hotel and asked for the room number for a man he knew only as Ace. A knock at Ace's door went unanswered. Jesse scouted the restaurant and again found no sign of Ace among the diners. That's when it occurred to him that the logical place to find a man of Ace's character was among the rabble at the Last Chance Saloon.

There in the far corner of the Last Chance sat the man Jesse had wasted twenty minutes looking for. Ace was seated at a blackjack table so engrossed in playing cards he failed to notice Jesse's entrance. What Jesse noticed as he walked in Ace's direction was the number of men wearing black bandanas.

Black bandanas. Jesse's eyes toured the room but did not find the two other men Ace normally hung out with among the black bandana-ed men in the saloon. *That's a good thing,* he thought. *Getting Ace out of here without shooting my way out will be challenge enough with Flapjack and Spence interfering.*

He neared the table where Ace played blackjack. No notice on Ace's part. At last he stood beside Ace. When the man playing next to Ace yelled, "Bust," Jesse bent down and whispered in Ace's ear. "I got a gun at your back, and want you to cash out your chips and walk ahead of me to the door."

Ace cocked his head over his shoulder and came face-to-face with Jesse.

"Now?" he whispered back.

"Right now," Jones answered. "Don't make any sudden moves or your blood will be splattered across this table." Jesse prodded Ace in the back with his LeMat revolver.

Ace turned his attention to the game in front of him. "I'm out this round. In fact, I think I'll call it a night. Wanna cash me out, Harry?" he asked the dealer. When the transaction was completed, Ace scooted his chair away from the table and stood up. "Do you really think you can get out of here alive?" Ace asked.

"I'm betting your life on it," Jesse replied. He nudged Ace in the back with his gun. "Now, make yer way to the door slow and easy like." Jesse walked behind and a bit to the left of Ace to make it look like two friends leaving the bar at the same time. He walked close enough to hide the pistol in Ace's back from public view.

"What do ya want with me, Jones?" Ace asked. "I ain't done nothin'. Can't a guy gamble some of his hard earned money without the law bustin' in?"

"Hey, Ace!" one of the men in a black bandana yelled. "Is everything alright?"

"Answer him," Jesse whispered. "But remember my gun is on you."

Jesse drew the hammer back on his gun. "Turn around slow like and tell him everything is just fine."

Ace turned slowly. "Yeah, Irv," Ace said. "Everything's fine. I'm a little tired so I think I'll call it a night."

"Night, Ace," Irv said. "Sleep tight and don't let the bedbugs bite."

The whole bar erupted in laughter.

That was all Jesse needed to turn Ace back around and head him through the swinging doors of the Last Chance and onto the wooden sidewalk outside.

Jesse uncocked his gun and holstered it.

"Would you mind telling me what this is all about?" Ace said.

"Sheriff Blanton wants you to come by for a little visit and he sent me to retrieve you," Jesse said. "He's got a couple questions about how J.F Coad's livestock ended up in Brody Belt's corral. Got any ideas?"

"He musta stole 'em," Ace responded.

Sheriff Blanton had prepared for Ace's arrival at the jail. He had shuttled Cynthia Belt and William over to Parson Abel's home. He also saw to it that Brody was locked behind bars. *Not because he was guilty,* he told himself, *but to make it look like we're taking Flapjack, Spence and Ace at their word.*

The door swung open. Jesse pushed Ace inside and closed the door. Sheriff Blanton was seated behind his desk.

"I finally found him, Sheriff," Jesse began. "He was over at the Last Chance soaking down some suds and playing blackjack."

"Have a seat," Blanton said. Ace plopped himself at the

table where an hour earlier Brody Belt had sat and answered questions.

"Where's that thievin' Belt fella?" Ace asked.

"I got him locked up," Blanton said.

"That's a good place fer a cattle thief. When ya gonna hang him?"

"That's for the judge to decide," Jesse said. He sat on Ace's right. Blanton came around his desk and sat on Ace's left.

Blanton noticed how nervous Ace became when the two lawmen fenced him in.

"Now, Ace," Blanton said. "Why don't you tell me your side of the story?"

Ace looked from side to side. There was no escape.

"It's hot in here," Ace said. "Is anyone else hot in here?"

"It's gonna get a whole lot hotter in here if you don't tell us everything you know," Blanton said.

"Ahhhh," said Ace. "Ahhh."

It was obvious to Blanton and Jones that Ace was carefully measuring every word.

"All I know is that Mr. DuFreeze told us about a rustlin' job and that Mr. Coad was missin' some cattle and me and Spence was to go out and look for 'em. We found 'em on that Belt fellas' place."

"You're lyin'," Jesse said.

"I am?" said Ace turning his head in Jesse' direction.

"We know you are," Blanton said with complete calmness.

"You do?" Ace's head snapped in Blanton's direction.

"We do," said Blanton. "We've got testimony from Belt and his wife that the man you work for—Mr. DuFreeze—was out at their place awhile back. He offered to buy them out, but they wouldn't budge."

"So, what does that prove?" Ace asked while he glared at Blanton.

"It proves that DuFreeze had a good reason to send you and your two pals to the Belt farm," Jesse interjected.

Ace turned on him. "It proves nothin'!" Ace spit out. "Nothin'!"

"Here's what I think happened," Blanton said. "You and your buddies got a hold of some of Mr. Coad's cattle and you waited until nightfall. After the lights in the house went out you waited some more. Probably a couple of hours. Then you put the cattle in the corral and waited until daybreak to spring yer trap. Isn't that how it happened?"

Ace's face turned as white as a sheet.

"Brody didn't steal Mr. Coad's cattle. The three of you did. And you planted them in Brody Belt's corral so Mr. DuFreeze could accuse Belt of stealing and get Mr. Belt's land. Didn't you?" Sheriff Blanton said.

Ace sat there staring straight ahead.

"Didn't you?" Blanton's tone of voice went from one of patience to one of insistence.

"It wasn't my idea," Ace said. He looked back and forth between Blanton and Jones.

"Probably not," Jesse said with a chuckle. "I don't think yer smart enough to come up with an idea like this on your own."

"I'm not," Ace agreed. "I'm really not." He turned his head toward Blanton. "And since it's not my fault, can I go now?"

"I have something else in mind," Blanton said.

"You do?" said Ace.

"Yep. How about you trade places with Brody Belt in my jail?"

"This ain't over!" Ace shouted. He grabbed the bars of the jail cell and shook them. "DuFreeze will get me out. You wait and see, Sheriff. This ain't over."

Sheriff Blanton opened the door of the cell next to Ace's. "You're free to go, Brody," he said. "Ace here just admitted that this whole incident was a frame up to get your farm like you said."

Ace wasn't finished yet. "Let me out, do you hear me!"

Jesse poked his head through the open doorway leading to the jail cell. "We all hear you, Ace. You need to be content with what you have."

"What do ya mean?" Ace replied in anger.

"Well, right now Ace, ya got it pretty good. You'll get three square meals a day and ya got a cot to sleep on and a roof over your head," Jones answered.

Sheriff Blanton led Brody through the door and closed the door behind them.

"I have a feeling that Ace is right about one thing," Blanton said.

"What's that?" asked Jesse.

"That this ain't over," said Blanton.

Body Belt sat at the table in Blanton's office. "This sure makes me a little apprehensive about going home. I got a wife and a little one to consider."

"I've always been in favor of standing up to bullies, but that's me," Jesse said. "Somehow we've got to get to the bottom of all this. Who's stealing the Coad brothers' cattle and what are they doing with them?"

"And why they want my farm." Brody added.

"And who are these guys wearing black bandanas?" said Blanton.

"Is DuFreeze behind all of this? If so, he's stealing from his employer," said Jesse. "Better still, if he is, can we prove it?

"We only have Ace's word on it," Blanton said. "And I don't

think his word would hold up in court if it were countered by Flapjack, Spence and, most likely, Bill DuFreeze. The only thing we've done so far is to set Brody free and lock Ace up."

"Right now that doesn't seem like much, does it?" Jesse pulled up a chair and sat next to Brody.

"It seems like a lot to me," Brody said. "That's the first time and I hope the last time I spend *any* time in a jail cell."

"Ah, quit complaining," Blanton said. "Like Jesse told Ace you'll get three square meals and a cot to sleep on and a roof over your head. Oh, and don't forget, you'll have companions. All the lice in the cot with you."

"That makes me itch just thinking about it," Belt answered. He involuntarily scratched himself.

"My question is," Jesse said, "how do we get whoever is pulling the strings to come out into the open?"

"You can bet that Flapjack and Spence are gonna want to break Ace out of jail," Blanton replied.

"More than anything, they're gonna want to kill Ace, especially if it leaks out that he is implicating Flapjack and Spence in the plot to take over the Belt place," Jesse said.

"But we need to smoke out the master mind," Belt said. "And I'll bet my life that DuFreeze is the mastermind."

"You've bet your life once already and you almost lost it," Jesse said. He paused to think things through. "Wait a minute," he said to Brody. "I think there is someone higher up than DuFreeze. Didn't you say that DuFreeze told you that his *boss* was interested in buying your place?

"That's right," Belt said.

"Then that means that DuFreeze has someone calling his shots. The question is who?"

"Because DuFreeze is J.F. Coad's foreman, my mind ran to J.F. as the *boss* DuFreeze was talking about," Belt said.

"We can find that out easy enough," Blanton joined in. "All

we have to do is ride out to the Coad ranch and ask J.F. if he's interested in buying out the Belts."

CHAPTER ELEVEN

With Ace in prison and Brody free to go, Jesse reunited Belt with his family at the home of Parson Abel. Sheriff Blanton stayed behind to guard his prisoner.

Brody had barely crossed the threshold of the Abel's front door when Cynthia wrapped her arms around him as if she'd never let him go.

"I knew you'd come for me this afternoon. I just knew it," Cynthia said.

"Where's William?" Belt asked. "I'd like to get back to the farm by supper time. There's livestock to care for."

"William is asleep in the kitchen," Cynthia said. "Adeline found a baby bed from when her children were little. I cuddled him and he fell right to sleep. He's all nestled in the bed. Martha's watching him."

"I'll put the tea on," Adeline called out. "Follow me into the kitchen. Oh, do be quiet about it since there's a baby asleep in there." She led the way and Brody and Cynthia followed.

Jesse hung back. He wanted to talk to Parson Abel about the day's events.

"Parson, can we talk?" Jesse asked.

"Of course," Parson Abel said. "Why don't you step into the parlor?" He led Jesse into his parlor where Doc already occupied his favorite chair.

"Well, Jesse, it didn't take long to free Brody," Doc said.

"It worked out better than I thought it would," he said. "I found one of the men who shot up the Belt place playing blackjack in the Last Chance and convinced him we needed his testimony at the sheriff's office."

"Come into my parlor said the spider to the fly," Doc said.

"Where in the world did you come up with that expression?" Abel wanted to know.

"Ah, it's just a saying my father used to say when I'd done something wrong and it was time for him to mete out the punishment," Doc replied.

Jones sat at one end of the settee and Parson Abel at the other.

"Between Sheriff Blanton and me we were able to get the truth out of Ace," Jones said. "He admitted that he teamed up with Flapjack and Spence to steal the cattle and plant them in Brody's corral."

"So who put them up to it? That's what I'd like to know," said Parson Abel.

"DuFreeze," said Jesse. "DuFreeze put them up to it."

"There's your man," Doc said.

"Not so fast," Jesse stopped Doc's thought dead in its tracks. He leaned forward to explain. "DuFreeze was at the Belt farm earlier and offered to buy them out saying that his boss wanted to buy it."

"His boss?" said Abel. "And who might that be?"

"DuFreeze works for J.F. Coad as his foreman," Jesse said.

"I can't believe that John Coad would be responsible for a plan to drive a man off his property," Abel said.

"He's as honest as the day is long," Doc added.

"Is that another of your homespun sayings?" Abel asked.

"Sorry, that one slipped out without any thinking at all," said Doc.

"And how is that different than usual?" said Parson Abel.

"We can substantiate that easily enough by riding out to the Coad brothers' spread," Jones interjected.

"That's a good idea," Doc said. "I've known John Coad for years. Delivered his children. His deceased wife was a wonderful woman."

"Doc, do you think you'd like to ride out there with me?" asked Jesse.

"Be happy to, Jesse," Doc said.

"There's also something peculiar, Parson." Jesse said. "Sheriff Blanton had a conversation with Mr. DuFreeze a while back and he used the expression God helps those who help themselves."

"That's the same expression Swan Holmes used over dinner the other night. Is that a coincidence?" Abel asked.

Sheriff Blanton opened his door to the sound of knocking. Flapjack and Spence pushed their way in.

"We understand that you got Ace locked up in here," Flapjack began.

"Yeah," Spence said.

"Wow, word sure travels fast," Blanton replied.

"We was over ta the Last Chance and some friends of ours told us that Jones walked out with Ace in front of him. All we done is put two and two together," Spence said, obviously delighted in himself.

"What's he doin' in jail, Sheriff?" Flapjack asked.

"Ya know, what you could do is go in there and ask him yourself," Blanton answered. "Look, I can make this all very easy for you. Give me your guns and I'll walk ya right back to his cell."

"That's mighty kind of you, Sheriff," said Flapjack. He unbuckled his gun belt and handed it to Blanton.

"Now yours, Spence. I believe that's your name isn't it?" Blanton said.

"Sure 'nuff, Spence is my name. I had no idea that you knew who I was," Spence said.

Spence unbuckled his gun belt and handed it to Blanton. He laid both gun belts on his office table.

"You boys can have 'em back after your visit. Doesn't that sound fair enough?" said Blanton.

"Sure, Sheriff," Flapjack said.

Blanton walked to his desk and retrieved his jail keys and opened the door that separated his office from the jail cells.

"Right this way, gentlemen. You'll find Ace in the first cell on your right."

"Is that you, Flapjack?" Ace asked.

"Yeah, Ace. And I brung Spence along," Flapjack said.

"That's right kind of ya to do that," said Ace.

Blanton unlocked Ace's cell door. "Move away from the door, Ace. These two men want to come in and see you," said Blanton. Ace moved back and Sheriff Blanton opened the cell door.

"Ok, fellas," said Blanton. "Go on in for your little visit."

"We thank you, Sheriff," Spence said. He and Flapjack walked into Ace's cell and Sheriff Blanton closed and locked the cell door behind them. A conversation between the three men was well underway when Blanton walked back into his office and closed and locked the wooden door behind him.

When Jesse arrived at Sheriff Blanton's office about an hour later Blanton had quite the tale to tell.

"You did what?" Jesse said.

"I captured Ace's two accomplices, Flapjack and Spence. They walked in here bold as brass and said they wanted to see Ace. I told them they could do that as long as they handed me their gun belts first. Which they did. Then I unlocked Ace's cell and told them to step inside. And they did," Blanton said. "It was the easiest arrests of my career."

"That's got to be the craziest thing I've ever heard," Jesse said. "Criminals coming in and inviting you to arrest them. They may be a bit upset when they figure out how you got the drop on them."

"I didn't really get the drop on them. They wanted to visit and I gave them the opportunity."

"Do you think you can handle the situation here for a couple of days?" Jesse asked. "Doc and I are riding out to the Coad spread to see if we can get some answers about who this *boss* is that DuFreeze is working for."

"I think so, as long as you can have Potter available for backup," said Blanton. "I sure haven't seen him around much lately."

"Neither have I," said Jones. "Ever since Elizabeth Archer showed up Potter's been conspicuous by his absence."

"I thought Potter said that he had no interest in women and would be a bachelor all his life," Blanton said.

"I think Elizabeth is changing his mind for him," said Jesse.

THE THOUGHT of Jesse being gone for several days again did not sit well with Martha and she told him so over lunch in the Moore Hotel. She kept her voice down out of courtesy for the other patrons eating there, but Jesse understood the demeanor of her voice very well.

"Why does it always fall on you to make these long trips?" she said. "There are other men who aren't married who could travel for you. Have you asked Potter?"

"I hardly see him any more. He comes in and works at Swede's when he's scheduled and then disappears. I've heard that he spends a lot of time with Elizabeth Archer. It's as if he can't stay away from her," Jesse said.

"They're not married and they most certainly don't have a little one. Besides, as the saying goes 'absence makes the heart grow fonder,'" Martha said.

Jesse looked across the table at Martha. "And what exactly does that have to do with Potter?" he asked. Although he hated to admit it, there was a tone in his own voice that he didn't like very much. "I'm sorry, that was out of line."

"Brody is taking Cynthia and William back to their farm this afternoon," Martha said. "I've already asked if Jesse Junior and I can stay with them until you get back. That's where you'll find us when you get back. I really don't want to spend another night alone in our cabin. It isn't the same there when you're gone."

"I hope this isn't too late for me to say this, but I love you," Jesse said.

"And I love you, too," she said. "But I need you around. You're my anchor, and Jesse needs a living role-model and not a dead one."

Jesse replayed that memory from the Moore Hotel restaurant several times on his trip north to the Coad brothers' ranch. Doc trailed along behind in his buggy providing Jesse with plenty of time to think. Jesse saw a watering hole in the distance and it wasn't long before his horse and Doc's we're side-by-side with their noses in the water.

"You know, Doc. This lawman business is putting a strain on things at home," Jesse began.

"It will do that," Doc said. "Yes, sir, it will do that. A woman needs safety and security and a man needs adventure. Sometimes there's a conflict and those individual needs butt heads like a pair of stag elk during rut."

"Are you saying that the stronger of the two elks wins and all I have to do is remain firm?" Jesse asked.

"Not saying that at all," Doc responded. "In fact, I'd go so far as to say that if you do insist on getting your own way all the time, you may win the battle but lose the war. When you got married you committed to God that you would care for Martha. I think the words Parson Abel said were to death do you part. So, from that day on the *me* of your old relationship became the *we* of a new relationship."

"So you're saying that every time I do something I have an additional life to think about?" Jesse said.

"Two additional lives because now you have a wife and a son," Doc said.

"You know, Doc, that all makes sense," said Jesse. "I've never thought of it that way."

"Well, that's the best advice I can give you," Doc said in an attempt to change the subject.

"Can I make one last comment?" Jesse asked.

"One last comment and then we need to move along," said Doc.

"When you said all those things a moment ago, you reminded me of Parson Abel."

"Whatever you do, don't share that with Parson Abel," Doc said. "It'll ruin my reputation."

A TWO HOUR ride brought Jesse Jones and Doc onto the lane leading to J.F. Coad's ranch house.

"Looks much the same as I remember it," Doc said when Jesse pulled his horse alongside Doc's buggy. "They've added several outbuildings, but that's to be expected as the ranch has grown through the years."

A couple of ranch hands rode out to meet the pair.

"I thought I recognized your buggy, Doc," one of the men said. "What are you doing way out here? Ain't nobody sick or nothing."

"I hadn't seen Mr. Coad since his kids were little, so when Jesse said he was coming out here, I decided to ride along, that's all," said Doc.

"You're timing is good, Doc," the man said. "Mr. Coad is packing for a trip back to Omaha. Business to handle. He's leaving in the morning."

By the time the two men rode into the front yard, J.F. Coad stood on the porch to greet them.

"Good to see you again, Doc," Coad said. "It's been a long time since you were out here last."

"Hardly recognized the place," Doc said. "The years have been good to you."

"Got one of the biggest ranches in Nebraska," Coad said. "Why don't you two step inside and tell me what brought you all the way out here."

"J.F., this here is Jesse Jones," Doc said. "Jesse, this is J.F. Coad, the man we rode here to talk to."

They shook hands. Jones noticed the firmness of his grip.

Coad brought the two men into his office. Above his desk was the head of a Texas longhorn with massive horns, the likes of which Jesse had never seen before. Coad caught Jones staring at the massive creature.

"That's Brutus," J.F. said while making his way to his desk.

"Brutus was the biggest longhorn bull I'd ever seen. Brought him up from Texas to sire my herd. Brutus was worth every nickel I paid for him. You might even say that he was worth his weight in gold. So, when he died I had to have a little reminder." Coad sat himself under the massive head. "Can I interest either of you in a cigar?" He gave them access to his humidor. Jones and Doc helped themselves. Soon the air was filled with aromatic smoke. "Have a seat, gentlemen." He waited until the two men were seated. "Tell me, how can I help you?"

Doc began, "Jesse has a couple of questions."

Jones felt J.F.'s steely grey eyes on him. "Can you tell me if you have any interest in buying the property of Brody Belt, east of the Camp Clarke road?"

"Never heard of him," Coad said.

"Your foreman, Bill DuFreeze, told Brody that *his boss* was interested in buying him out. I assumed that the man who authorized him was you."

J.F. Coad took a long drag on his cigar and blew out the smoke. "I never authorized any such thing. I got all the land I need and then some on the west side of the road. DuFreeze did tell me about a man he ran into that had some of my stolen cattle in his possession. I don't remember the name."

"Stolen cattle, huh?" Jesse replied.

"About a thousand head," said Coad.

"I have a stinkin' feeling that DuFreeze is using your stolen cattle to drive Brody Belt off his farm," said Jesse.

"Did DuFreeze steal my cattle?" Coad asked.

"I'm afraid I can't prove that," Jesse said. "Not yet anyway."

CHAPTER TWELVE

Kodiak stood at the bar gulping down a whiskey shot, warming his innards. Not far from him a young cowboy swayed forward and smacked his chin on the bar. Blood splattered everywhere. The cowboy's limp body slid down the bar and thudded to the floor. Two men grabbed the young man's arms and a third took his feet and tossed him unceremoniously into the street. None of the Last Chance's patrons seemed to notice but Kodiak.

"I'll have another." Kodiak slid his shot glass in the bartender's direction. He faced away from the bar where the gambling hall was filled with cigarette smoke that hung like an acrid veil.

"Here's yer whiskey, mister," the bartender announced. "That'll be two-bits."

Kodiak dropped the money into bartender's waiting hand and slammed down the second shot like the first.

"Are you Kodiak Crabtree?" a quivering voice behind him asked.

Kodiak's right hand instinctively dropped to his revolver.

"I am," Kodiak said. He wheeled about to face the voice, one that belonged to an unarmed kid half his height and not yet old enough to shave. "What can I do for you, son?" he asked.

"I got a message for you from Bill DuFreeze. Is it okay if I reach into my pocket, Mr. Crabtree?" the kid asked.

"Go ahead, but don't make any sudden moves." Kodiak wondered if the kid had a hidden derringer so he kept his gun hand free.

The kid struggled to withdraw a slip of paper from his pants pocket and when the note was partially visible Kodiak snatched it with his left hand. He unfolded the note and read: *Free Flapjack and Spence by any means necessary.*

The kid held out a hand expecting a tip.

Kodiak flipped him a quarter. "You can tell Mr. DuFreeze his message is received and I'll take care of it."

The kid was gone.

KODIAK WALKED two blocks west and stopped at the door of Sheriff Blanton's office. He removed the note from his trouser pocket and read it again. Four words stood out on the note--*by any means necessary.* To Kodiak that meant whether the Sheriff survived his visit or not did not matter in the least to Bill DuFreeze. Kodiak wondered how this whole scene would play out. If Sheriff Blanton wanted a gunfight, Kodiak would oblige him. He checked the chambers of his revolver in anticipation. Five rounds. Kodiak spun the empty chamber to the top so the hammer rested on it to prevent a misfire. He holstered his gun and knocked on Sheriff Blanton's door.

"What do you want?" Kodiak heard the voice inside say.

"It's Kodiak Crabtree, Sheriff. Open up. I want to talk to yer prisoners."

Footsteps moved toward to the door. Kodiak was tempted to shoot Sheriff Blanton on the spot. His right hand wrapped around the gun butt, but he resisted.

The deadbolt slid with a soft click and the doorknob slowly turned. Blanton cracked the door just wide enough for him to eyeball Kodiak. "What do you want with my prisoners?"

"Bill DuFreeze sent me to check up on 'em," Kodiak replied.

"Take off your gun belt and hand it to me through the door."

"You do know that I could give this door a push and you wouldn't be able to hold me back," Kodiak announced.

"You could do that," Blanton said. "But I'd advise against it. Adam Potter's got his shotgun trained on the door. Just pop yer head in and he'll blow it clean off."

Kodiak heard the hammer of a shotgun click into place. *Well, so much for getting the drop on the Sheriff.* He removed his gun belt and handed it to Blanton.

The door swung open and Kodiak stepped inside.

"You two act like yer expectin' trouble." Kodiak nodded a greeting to Potter. Potter nodded back but his shotgun followed Kodiak's every move.

"You can pick your gun up on the way out," Blanton said. "The prison cells are in the other room. Go right through that door." Blanton pointed the way. "You got five minutes."

"That's not enough time," Kodiak pleaded.

Blanton pulled out his watch and gave it a glance. "Time's a wastin'."

Flapjack was glad to see Kodiak. He made a bee-line from his bunk and stood at the cell door. "Did ya come to get us out?"

"Yeah. DuFreeze sent me," Kodiak said.

"So, did ya git the key?"

"No," Kodiak said. "That stupid sheriff outsmarted me. I had no idea that he'd be waiting for someone to bust you out."

Ace sat up in his bunk. "He outsmarted Flapjack and Spence, too."

"Sure 'nuff," Spence added. He remained stretched out on his bunk with his hands behind his head like a contented child. "We said we wanted to see Ace so he opened Ace's cell and we walked right in, and he closed the door after us."

"Me and Spence don't want out," Ace added. "We like it here 'cuz we know where our next meal's comin' from."

"'Sides we like not havin' to work for a livin'. We can lay in bed if we want ta and only have to get up for meals," Spence said. "Or at least that's what the sheriff told us. Ain't that right, Ace?"

"Yep. That's what he done told us," Ace said.

"For the time being I want the three of you to sit tight. I'm goin' to get the night riders and we're gonna bust you out of here," Kodiak said. "DuFreeze has got work for you to do and you can't do it flat on your backs in jail."

Kodiak pounded on the door and Sheriff Blanton opened it.

"DuFreeze wants these men freed and Brody Belt locked up," Kodiak announced.

"Well, that ain't gonna happen." Potter leveled his shotgun at Kodiak's mid-section. "Ace told us that the plan was to frame Brody so DuFreeze could get his land."

"Ace said that, did he? Well, I'm sure DuFreeze will take that under consideration when Ace is free. The way I hear it is DuFreeze has killed men for less."

Sheriff Blanton handed Kodiak his gun belt. Kodiak strapped it on and in one swift motion grabbed Blanton and put a pistol to his head. Kodiak motioned for Potter to put down his shotgun.

Potter didn't move. His shotgun remained aimed at Kodiak.

"Put the gun down or Sheriff's Blanton's wife becomes a widow," Kodiak barked.

Potter never moved.

"Did you hear what I said?"

"I did," Potter said.

Kodiak cocked his revolver. "I'm serious. Dead serious!"

Still Potter did not move.

"I warned you!" Kodiak pressed the barrel of his gun to Blanton's head and pulled the trigger. It clicked as the hammer fell on an empty chamber. He tried again. Another click.

Potter laid down his shotgun. He extended his hand to reveal five cartridges. "Are you looking for these?" he asked with a smile. "Now, get out! And don't let the door hit you in the backside as you do. I'm lettin' ya off this time. Don't you ever trample on our hospitality again."

Kodiak stormed out and slammed the door behind him.

JESSE JONES WAS THINKING about DuFreeze on the ride home. In particular he wanted to know the name of the puppet master who pulled DuFreeze's strings. It wasn't J.F. Coad. He was certain of that. The look on Coad's face said it all when he asked Jesse if DuFreeze was stealing his cattle. No, Coad couldn't fake that expression of surprise and disappointment. Jesse pulled up his horse so Doc's surrey could catch up with him. They rode side-by-side on the Camp Clarke road.

"You know J.F. better than I do, Doc. What's his next move?"

Doc did not answer at first. Jesse imagined Doc was lost in thoughts of his own. "What did you say?"

"I asked what you thought J.F.'s next move would be. Would he ask Sheriff Blanton for help?"

"That wouldn't be J.F.'s style. I'd say that J.F. will do some digging around on his own. He didn't get to be the largest landowner in Nebraska without good instincts. All I can say is God help DuFreeze if he's stealing from J.F. Coad. He'd most likely kill DuFreeze and there ain't a jury around who would convict J.F. of anything."

An hour of silence passed between the two men.

"Doc, do you think you can ride the rest of the way into Sidney alone?"

"If you had any idea how many times I've driven over this road alone you wouldn't ask me such a stupid question. I like my company and next to you I am the greatest conversationalist I know."

"I wanna play a hunch. If someone is running stolen cattle they'll need to rebrand before they can sell them. A thousand head don't disappear into thin air. There has to be hoof prints. I'm gonna nose around the hills to the east on the chance I can find some evidence."

"Come to think of it," Doc said, "I remember seeing lots of tracks meeting up with the road a bit further up the line."

"Don't know why I didn't notice 'em," Jesse said.

"Probably had your mind on something else."

"Out here that kinda mistake could get a guy killed."

A short time later, Doc found the spot he'd remembered seeing. "Is this what you're looking for?"

Jesse saw hoof prints in abundance. This was the spot alright. The hoof prints came from the east as he suspected they would. All he had to do was follow where they led. If someone was hiding cattle back in the sandhills, these tracks would lead him there. "This is exactly what I'm looking for.

What's even better is the Belt homestead is about three miles to the southeast as the crow flies."

"That would make it possible for cattle to wander and end up in the Belt's front yard." Doc pulled the slack out of the reins. "Looks like this is where we part company. See ya in Sidney," Doc said.

Jesse nodded.

"Giddy up." Doc's horses lunged into action and soon carried him out of sight.

The afternoon sky darkened overhead. There was bad weather brewing. Jesse nudged his horse forward, off the road and onto the trail pockmarked by hoof prints and cow pies. In a clearing between sandhills and only a mile or so north of the Belt place, he found what he was looking for. Someone had erected a makeshift corral. He kicked around what once was a branding fire and something caught his eyes. A piece of dark metal. Partially buried. Left behind. With a well-worn boot he kicked away the dirt. A branding iron. A Double-B Bar branding iron. Who was this brand registered to? Sheriff Blanton would know. Jesse put the branding iron across his saddle, mounted, and rode in the direction of the Belt place.

BRODY BELT LOOKED up from his chores. He watched the distant rider come down the hill toward him. He sat the feed pail down and walked toward the fence. His tiny Hereford herd would have to wait. Brody slowly walked to where he had propped his rifle against a fence post. Since the attack by Flapjack and his henchmen, he was taking no chances. He grabbed his rifle and was about to chamber a round when the horsemen yelled at him.

"Put yer gun down, Brody. It's me. Jesse."

"Scared the devil out of me riding in from that direction," Brody said after Jesse joined him at the fence and dismounted. "I thought you'd head into town before coming out here."

"Took the long way around." Jesse tossed the branding iron at Brody's feet. "What do you make of this?"

"Double-B Bar brand? Have no idea who this belongs to. Where did you find it?"

"In a clearing not too far north. Looks to me like whoever it was that rustled J.F. Coad's cattle rebranded them. Isn't his brand the Double F Bar?"

"That's what I've heard," Brody replied.

"It wouldn't be that hard to stamp the Double-B Bar brand over it. That's what I reckon they did."

"The question is who are they?"

"Is this a new fence?"

"Yeah. Switched out the wood lathes and strung up barbed wire. The salesman said it would outlast wood making it more economical."

Jesse fingered one of the barbs and it pierced the skin. He stuck his bloody finger in his mouth. "Doggone if that barb ain't sharp. Who was this salesman? That sounded like some-thin' Potter would tell you."

"You didn't think that I'd buy anything anywhere other than Swede's Mercantile did you?"

Cynthia appeared on the porch. "Supper's ready!"

"Better put another potato in the pot. Jesse's back."

"Martha will be glad of that. She's been on pins and needles all day waiting for you to come back, Jesse."

Brody led the way to the side of the house where a washtub and a bar of lye soap removed the dirt from working hands. Cynthia often complained that Brody never used soap; that he only wet his hands and dried them with the towel. His muddy handprints were on display for all to see.

When Jesse stepped over the threshold and came into Martha's view, she bounded from the rocking chair and into Jesse's arms. "I've missed you."

Jesse pushed his hat back to reveal brown hair now sprinkled with flecks of gray about his temples. "I missed you, too, Mrs. Jones." They kissed.

"Where's Jesse Junior?" Jesse looked around the room hoping to catch a glimpse of him.

"Down for a nap. He should be waking up anytime now," Martha said.

Cynthia hurriedly set a fourth place setting at the table. "We weren't expecting you until tomorrow, Jesse. So what that's gonna mean is that Brody will have to stop at second helpings tonight, otherwise you won't get anything to eat."

"Ouch!" Brody retorted with a smile.

Cynthia gave the table settings one long last look. "Okay, everyone take a seat. I'll grab a hot pad and bring everything to the table."

Jesse pulled Martha's chair out and held it firm while she sat down.

"There you go, Jesse. Making me look bad again," Brody chided.

"Well, at least one of you men has learned to be a gentleman," said Cynthia playfully.

With the meal on the table, Brody stood and helped Cynthia into her chair.

"That wasn't so hard, was it, brother dearest?" Martha asked.

"Oh, so now the two of you are ganging up on me?" Brody chuckled out loud. "Ok, now that we are gathered together over this meal, allow me to pray."

CHAPTER THIRTEEN

Jimbo Livingston ducked to enter Swede's Mercantile. Being nearly seven foot tall came with disadvantages.

"Jimbo, what are you doing in town so soon? We weren't expecting you until the day after tomorrow." Adam Potter stood behind the counter.

"Mr. Clarke sent me in for supplies. With the fall rain holding off, the bridge is going up faster than he expected. Here's a list of supplies I need before I start back in a couple of days."

Jimbo handed the list to Potter who perused it. "You'll find most of these items at the warehouse. You remember where it is, don't you?"

"Yep," Jimbo said. "We'll make our way there."

"And I'll send Jesse to unlock the door," Potter said.

Jimbo and his teamsters navigated their wagons through the busy streets, arriving at the same time as Jesse.

"Did you have a good trip, Jimbo?" Jesse asked.

"I know the way like the back of my hand. Only thing I saw that I hadn't seen before was hoof prints all over the road.

Looks like somebody drove their cattle down the road instead of beside it. I'm guessing the tracks were from the cattle drive that came through Camp Clarke a while back."

"You had a cattle drive through Camp Clarke?" Jesse said as he fumbled to find the correct key among others on his large key ring. "Here we go," Jesse said as the padlock unlocked. "Do you need any extra men to help you? I've got 'em if you need 'em."

"Don't think so, but thank you."

While the teamsters went to work loading their wagons, Jesse and Jimbo returned to the topic of a cattle drive through Camp Clarke. "You've never had a cattle drive through Camp Clarke before?"

"This was the first time. Usually J.F. Coad has his men drive their cattle through the hills further west, but not this time. There's something else I noticed."

"What's that?"

"Well, the cattle looked like Coad cattle I've seen in pens around town, but the brand was all wrong," Jimbo continued. "Instead of the Double F Bar brand, these cattle wore the Double-B Bar brand."

"That Double B Bar is the same brand my brother-in-law Brody Belt found on cattle on his place," said Jones. "I think it's time we got to the bottom of this and find out who owns the Double-B Bar brand."

Jesse's quest took the two men the Sheriff Blanton's office. They found him feeding his three prisoners. Blanton turned and noticed his new arrivals.

"Give me a minute," Blanton said.

"And it looks like for the second day in a row we get split-pea soup and ham hocks," a voice shouted. "Except there ain't ham in it."

"Yeah, Sheriff. Ace is right," another voice said. "How can

you call this soup split-pea and ham hocks if there ain't no ham?"

"Will you boys keep quiet?" Sheriff Blanton said. "The café up the street is doing the best they can. I can't remember the last time I saw a pig around here."

"Then they shouldn't advertise it as split-pea and ham hocks," said a third voice.

"Suit yerself. I'll just take this soup back to where it came from and tell 'em you ain't hungry," Blanton said.

"No, don't do that," screamed a voice Jesse finally recognized as Ace. "We didn't say we wouldn't eat it. We're only saying that there should be ham in split-pea and ham hocks soup. That's all."

With his prisoners occupied with their soup, Blanton stepped into the main part of his office and closed the door. "These three prisoners are a pain where a pill won't reach." He broke into a smile when he saw Jesse and Jimbo. "What can I do for you two?"

"Jimbo and I have a question. Do you have a registry of all the cattle brands in the county?"

"I think so. If I do it'd be in my desk." Blanton made his way to his desk and soon produced the registry Jesse and Jimbo sought.

Jesse sat at the lone table in the room and thumbed through the alphabetically ordered pages. Jimbo and Blanton stood over him. At last Jones found what he was looking for. He spread the registry wide open for Jimbo and Blanton to see the handwritten entry:

BB Bar Registered to Swan Holmes April 5, 1875

DuFreeze sat alone nursing his beer. His index finger tapped the table nervously as he waited for Kodiak who was already ten minutes late. The Last Chance Saloon satisfied his need to be near people yet alone. DuFreeze liked to be alone since his days of riding with William Quantrill when another raider had betrayed him at the cost of his left arm. A man named Curtis Leaver. Because of that betrayal he made it his practice never to confide in anyone. Some men accused DuFreeze of being standoffish, but he'd determined it was better to be accused of being standoffish than to be dead.

Kodiak parted the swinging doors and stepped inside the Last Chance. It was filled with men wearing black bandanas about their necks. DuFreeze hailed him with his right hand. Kodiak nodded and pushed his way between occupied chairs to where DuFreeze sat.

"You kept me waiting," DuFreeze said. His voice hissed like a rattler before it strikes.

Kodiak made the mistake of shrugging his shoulders.

In an instant DuFreeze drew his revolver and slammed it on the table. Heads turned in their direction. There was no ignoring his anger. "Get back to what you were doin!'" he bellowed. Some still stared. "All of you, back to what you was doin! This is between me and Kodiak." At that moment no one in the saloon wanted to be Kodiak.

DuFreeze glared up at Kodiak who bowed his head and never looked up. He didn't dare.

"I'm not in the mood," he growled. "When I say meet me at high noon, I mean meet me at high noon. Do I make myself clear?"

Kodiak sheepishly nodded.

"Now, sit down."

He did, but still never looked up.

DuFreeze's voice took on the tone of a condemning parent.

"I gave you an assignment. I sent you to the Sheriff's office with orders to get Flapjack and Spence out of jail. Did you do that?"

Kodiak didn't dare move.

"I asked you a question and I expect an answer."

Kodiak sighed and let out a barely audible, "No."

"Look at me," DuFreeze commanded.

Kodiak sat unable to move.

"I told you to look at me!"

Reluctantly Kodiak raised his head and fixed his eyes on DuFreeze.

"I'm going to tell you this once, and once only. I want Flapjack and Spence out of jail by midnight tonight. I don't care what you have to do or who you have to kill in the process. I want them out of jail."

DuFreeze waited for Kodiak's reply. There was none.

"Did you hear me or have you gone deaf or somethin'?" DuFreeze belched out.

Again heads turned. DuFreeze motioned them to turn around.

"I heard you," Kodiak softly replied.

"Let me be very clear. I want Flapjack and Spence released." DuFreeze waited for the question he knew was coming.

"And what about Ace?" Kodiak asked.

"Hang him. Take him out of the jail and put a noose around his neck. Let his hanging be an example of what happens to any man who dares to cross the Night Riders. Ace disobeyed my orders and got caught. This isn't the first time Ace was careless, but it will be the last time."

DuFreeze stared Kodiak down. "This is a lesson to you, too. You've disappointed me once, don't let it happen again. Now, get out of here before I change my mind."

Every eye in the saloon followed Kodiak to the door.

JIMBO RETURNED to the warehouse to help load freight. Jesse walked with him. Both men tried to make sense of what they learned from Sheriff Blanton. Was it possible Swan Holmes was behind the theft of J.F. Coad's livestock? Was Holmes using Bill DuFreeze, Coad's foreman to ramrod this scheme? To what end?

Jesse's mind turned to the branding iron he'd discovered. He was in possession of a major piece of evidence. Could Jesse use that evidence to smoke Swan Holmes out?

Parson Abel and Doc met the two men on the warehouse dock. Abel was bubbling with excitement. "Doc and I have been doing some talking."

"More like thinking out loud," Doc interrupted.

"And what have you two geniuses come up with?" Jesse said with all the sarcasm he could muster.

Doc turned on Parson Abel. "Now look what you started. You got Jones sounding like you, sarcasm and all."

"Ah, I didn't mean anything, Doc. I just felt like poking the bear a little to see what would happen." Jesse chuckled.

"Excuse me gentlemen, but I got work to do." Jimbo walked away in disgust. He had no time for idle chit-chat and was soon manhandling one end of a massive crate while three men half his size struggled with the other end.

"Anyway, Doc and I were talking about the phrase we keep hearing. The Good Book says that God helps those who help themselves."

"I told Parson I've heard that phrase a lot and he tells me that it's not in the Bible."

"It's not. But that's beside the point. The point is there are two men who are using that phrase. Remember, we heard Swan Holmes say that when he and his wife Beatrice were in our home? The other man is Bill DuFreeze."

"Parson and I have come to the conclusion that these two are in cahoots with each other," Doc said.

"I've come to the same conclusion," Jesse said.

"You have?" Doc's mouth flew open in amazement.

"Did you think the two of you have the market on think-ing?" Jones asked.

"The question is, if the three of us are thinking Swan Holmes is involved in cattle rustling, how do we prove it?" Parson Abel added.

"Let me show you what I found north of the Belt farm. It's in my saddlebag at the livery stable."

Doc and Parson Abel walked with Jesse the four blocks and were soon standing over Jesse's saddlebag near the stall holding his horse. A metal handle poked out of the saddleback but a cloth flap hid the object from view. Jesse undid the buckle on the saddlebag and produced a branding iron. He held it so both men could see the business end.

"What do you see?" asked Jones.

"A double B with a bar under it," said Doc.

"Yeah, this is a Double-B Bar branding iron. I found it a couple of miles north of my brother-in-law's place, buried under the sand. And you'll never guess who it's registered to. This here is the registered brand of Swan Holmes. I confirmed that with Sheriff Blanton a few minutes ago."

"That makes sense, Jesse." Parson Abel held the branding iron and pressed the brand into the dirt floor. It left an imprint. "The B stands for Beatrice, Swan Holmes' wife."

Someone darted from the stall next to Jesse's and hurriedly exited the stable. Jesse saw enough of the intruder to identify him.

"Slim Montrose. Gentlemen, things are about to get interesting."

THE SUN PLUNGED behind the sandhills. Spectacular colors reflected off the windows in Sheriff Blanton's office and set prisms of light dancing on his desk. Isaiah Blanton cleaned his revolver, giving his hands something to do.

Kodiak's visit unnerved him. He'd gotten the drop on him but wasn't placing much hope in doing so again. Blanton had no idea what Kodiak would do next. This not knowing set Blanton's nerves on edge and he was taking his nervousness out on his revolver.

"How many times are you gonna run your cleaning rag through the barrel?" Adam Potter sat at the table and while his body faced the door, his eyes were on Blanton. "I've counted five times so far."

"A clean gun is a reliable gun." Blanton never looked up from his cleaning.

"If it makes you feel any better, I'm nervous too," Potter said.

"You better be," Ace shouted from his jail cell. "You better be nervous. Kodiak's a comin' and all hell is comin' with him."

Flapjack and Spence laughed.

"Yeah. Why don't you save yerselves a lot of trouble and turn us loose," Flapjack yelled.

"And why don't you just shut yer mouth!" Potter fired back. He slammed shut the door separating the jail cells from the office. The door muted the taunting, but didn't eliminate it.

Two quick knocks on the front door drew the attention of Blanton and Potter. Potter laid his revolver on the table while Blanton fumbled to put his revolver together.

The door knob quickly turned.

Elizabeth Archer burst into the room.

"I brought you some supper." Elizabeth set the food hamper on the table and began emptying it. "It isn't much, but it will keep you from walking down to the Moore Hotel and getting ambushed." Her eyes met Potter's. "There are of lot of men with black bandanas in the streets. It's like they're waiting for something to happen."

"Liz, you shouldn't be here. This is a dangerous place," said Potter.

"Potter's right. It's not safe in here." Blanton finished reassembling his gun and looked up. "Go on back home."

Blanton looked out the window. "Trouble's brewin'." He rushed to shutter both windows, one on either side of the door, attempting to put a wooden barrier between the glass and his office.

"You, inside the office," someone shouted.

"What do you want?" Blanton answered.

"Send out yer prisoners and no one gets hurt."

"That ain't gonna happen," Blanton replied. He snatched a shotgun from the gun rack and loaded it. "I'm going outside."

"Liz, go out the back way," Potter said.

"But--" she said.

"Look," Potter interrupted, taking her in his arms. "I love you and don't want anything to happen to you."

Potter escorted Elizabeth to the back door, searched outside to discover the coast was clear and then ushered her into the alley. "Get as far away from here as you can. I'll come and get you when this thing blows over." He slammed the door in her face and turned in time to watch Blanton open the front door and step outside.

Someone outside grabbed Blanton's shotgun and it roared to life, hitting no one.

Four men shoved Blanton back inside. They cold cocked him and he dropped like a discarded rag doll.

Potter attempted to draw but the men were on him in a heartbeat. Steely fists pummeled his face. Blood spattered. Potter's head throbbed. The pain was excruciating. He felt his nose. It was askew.

Reeling and dizzy, he pitched forward and fell. His face met the floor.

Boots kicked into his ribs and belly.

His breath wheezed out.

He couldn't breathe in.

Everything went black.

CHAPTER FOURTEEN

From inside his office, Doc heard the shotgun blast. Bookwork could wait. He grabbed his hat, coat and medical bag, descended the stairs and followed the flow of townsfolk running in the direction of the sheriff's office.

"What's all the ruckus, Mayor?" Doc asked as he passed Claiborne Truax.

"There's been a lynching in front of the jail." Truax stopped to lean against a storefront. He was having trouble breathing.

"Are you alright, Claiborne?"

"Yeah. I just need to—catch my—breath—that's all."

Doc checked Claiborne's pulse. "I want to see you first thing in the morning."

"But, I'm alright, Doc. I'll rest here a minute and I'll be fine."

"If you don't take better care of yourself, you'll find yourself pushing up daisies on Boothill. Go along home now and be in my office at eight a.m."

Doc pushed his way through the crowd outside of Blanton's office. Someone in the crowd motioned to a lamppost nearby. A man was hanging from it, eyes wide open, but no longer seeing.

"Someone cut that man down," Doc yelled. "Take him over to the undertaker. I'll be over in a little while to confirm the cause of death."

Parson Abel arrived.

"That one won't need you tonight, parson. He's dead." Doc pointed in the direction of the men cutting the corpse down.

"What about inside?" Abel asked.

"Haven't made it in there yet." Doc stepped inside. Abel came in after.

Doc found Sheriff Blanton sprawled out near the door. He bent down to assess the injuries.

Parson Abel spotted another man behind the table. "Adam Potter's over here, Doc. He's taken a beating."

"Is he alive?"

Parson Abel got down on his knees. He gripped Potter's wrist and searched for a pulse. "Got a pulse, Doc."

"That's good. Blanton's got a big 'ol goose egg on the back of his head, but he's gonna be alright. He'll have a nasty headache for a few days."

Blanton tried to sit up, but Doc forced him to lie back down. "Stay put for a bit. You've got a nasty knot on your skull. I'm gonna go over and give Potter a look."

Doc found Potter in worse shape. He assisted Parson Abel in rolling Potter onto his back. Potters eyes were swollen shut. His nose broken. Blood everywhere. Doc spotted bloody boot prints all over Potter's midsection and thought *Dear God, it's a wonder he's still alive.*

Elizabeth Archer burst through the front door. "Adam?" she called out.

Parson Abel stopped Elizabeth from going any farther. "He's alive, Elizabeth, but he's taken one heck of a beating."

Elizabeth struggled to free herself. "Let me go to him. I want to see him."

Parson Abel held her fast. "Not right now you don't. Whoever it was kicked the snot out of him. You don't want to see him like that."

Doc looked up. "Elizabeth, go along home now. I'm gonna have to patch him up. It won't be pretty."

Elizabeth broke free from Parson Abel to join Doc on the floor. Her tears fell on Potter's disfigured face. "Adam. Adam, I love you. Don't die, Adam."

Doc pleaded with the distraught woman. "Elizabeth, he's going to be alright, but I have got to get him out of here. Abel, will you take care of her?"

Parson Abel took Elizabeth by the arm and coaxed her away. "Come on, let's give Doc some room."

"I need a couple of men in here to carry Potter to my office," Doc yelled at no one in particular. Three men soon lifted Potter from the floor and carried him from the building.

Doc knelt over Sheriff Blanton and helped him slowly to his feet before following the others.

KODIAK PLOPPED Ace's hat in the center of Bill DuFreeze's table. The one-armed man looked up at him and smiled.

DuFreeze took the hat by its rim and examined it. Sarcasm dripped from his lips like venom. "Where did you find this hat? And what is the man doing now that once wore it?"

Kodiak pulled out a chair and sat down. "Well, I found this hat in the street. It fell from the head that wore it. And what is the man doing now? Not much. He's just *hangin'* around."

DuFreeze burst into a belly laugh. This was his kind of humor. "Wonderful. Absolutely wonderful. I have to admit that your reply caught me off-guard. 'He's just hangin' around.' That's wonderful."

"I've got somethin' else for you," Kodiak announced.

"You do? Whatever could that be?" DuFreeze delight was child-like.

"Show him, boys," said Kodiak.

The mob in the Last Chance Saloon parted like the Red Sea. Flapjack and Spence paraded through.

DuFreeze stood. "Boys, I gotta tell you that Kodiak proved his worth tonight. In fact, all you Night Riders did. Belly up to the bar, boys, the drinks are on me. We're gonna take over this town and there ain't a man around who's gonna stop us."

The hootin,' hollerin,' and drinkin' lasted well into the night.

SHERIFF ISAIAH BLANTON opened his eyes. He looked around the room, unable to identify his surroundings. Where was he? At last his eyes focused on someone slumped in a nearby chair. It was Doc. He must be in Doc's office, but how did he get here? Blanton's head throbbed like the pounding of Indian tom toms. He fingered the lump on the back of his head. The pain was instantaneous and almost sent him through the ceiling. A wave of nausea flooded over him. He looked for a pan he could get sick in and tried to sit up.

"Whoa, hold on a moment." Doc was awake now and sitting up in his chair.

"I think I'm going to be sick," Blanton uttered.

Doc hurried across the room to stand over him. "Then lay yourself back down and close your eyes. You've got a knot on the back of yer head about the size of a half dollar."

"Yeah, I felt it." Blanton did as Doc instructed him. He squeezed his eyes closed in an attempt to stifle the queasiness.

"Keep your hands away from there you'll only make the nausea worse."

"I noticed that, too."

"Do you have any idea who did this to you?" Doc asked.

"I couldn't pick anyone out specifically, Doc. They were all wearing black bandanas over their faces."

Blanton thought for a moment and continued. "Wait a minute. I remember. Across the street there was someone I thought I knew. But everything happened so fast. I opened the door and next thing I know I'm waking up here."

"You said you thought you recognized someone?"

"Across the street." Blanton paused. "I think I'm gonna be sick, Doc."

"Remember to keep your eyes closed and stay still until the nausea passes."

Several minutes passed before Blanton could continue without gagging. "The man I saw. I think it was Kodiak. He had a black bandana. His face was hidden, but I recognized his clothes."

"That's a start," Doc said. "I sent a rider out to Jesse's cabin to fetch him. He should be here at any moment. I want you to rest."

Blanton tried to do as Doc suggested but a wave of panic set in and he tried to sit up again. "What about Potter, Doc? Is Potter alright?"

Hands on his shoulders, Doc forced him down. "Potter is in bad shape. I got him in my recovery room. It looks like someone used his face as a punching bag. He's got a broken nose. I sewed shut the gash over his right eye. He's got at least four broken ribs and God knows how much internal damage. I've given Potter laudanum so he can sleep."

"Will he pull through, Doc?"

"He's young. He's got that going for him, but it's gonna take a while before he's up and around. Can't say that for one of your prisoners."

"What do you mean?"

"The mob freed Spence and that other fella—"

"Flapjack."

"That's the one. Flapjack. But they strung Ace up. It's like they were making an example of him or somethin'."

"And I let it all happen." Blanton covered his face with his hands.

"I'm sure you did everything you could to prevent it."

"I should never have stuck my nose out the door. It all happened so fast. Someone grabbed my shotgun and it was lights out. If I'd have barricaded the door and stayed inside everything would have been different."

"You don't know that."

Sheriff Blanton struggled to sit up. This time Doc was unable to hold him down.

"I've got a job to do and I can't do it laying around in here."

Doc clamped his hands on Blanton's shoulders preventing him from standing. "Now, you listen here. You are in no shape to go chasing after anyone. When are you gonna get it through that thick skull of yours? You need to rest. Let Jones handle it when he gets here. Right now you're outmanned and outgunned. All you're gonna do is get yourself killed."

Jesse Jones burst through Doc's door. He had fire in his eyes. "Where is he, Doc?"

"Potter's in the other room, Jesse. He's hurt bad. I've done everything I can. He's still hasn't come to. Elizabeth has been with him the last hour or so."

Blanton sat up. This time Doc didn't try to hold him down.

"Jesse," Blanton said. "There was nothing we could do, there were too many of them."

Jesse stood next to the operating table where Blanton was doing everything he could to remain upright. "That's what I heard. I wish I'd stayed in town last night."

"Don't beat yourself up over this. No one knew this was coming." Blanton rested himself on one arm.

"That doesn't make me feel any better. I wasn't here to help my best friend when he needed me most."

"You're here now, aren't you?" Doc joined in. "You can't undo the past, Jesse, but you can impact the future."

Elizabeth Archer came through the recovery room door. Tears made a path down her cheeks. "He's asking for you, Jesse."

Doc took hold of Jesse's arm. "He's taken a beating. You may not recognize him under all my bandages."

"He's still my friend, Doc. Regardless of what he looks like." Jesse broke free of Doc's grasp and followed Elizabeth.

Doc was right. Jesse did not recognize his friend. Adam Potter's face was puffy and swollen under his blood-stained bandages. The flesh around his eyes was blackened by bruising and his hair matted with blood.

"Jesse." Potter's voice was forced and raspy.

Jesse knelt by Potter's bedside. "I'm here, Adam."

"I want you to promise me something, Jesse." Potter rested an injured hand on Jesse's head.

"Anything."

Potter drew in a heavy breath. His chest rattled. "Don't do anything stupid. Wait for me, okay?"

Potter's eyes closed. His hand fell limp at the side of the bed.

"Doc!" Elizabeth cried out.

Doc rushed in. Took one look at Potter and shoved Jones out of the way. He took Potter's limp arm in search of a pulse.

The room was bathed in silence.

Doc turned to Elizabeth. She covered her face with her hands and wept openly.

"He's not dead," Doc said. "I've got a pulse. It's faint, but it's still there. The best thing for him is rest. I want the two of you out of here." Doc shooed Jesse and Elizabeth from the room, followed, and closed the door behind them.

Jesse didn't know what to say. He wrapped Elizabeth in his arms. Her warm tears fell on his neck.

"It's going to be tough for the next week or so," Doc said. He sat at his desk and rubbed his chin. "I've done all I can. The healing is up to God."

"Jesse," Blanton said weakly. "I want you to bring Mayor Truax in. I want him to swear you in as acting sheriff until I'm up and around."

JESSE KNOCKED on the mayor's front door. It took several minutes of persistent knocking before Claiborne Truax peeked out the partially opened door.

"Do you have any idea what time it is?" Truax asked.

"Sheriff Blanton wants you to swear me in as acting sheriff," Jones announced.

"At three-thirty in the morning? All the ruckus at the Last Chance has kept me up. Can't this wait until morning, say ten o'clock or so?" Truax attempted to close the door, but Jesse wedged his boot between the door and doorframe preventing it.

"Blanton was hurt in the raid on his office last night."

"I know all about it. I was on the way there when Doc sent me home. I was having breathing troubles 'n Doc thought I was about to have a heart attack. Now, if you don't mind, remove your foot so I can go back to bed."

"Look, Mr. Mayor, right now I'm the only one standing in the way of an attack on the city."

"I think that's overly dramatic."

"Look there was a raid on the sheriff's office. Prisoners freed. There was a lynching. Sheriff Blanton was pistol whipped and Adam Potter beaten half to death. Someone's gotta be held accountable."

"In the middle of the night?"

"From what Blanton has told me, all the men were wearing black bandanas. And this isn't the first time these men have been involved in illegal activities. Men dressed like this were seen rustling cattle."

"Oh, for Pete's sake already, let's get this swearing in over with. I'll slip my boots on and be right out."

Mayor Truax followed Jesse. Truax attempted to tuck his nightshirt into his pants, but failed miserably. In the process the suspender over his right shoulder fell about his waist. He puffed his way up the boardwalk like a freight train pulling a heavy load.

Jesse bounded up the stairs to Doc's office. He turned around on the landing and saw Truax grab the railing.

"Steps. I hate steps." Truax had stopped. He wasn't going another step. He looked up at Jesse and yelled, "Can't we do the swearin' in down here? These steps will be the death of me."

"I'll see if Doc can get away long enough to serve as a witness," Jesse said.

"We need two witnesses. If you don't have two witnesses I'm going home," Traux puffed out.

In the middle of the night and in the middle of the street, Doc Hardesty and Elizabeth Archer stood on either side of Jesse Jones.

"Raise your right hand," Mayor Truax commanded. Jesse complied and Claiborne Truax continued, "Do you, Jesse Jones, swear to uphold the laws of the city of Sidney, in the State of Nebraska, so help you God."

"I do."

"Then by the authority vested in me by the citizens of this city, I appoint you acting sheriff."

Mayor Truax pinned a tin star on Jesse' chest.

CHAPTER FIFTEEN

Jesse took an uneasy cat-nap in Sheriff Blanton's office. The cot was hard and the only position he found comfortable was to sleep on his back. When he did sleep, Jesse's mind played scenes of things that could befall him if he chose to go against DuFreeze. It seemed the dream of his widowed wife and fatherless son was meant to dissuade him from the job he knew he had to do. He woke in a cold sweat.

The sun wasn't up when Jesse threw off the skimpy blanket that provided little warmth. He sat upright. His back ached. He wondered to himself if this ache was caused by the cot he slept on or if he was getting old?

Jesse found his answer in the mirror. The man looking back at him was familiar, but the furrows in his brow and flecks of grey in his hair and un-shaven beard were not. Neither were the pouches under his eyes or his bristly eyebrows. *Is it the years in my life or the life in my years?* he wondered.

He splashed water on his face. When Jesse opened his eyes again the tin star pinned to his shirt revived him. He had no time to waste thinking about aches and pains or contemplating life. There was a job to do. Justice to be meted out.

But, he was alone. Potter and Blanton were flat on their backs in Doc's office. They could not help against an army of desperados.

In the distance a trumpet sounded reveille. Jesse was not sure why he hadn't noticed the trumpet call lately. It had been an integral part of his life as a cavalryman. Maybe he didn't notice because he was a civilian now. He didn't know. But, he heard it today. Fort Sidney was awakening. Soldiers were readying themselves for breakfast.

Jesse was no longer alone. The help he needed was a mile away.

Arriving at Fort Sidney, Jesse was greeted by the sentry on duty. The sentry passed him off to a trooper to escort Jesse to the commanding officer's quarters. Jones was pleased that the sign above the commanding officer's door read Colonel Englewood, the officer in command who he had served under.

He knocked.

An orderly answered. "May I help you?"

"Jesse Jones to see Colonel Englewood."

"Do you have an appointment?" the orderly asked.

"It's alright, Arthur," a voice boomed. Colonel Englewood stood in an adjacent doorway. Englewood slid his suspenders over his shirt and extended his right hand.

"Good to see you, Jesse." The two men shook hands. "Does that star on your chest mean you're here on official business?"

"It does. I'm going to need your help. You've probably heard by now that some men stormed the jail and that Potter and Blanton were injured in the fracas."

"Yeah, I heard. Let's talk about that over some breakfast. You hungry? Wasn't there a lynching?" Englewood led the way into the dining room.

Jesse followed. "A man named Ace."

Colonel Englewood pointed to a chair. "Have a seat, Jesse." Jesse sat and Englewood poured coffee. "So how can I help?"

"I wonder if you can spare a few men? Someone is rustling cattle from the Coad brothers and I'd like to find out who's behind it and what they're doing with the cattle."

"Must be running them north to the Red Cloud Agency." Englewood sat down and helped himself to a bowl of scrambled eggs.

"That makes sense because they're not shipping cattle east from town or selling them to you." Jesse sipped his coffee. "Can you send a couple of men north to check into that?"

"Absolutely. If someone is rustling cattle and selling them to a government agency, I can involve my troops in a civilian matter."

Colonel Englewood sent an orderly to fetch Sergeant Major Kelly. Within minutes the rotund Sergeant Major joined Jones and Englewood.

Kelly snapped to attention and saluted. He stood ramrod straight and held his chest high.

"At ease, Sergeant Major," said Englewood.

The Sergeant Major's chest fell. "Thank you, sir."

"Did I take you away from mess this morning, Sergeant Major?" Englewood asked.

"No, sir. But I will take a wee nip of your coffee, sir. I missed my second cup." Kelly spotted Jones. "Jonzie, my boy, how are ya? I haven't seen you in a long while."

Jesse extended his hand and Kelly took it. "Sergeant Major," he said.

"So what brings you to Fort Sidney?" Kelly asked.

Englewood handed Kelly a cup of coffee. "Jones and I have been talking about that. Let's be seated, gentlemen."

After everyone was seated, Englewood looked across the table at Kelly and continued. "Sergeant Major, Mr. Jones has brought to my attention a little matter that now involves the U.S. Army. Do you want to tell him, Mr. Jones?"

"Yes, sir," Jesse began. "Someone is rustling J.F. Coad's cattle. I got a hunch that the rustlers work for a one-armed man named Bill DuFreeze. What I think they're doing is rebranding the cattle and selling them."

"I've seen that man around town," Kelly said. "Usually hangs out with a bunch of men all wearing black bandanas."

"That's the one," said Jesse. "Since the rustlers are not selling the stolen livestock in town, then the next logical place is up north at the Red Cloud Agency. I know that one large herd wearing the Double-B Bar brand went through Camp Clarke awhile back. That brand belongs to Swan Holmes."

"The banker?" Englewood asked.

"Yes," said Jones.

"Beggin' your pardon, Jonzie. If the rustlers drove the cattle through Camp Clarke couldn't they follow the Oregon Trail and be a-drivin' the cattle to Fort Laramie?"

"Don't think so, Sergeant Major," Jesse responded. "I'm thinking they want to sell the cattle as far away from here as possible. But, I could be wrong."

"You can look into that when you lead some men north. Take a couple of Indian scouts with you and see if they can find the rustler's trail," said Englewood. "Find out where they're selling their cattle."

"At this point," said Kelly, "it looks like we have two options for where the rustlers are takin' their herd. They're either takin' them to Fort Laramie or to the Red Cloud Agency."

"Fort Robinson is near the Red Cloud Agency. So, Sergeant

Major, if your scouts find that the rustlers headed north, ride into Fort Robinson. Start your investigation from there," Englewood said.

"And when would the colonel like me to begin?"

"Sergeant Major, I would like you to report to the quartermaster and draw two-week's rations, a supply wagon and ammunition.

"Beggin' yer pardon, sir. What company would you like me lead?"

"That's entirely up to you, Sergeant Major."

Sergeant Major Kelly looked at Jones. "Sir, if you don't mind I'd like to ride in front of Jonzie's old company."

"Company A," Jesse said with a nod.

"Company A," Kelly repeated.

Jesse was present that afternoon when Sergeant Major Kelly stood before Colonel Englewood.

Sergeant Major Kelly saluted. "Sir, I have assembled the men of Company A and drawn the supplies as ordered. I'm requestin' permission to lead these men on the mission assigned to us."

Englewood returned Kelly's salute. "Permission granted, and may God speed, Sergeant Major."

Sergeant Major Kelly mounts and rode to the front of his men. He looked down and gave Jesse a wink before facing forward. "Company A by twos. At a trot," he shouted.

Jesse watched Sergeant Major Kelly lead the men of his old company north in search of answers as elusive as dust in the wind.

Bill DuFreeze stood in front of the Last Chance Saloon watching from a distance as a company of troopers headed north through town. It was not unusual for troopers to leave town. There were reports of isolated bands of Indians raiding settlers along the Mormon Trail.

DuFreeze pushed through the swinging door and stepped inside the saloon. The place was busy. Faros tables were full. Men stood two-deep at the bar. A cigarette haze burned the eyes of those not accustomed to it. One-armed Bill DuFreeze was accustomed to it. He pushed his way through the crowded saloon and found his usual table. Kodiak Crabtree, Slim Montrose and Stetson Burnett were already seated. Only one chair remained. His chair.

"Got some troopers headed north again." DuFreeze pulled his chair and sat.

"My bet is on an Indian hunting party killing livestock," Montrose said.

"Won't be long and they'll all be on a reservation," said Stetson. "I'm hearing that Custer is leading the Seventh Cavalry on a mission to round up Sitting Bull and Crazy Horse."

"Custer is an arrogant cuss. Thinks he's invincible. That's what I heard," Kodiak added. "He's more apt to be killed than anything."

"Wanna bet?" Montrose said. "Two to one that Custer gets 'em all."

Bill DuFreeze put a halt to any further arguments. He pounded his fist on the table. "Do your arguing on your own time. We got work to do."

DuFreeze took a folded piece of crisp white paper from his pocket. He unfolded it and placed it on the table.

Stetson stood next to DuFreeze and peered over his right shoulder. "So what am I looking at?"

"A layout of the bank."

"Which one?" Montrose peered over DuFreeze's left shoulder.

"Swan Holmes' Bank. Got a source inside the bank that drew this for me."

"Are we gonna rob it?" Stetson asked.

"There's a shipment of gold coming out of Deadwood in a week. My sources say about two-hundred thousand dollars worth. It'll be too heavily guarded for us to rob in route. But, once it's in the bank, that'll be another story."

"I'm thinkin' that's your explanation for where the troopers are headed," Kodiak joined in. "They're riding north to accompany the gold."

"The gold arrives in Sidney and it stays here three days before heading east on a train. We gotta get into the bank overnight on the third day," DuFreeze continued.

"And make a withdrawal," said Montrose. "I like it. I like it a lot."

"Mind if I take a look at the layout?" Kodiak asked.

DuFreeze slid the map in front of Kodiak.

"Did any of you notice the number of guards stationed inside the bank the last time we were there? I count six in the main part of the bank and four in reserve. We can't just go waltzing in there. It would be committing suicide," Kodiak said.

"Kodiak's right," said DuFreeze. "But God helps those who help themselves. And we're gonna help ourselves to all that gold. We'll need a diversion. Something to get the guards out of the bank so we can do our job."

"It's got to be something inside the bank that chases them out into the street," Montrose said.

"Once in the street the guards will be sittin' ducks for our rifles." Stetson smiled to himself.

"A fire," Kodiak announced. "A fire inside the bank will chase everyone out."

"You know, Kodiak," DuFreeze said, "I like the way you think."

"Now the question becomes how do we get a fire started inside the bank?" Kodiak asked.

A young man approached the table. DuFreeze recognized the young man as J.F. Coad's teenaged son. DuFreeze attempted to fold the layout of the bank with one hand, but failed. He wadded the paper and stuck it in his trouser pocket.

"Mr. DuFreeze," the young man said.

"Yes, Ben, what is it?"

"My father's over at the Moore Hotel. He'd like to have a word with you."

DuFreeze walked down the street toward the Moore Hotel with J.F. Coad's son by his side. DuFreeze noticed that the young man was trying to grow out his beard.

"You got a great stand of peach fuzz on yer face, Benjamin." DuFreeze couldn't resist tormenting J.F.'s youngest son. "What does yer pa think of you attempting to grow a beard?"

"He thinks I should wait until I'm a couple of years older."

"Your first attempt at defiance, huh?" DuFreeze replied. "I'm betting that you're not man enough yet to win that argument. Besides, I don't blame him for that. You got a lot of bald spots on yer face. Makes everyone wonder if you're part Cheyenne. Their beards always come in all splotchy like."

Ben stopped walking and looked directly into DuFreeze's eyes. "Pa wouldn't like it if he knew you were talking to me like this."

DuFreeze stared Ben down. "Yeah, but yer pa ain't here and you ain't gonna tell him. Ya know that if you do, I'll kill ya."

Ben made a crude attempt to draw his gun. DuFreeze swiftly slapped it out of his hand and into the street. "Don't you ever try that again, sonny boy. I don't care who yer pa is. Now, pick it up."

The two men walked in silence the remainder of the walk. DuFreeze turned his head occasionally to get a glimpse of Ben. DuFreeze smiled contentedly to himself. Ben never turned toward him, but kept his eyes looking straight ahead.

J.F. Coad waved the men to his table in the restaurant of the Moore Hotel.

"Have a seat," Coad said.

DuFreeze noticed Coad's steel grey eyes. *Doggone if that little pip-squeak of a son ain't got his daddy's eyes.*

A waitress hustled over to Coad's table. "Are you ready to order now, Mr. Coad?"

"Give me a thick cut of steak with mashed potatoes and some of your white gravy," J.F. responded.

The waitress turned to DuFreeze who had seated himself next to J.F. "And you, sir?"

"Steak sounds good to me, too," DuFreeze said.

"I'll have the same," Ben announced before the waitress could ask him. She disappeared into the kitchen.

"Well, Mr. DuFreeze, how are you progressing on getting my cattle back?" Coad asked.

The question caught DuFreeze off-guard and he fumbled around for an answer. "What cattle, sir?"

"The thousand or so head that someone rustled from me. You do know about that, don't you? That's why I pay you so handsomely. You would tell me if there were missing cattle."

"I don't have any idea what you're talking about."

DuFreeze caught himself squirming in his chair and forced himself to sit still.

"Doc Hardesty was out at the ranch a few days ago," Coad began. "He brought a man with him named Jesse Jones. Jones said he suspects that you stole my cattle and are trying to frame his brother-in-law to get his ranch."

"Why would I want to do that?"

"That's what I'd like to know. Is Mr. Jones telling me the truth or not? I've known Doc Hardesty a long time and he's not known to frequent with liars. Is Mr. Jones lying, Mr. DuFreeze?"

DuFreeze made no reply.

"Mr. DuFreeze, you were supposed to drive my cattle north to the Red Cloud Agency and sell them. Did you do that?"

DuFreeze noticed how much Ben was enjoying watching him squirm. He didn't dare not respond.

"Yes, sir. We did."

"Then why didn't you bring the money back to the ranch as I asked you to do? You do have my money, do you not?"

"Uh, not on me, sir." DuFreeze was trapped and he knew it. "I gambled some of it away," he said at last.

"I'm leaving town in four days," Coad said. "I'll give you until then to return all of my money. After that you and I are through. Now get out of my sight."

As he left the restaurant DuFreeze heard the waitress ask what she should do with DuFreeze's steak and Coad said, "Throw it to the dogs."

And Ben was laughing.

CHAPTER SIXTEEN

DuFreeze tossed and turned in his squeaky hotel bed. He tried desperately to get comfortable, but couldn't. No matter what he did he could not wipe away the sting of his mistreatment. Coad had fired him. Worse still, Coad's puppy of a son had laughed at him. Compounding the memories of his mistreatment, a stifling humidity hung over the night. DuFreeze's clothing clung to him like stink on a skunk.

The air in his room was so thick he found it hard to breathe. He opened a window to let in some air.

Nothing.

No cool breeze.

Only stillness.

A humidity laced stillness.

The autumn moon peeked from behind a wisp of clouds and lit up his room as if to mock his inability to sleep.

DuFreeze heard the unmistakable buzz of mosquitoes and horse flies. They flew about his face looking for a place to land and administer welt-raising bites.

With the only arm left to him he slammed the window

shut with a thud. The window pane cracked under the weight of his anger.

"Would you knock it off up there?" someone yelled.

"Yeah. You woke me up," yelled someone else.

Everyone else is sleeping and I'm in agony and can't sleep. Everything annoys me. This must be what hell is like.

DuFreeze left his dingy hotel room and found Kodiak Crabtree's room in the same hotel.

He knocked several times before someone stirred.

"Go away," a sleepy voice said.

"Kodiak, its DuFreeze. Let me in."

"Why should I?"

"'Cuz if I'm miserable someone is gonna be miserable with me."

The door opened a crack and DuFreeze saw two eyes looking at him from inside the room. He pushed himself in.

"I can't sleep," DuFreeze announced.

"What does that have to do with me?"

"I wanna get rid of that little peck 'a wood." DuFreeze spun the lone chair in the room around and sat on it. "He laughed at me."

"Who did?"

"Coad's sissy of a son, Benjamin."

"Earlier in the evening you were more interested in the bank job and using some of the money to pay back Coad. You've changed your mind?" Kodiak asked.

"When I was trying to sleep all I could see was that little imp laughing at me. Coad told the waitress to throw my steak to the dogs and that little brat sat there and laughed."

"Maybe we can do several things at once. Maybe we can rob the bank, kill the kid in the crossfire, and Jones, too."

DuFreeze thought a moment. "Why in the world should I consider paying Coad back? He fired me. I don't owe him anything. I got manpower and guns enough to get what I want."

"Now you're talkin."

"Here's what I want you to do. First thing in the morning send a message to all the Night Riders. Have them meet me at the brandin' spot at midnight. We're gonna pull off the most spectacular raid; a raid so spectacular future generations will read about what we done. What I'm thinkin' about will make Quantrill's raid on Lawrence, Kansas look like child's play by comparison."

"What do you have in mind?"

"No, sir. I ain't a gonna tell nobody just yet," DuFreeze announced. "I gotta run the whole thing by my boss first. He may have other plans, but I think I can talk him into somethin' that will put Sidney on the map and make him the wealthiest man in Cheyenne County."

"Wealthier than J.F. Coad?"

"Yep."

"Then Henry T. Clarke?"

"Wealthier than the two of 'em put together." One-armed Bill DuFreeze walked over to Kodiak's bed and sprawled out on it. He tucked his arms under his head and smiled up at the ceiling. "Now get outta here. I'm gonna take me a snooze and then walk on over to the bank."

ADAM POTTER WOKE in Doc's recovery room. He had spent his night in pain. His broken ribs kept him painfully aware of their existence by making breathing a chore. Doc had cautioned Potter's visitors to not make Potter laugh but that only encouraged Jones and Parson Abel to do just the opposite. Sneezing was worse than laughing. Potter tried to stifle them. Yet even the tiniest sneeze doubled him over with pain.

There were headaches as well. Nasty headaches accompanied by waves of nausea. Doc had placed a chair at Potter's bedside. That chair held a white enamel basin within arm's reach for those times when nausea overwhelmed him.

Doc dispensed laudanum to assuage Potter's pain. He discovered the reddish-brown liquid to be extremely bitter and this morning he refused to down the spoonful Doc offered him.

"I don't mind your refusal at all," Doc said. "I've been reading medical articles saying laudanum is addictive. They say Wyatt Earp's wife is addicted to the stuff. Got someone in my outer office who has been waiting since before sun up for you to wake up. Do you want me to send her in?"

"Elizabeth?"

"I know a confirmed bachelor like you ain't gonna want ta hear this, but I think she's stuck on you." Doc waited for Potter's reply. Instead Potter sighed. "Yep," said Doc. "Yer twitterpated alright. I'll send her in."

Elizabeth peeked around the door. "Can I come in?"

"Please do," Potter replied.

"Your friends Jones and Parson Abel have been here a lot. I almost got the impression that you didn't have time for me. So I got up early to get here before the others. How are you feeling?"

Elizabeth stood at Potter's bedside.

Potter took hold of her hand. "I'm feeling much better now that you're here."

"Doc says that you'll be up and about in a day or two."

"That's if the nausea goes away."

"You're best friends with that basin, are you?"

Potter looked up into Elizabeth's eyes. "Yea, that basin is my constant companion."

"Things sure got a little crazy the other night. Did you know they hung one of the men Blanton had in jail?"

"Yeah, Jesse told me." Potter remembered the night. "They overwhelmed us and there was nothing we could do to stop 'em."

"You're just lucky to be alive." Elizabeth bent down and kissed Potter. "And I'm glad you are."

"Me, too," Potter replied. "What do you think your mother would say if I asked you to marry me?"

"Is that the laudanum talking or are you serious?"

"Didn't take any laudanum this morning."

"I thought maybe you had, because everyone around here seems to think you're planning to stay a bachelor."

Potter smiled. "I think I know my own mind."

"If this is you in your right mind, then I accept."

They kissed carefully because of his broken nose.

Doc entered and removed the romance from the room. "I hate to interrupt your attempt to convert a bachelor into a married man, Elizabeth, but Jesse is here to see him."

Jesse barged in. "How ya feeling? Doc says you'll be up and around in a day or two. Gonna need your help."

"Whoa! Hold your horses, Jesse," Doc said. "I said he'd be up and around. What I didn't say is that it would be another week or two before he's worth anything."

"C'mon, doc. I'll be alright once this nausea goes away," Potter replied.

"And that may take another week or two. That's what I'm trying to tell you."

"You're really going to try to be ready in a day or two?" Elizabeth asked.

"I am. Jesse and I have been through a lot together. I'm not about to let him down."

"What about me?" she asked.

Potter tugged on her hand until she bent and he kissed her again. "I won't let you down, either."

THE HOME of Wade and Esther Blanton was snuggled among the elm trees a mile west of town. Wade had purchased the land and the home from an early Cheyenne County settler when he moved further west to get away from all the people. Originally the house had been no more than a fur trapper's cabin. Wade had squared up the walls and reinforced them. He'd added two rooms and seamlessly attached them to the old cabin. From any angle it was viewed it looked as if the old cabin and the two new rooms were constructed at the same time. It was Esther's touch that made this house a home.

Wade sat on his front porch alone with his thoughts. Doc had sent him home to recuperate from the beating he'd sustained during the raid on his office. Being laid up gave Wade a chance to contemplate his life as Sidney's lone peace officer. Sure, he'd been fortunate to have several deputies working under him, and none more dependable than Jones and Potter. But the responsibility of keeping the peace had always rested on him.

Wade remembered Parson Abel telling him years ago 'uneasy is the head that wears the crown.'

"What does that mean?" Wade had asked.

"It means that men entrusted with great responsibility carry a heavy burden and that heavy burden makes it difficult to rest," Abel had told him.

Wade took a wad of tobacco and pressed it into his pipe. With a single strike, a match head sparked to life to set the tobacco afire. A blue halo surrounded his head before disappearing.

"You look comfy," Esther said. She sat in a nearby chair.

"I've been doing a whole lot of thinking lately."

"I'll bet that hurt," said Esther as an impish smile crossed her lips.

"Your sense of humor is one of the many things I love about you," Wade replied.

Esther took his hand in hers. "What have you been thinking about?"

"About us." He took another drag of his pipe and blew two perfect smoke rings. "Life is kinda like smoke rings."

"What do you mean?"

"Well, smoke rings start out well, but soon disappear. Life starts out the same way. Perfect. Grand. But, the next thing you know life disappears and it's over."

"What are you saying? Do you think your life is over?

"No, I'm not saying that. What I am saying is that I'm starting to question what my life has been all about. What do I have to show for it?"

"You have a town that respects you."

"That's true. But I'm beginning to take stock of my life. I've come to realize I haven't been home very much over the last ten years."

"I haven't complained about that, have I?" she asked.

"No, you haven't. And I love you for that. But being married to me hasn't been easy. All those evenings you prepared a meal and I never came home. Those times I promised to take you to North Platte to see your sister and I couldn't go with you because I had to work."

"You really have been thinking, haven't you?"

"I've just realized what Parson Abel meant when he said 'uneasy is the head that wears the crown.' I'm tired, Esther. I'm ready to let another man wear the star. Tomorrow morning I'm going to ride into town and let Mayor Truax know I'm quitting." Wade Blanton turned to his wife. "Does that scare you?"

"No, Wade. This is what I've wanted for a long, long time."

"That decides it. I'll ride in tomorrow and tell the mayor he can change Jesse's title from acting sheriff to sheriff." He took a drag on his pipe and breathed out a smoke-filled sigh.

JESSE HAD SPENT another night alone in the jailhouse. He tried unsuccessfully to make the cot comfortable. None of the thin blankets removed from the jail cells padded the cot enough to allow him to sleep. Somewhere in the middle of the night he'd determined the futility of his effort. He'd struck a match to the lantern and spent his sleepless hours playing solitaire.

After sunrise, Jesse walked the streets of town to make his presence known among the citizens as they went about their workaday lives. About noon he paused for lunch in the restaurant of the Moore Hotel.

"May I join you, Jesse?" Jesse recognized the voice of Mayor Truax and turned in his chair to face him. To his astonishment the mayor was not alone. Bill DuFreeze and Kodiak Crabtree were with him.

"What are these two men doing with you?" Jones asked.

"May we join you?" Truax asked a second time.

"Suit yourselves," Jesse replied returning to his lunch.

After the men seated themselves Mayor Truax began. "Jesse, I had a nice long talk with Wade this morning. It seems that he's decided to resign as sheriff."

"That comes as a bit of a surprise," Jesse said.

"It did to me as well," Truax said. "Wade said it's been a long time since he had much in the way of time off. That he's tired. It took the incident of a few nights ago to make him realize he's ready to give up his star."

"So, what are these two men doing here? Wade told me that one was involved in the scuffle." Jesse nodded toward Kodiak.

"That's a lie!" In a heart-beat Kodiak stood to face Jesse, hand on his gun. The commotion drew the attention of everyone in the restaurant.

"Now, now, Mr. Crabtree," said Truax trying to calm Kodiak. "It's all a simple misunderstanding."

"Are you calling Sheriff Blanton a liar?" Jesse countered.

"Ex-sheriff, Mr. Jones," Truax said. He returned his attention to Kodiak. "Do sit down, Mr. Crabtree. You are attracting a lot of needless attention."

Kodiak plopped himself down in his chair and continued to glare at Jesse.

"I think it's high time I cut to the chase, Jesse. The city council met this morning to consider Wade Blanton's resignation. Our newest council member suggested that we reluctantly accept his resignation. Which we did. Wade has served us well the last ten years."

"And just what does all of this have to do with me?" Jesse asked.

"I'm afraid, Jesse, that I am going to have to ask you for your badge."

"Wade asked me to step in until he was healed."

"And Wade resigned this morning," DuFreeze butted in, "and that means you are out of a job. The job of lawman, that is. You can go back to working fulltime in your measly little mercantile."

"Wade resigned and I'm out. Is that it?" Jesse asked. "Sounds like I've been railroaded. And I don't like it."

"Whoa. Hold on, Jesse," Truax interrupted. "It's not like

that at all. Why, it was all nice and legal. Wade resigned. The city council met, and I was asked to appoint, Mr. DuFreeze as the city's new sheriff. I'm simply carrying out the will of the city council."

"I know for a fact Wade wanted me to succeed him as sheriff if and when he decided to call it quits."

"That's well and good but the city council and the mayor has decided otherwise," Kodiak joined in.

"I'm sorry, Jesse, but I'll have to ask for your badge." Mayor Truax extended his hand to retrieve the tin star.

Jesse saw Kodiak slide his hand off the table and rest it on his gun butt.

"Alright, Mr. Mayor, as you wish." Jesse took the star off his shirt and tossed it onto the middle of the table. "So just who is this councilman who has so much influence?"

"Swan Holmes," Truax answered. "Don't cross him, Jesse."

CHAPTER SEVENTEEN

Parson Abel's parlor served as an impromptu meeting place where Jesse Jones gathered his friends to discuss the morning's events. Doc and the parson sat side-by-side on the settee. Potter made himself comfortable behind Abel's desk, while Wade Blanton stood in the middle of the room with Jesse.

"I'm not sure how this all happened," Jesse said. "But sure looks like Swan Holmes is making a bid to take over the town."

"And if it looks like a duck and walks like a duck, I'd say chances are pretty good that it is a duck," Doc added.

"So, Mayor Truax and the city council are in Swan's pocket?" Abel asked.

"That's the report I'm hearing around town," Jesse said.

"I'm hearing the same thing," added Blanton.

Parson Abel shook his head. "I knew there was something peculiar about Swan Holmes from the get-go. Anybody who believes 'God helps those who help themselves,' can't be trusted any further than you can throw them."

"There is one good thing that's come out of all of this," Potter said. "At least now we know the lay of the land."

"That we do," said Jesse. "What we don't know is what it all means…"

"…or what to do about it," said Doc.

"How long do you think it will be before Holmes comes after us and our lucrative contract to run supplies to Camp Clarke?" Parson Abel said.

"Not very long," Blanton said. "I'm getting reports that DuFreeze has named Kodiak as his deputy. That means Holmes is consolidating power. How long before all those men wearing blank bandanas will fan out to do Swan's bidding?"

"We got us a problem bordering on a conundrum," said Doc.

Parson Abel wasted little time in finding this an appropriate moment for some verbal sparring with Doc. "Why, Doc," he said. "That's out of character for you. I had no idea, no idea at all, that you knew a three-syllable word."

"It may surprise you to know that I know a whole passel of three-syllable words. I went to medical school you know."

"I can vouch for Doc," Potter joined in. "He went to medical school alright. He patched me up pretty good."

"And me, too," Blanton added.

"Well, how about that. Not only does Doc know a three-syllable word, but he's got friends, too. Who would have thunk it?" Abel grinned and even Doc laughed.

"The question seems to be how will all of us as Doc's friends respond to the take-over of our town?" said Jesse.

"Great question," Blanton said.

"We need a trump card of some kind. An ace up our sleeve," Potter joined in.

"And what might that ace up our sleeve look like?" Doc asked.

"We need a lawman with more authority than can be given by a local municipality," Abel wondered aloud.

"A federal lawman," Potter said.

"That's it!" Blanton announced. "We need a federal marshal with the authority to clean up this mess."

"Now, just how do we go about getting a federal marshal in here?" Doc asked.

"I've got an even better idea. How about we send Jesse to Omaha to visit with the federal judge there and seek an appointment as a federal marshal? All of us can write a brief letter of recommendation expressing the need for federal intervention," Blanton said.

"You know that might work except for the fact it will take more than one man to face down Swan and his gang," Abel said. "Besides we haven't really asked Jesse if he felt he was up to the task. He's got a wife and a little one."

Jesse Jones became the focal point of every eye in the room.

"There comes a time when someone has to stand in the breach. Martha understands," Jesse said.

WITH THE GOLD shipment arriving in five days, Swan Holmes moved swiftly to consolidate his power. The unforeseen resignation of Sheriff Blanton had sped up the process. The city had obliged Holmes by appointing 'One-arm' Bill DuFreeze as Blanton's replacement. That appointment put the law in Holmes' hip pocket.

"And I intend to make full use your appointment." Swan Holmes looked up from the paper he was writing on.

"What do you have in mind?" DuFreeze asked with a wry grin.

"I want you to deliver these papers to Jesse Jones over at

Swede's Mercantile. Tell him the bank wants him out of the warehouse. We're foreclosing and I want him out. Put Kodiak in charge there. Have him send a rider north to let Henry T. Clarke know that from now on we're supplying his bridge project and we're upping the price one hundred percent."

"Yes, sir."

"And, Sheriff." Swan Holmes handed DuFreeze a second piece of paper and a key. "Our little plan to rob the bank when the gold arrives is still on. Here's the combination to the vault and a key to the back door. I like the idea of starting a fire to get the guards outside. Bring the chuck wagon and load the gold in it. Have Montrose drive Coad's cattle that remain in town north through town that night. That'll give us extra cover as we pull off the bank job."

"I get it. The chuck wagon with all the gold will look like it's part of the trail drive."

Holmes nodded. "Have Montrose rebrand the cattle in the usual spot and drive them north and sell them at the Red Cloud Agency. But, send the chuck wagon east with a half dozen men to North Platte to where it hits the Oregon Trail. We'll split up the gold and divide the cash when I arrive at North Platte."

"Doesn't sound to me like you plan to stay in Sidney."

Swan Holmes chuckled aloud. "Never did like this little piss-ant town. My wife and I plan to move back to southern Missouri, somewhere around Joplin. You know what you need to do, DuFreeze, and you've got five days until the gold arrives to coordinate everything."

"I'm headin' south as well. Gonna settle around St. Joe. Us southern boys need to stay in the south."

Holmes led DuFreeze to the door of his office and opened it. "Yes, well that's all very well and good. But for now, Mr. DuFreeze, I bid you a very pleasant adieu."

BILL DUFREEZE LIKED the idea of kicking Jones out of the warehouse himself, but thought better of it. Not that he wouldn't enjoy the task, but knowing Kodiak would enjoy it far more. After all, Kodiak had been nursing a grudge against Jones and often talked about the standoff at the warehouse. Yes, DuFreeze thought, this would be a fitting opportunity for Kodiak to remove Jones once and for all.

Kodiak arrived at Sheriff DuFreeze's office.

"I'm deputizing you and givin' you an assignment," said DuFreeze. "So raise yer right hand."

Kodiak did.

"Do you, Kodiak swear to uphold the law to the best of yer ability, so help you God?"

"I do."

"Pin this badge on ya so everything is all legal like." After Kodiak finished pinning on his badge, DuFreeze handed him the paper Swan Holmes gave him. "The bank has changed its mind about Jesse Jones leasing their warehouse. Swan Holmes wants him out. We're taking over selling supplies to Camp Clarke. See to it that Jones is out of the warehouse by this time tomorrow."

"With pleasure. Been lookin' for an excuse to put Jones in Boot Hill. This looks like the perfect reason."

"And legal, too," DuFreeze added. "I want you to send a couple of riders to Camp Clarke and break the news of the change to Henry T. Clarke. Tell him we're doubling his prices."

"That ain't gonna make Mr. Clarke very happy," said Kodiak.

"Tell him he can take it or leave it. It's up to him. If he

wants to build a fancy bridge an all, it's gonna cost him more to do it."

DuFreeze reached into a desk drawer and drew out a handful of tin stars. "Take a few of the night riders with you when you go to see Jones."

"Don't need anyone to help me."

"You never know what you might run into," said DuFreeze. "It might be that Jones tries to resist arrest. We want this to be nice and legal. You may need a witness or two if ya gotta kill him."

"I would feel terrible if I had to kill him." Kodiak smiled. "That would be a shame."

"Yeah, and it could be that Adam Potter gets in the way, too."

"It could happen."

"But you will have witnesses, legal witnesses who will swear that you killed them in the line of duty, won't you?"

"All neat and tidy."

"Neat and tidy and completely legal," DuFreeze added.

Kodiak took Slim, Stetson and a half dozen other men on the five block walk from the Last Chance Saloon to the warehouse Jones had leased from Swan Holmes. The men stood shoulder-to-shoulder and all carried rifles except Montrose who toted a scatter gun. There was no mistaking these men were serious about the business they had in mind. Townsfolk scattered. Some peered through windows to get a look at what all the fuss was about.

Jimbo Livingston was overseeing a crew of men loading four wagons bound for Camp Clarke when he saw Kodiak and his gang bearing down on them.

"We got company, boys," Jimbo shouted. In response the men dropped what they were doing and looked up the street. Jimbo noticed that one of the men wore a badge. Grabbing his gun belt and putting it on, he stood in the street to await the lawman's arrival. His teamsters gathered behind him. They had armed themselves with pieces of lumber.

"Greetings, Sheriff. What can we do for ya?" asked Jimbo.

"Let me be clear, I ain't the sheriff," Kodiak indignantly fired back. "I'm deputy sheriff and I want you and your men to drop your weapons."

Jimbo unbuckled his gun belt and it fell to the ground. "Do as yer told boys." Behind him the teamsters did as Jimbo commanded. "Now, what's this all about?"

Kodiak removed the paper DuFreeze had given him and handed it to Jimbo. "You and your men are to vacate the premises at once by order of Sheriff DuFreeze. That there paper says that the bank is withdrawing its lease to Jesse Jones and his business known as Swede's Mercantile."

"I'm gonna have to take yer word for that," Jimbo replied, "cuz I can't read. I can see to it that Jesse gets this paper."

"You do that. And tell that highfalutin' boss of yers," Kodiak spit out the words, "that Mister Henry T. Clarke from now on is buying his supplies from Mr. Swan Holmes, who owns this here warehouse. I want it to be made very clear. From now on any shipment of supplies heading to Camp Clarke will cost double. And that includes anything you got aboard these wagons."

"That ain't gonna make Mr. Clarke very happy," Jimbo announced.

"Well, you tell Mr. Clarke for me that anytime he doesn't pay what's owed, me and the boys will ride north to take it outta his hide."

JESSE WAS NOWHERE near the warehouse when Kodiak issued his ultimatum. He had returned home following his request to meet with a Federal Judge in Omaha. Although he and Martha had discussed his probable appointment as sheriff, they had not discussed an appointment as Marshal.

With Jesse Junior snuggled in his bed for his afternoon nap, Jesse broached the subject.

"I want to let you know that Mayor Truax has not appointed me Sheriff," he began.

"I thought something was up when you came home without your badge. Oh, Jesse, I'll bet you are terribly disappointed." Martha wrapped her arms about his neck. "So, did they appoint Potter as sheriff instead?"

"No, it seems that a new member of the council took them in a different direction entirely. The city council appointed Bill DuFreeze instead."

"Wasn't he John Coad's right hand man until recently?"

"That the one alright. Now he's the new sheriff. He's already appointed Kodak his deputy. I see nothing but disaster ahead."

"So, who was the councilman that swayed everything Bill DuFreeze's way?" Martha asked.

"Swan Holmes."

"The owner of the bank?"

"One and the same. I've got a feeling his phrase 'God helps those who help themselves' has taken on a whole new meaning."

"Isn't Kodiak the man behind the sheriff's office raid that injured Sheriff Blanton and nearly killed Adam Potter?"

"You are doing a good job of putting two and two together."

"But, that doesn't mean that this whole thing adds up. Kodiak is also associated with the gang that hangs out at the Last Chance Saloon."

Jesse smiled down at Martha.

"Something has to be done to prevent the takeover of Sidney. Has anyone thought of that?" she continued.

"That's what I need to talk to you about," said Jesse. "Let's sit down at the table and talk through the suggestion Wade Blanton made this morning."

They sat and Jesse took her hand.

"Wade suggested that I travel to Omaha and seek an appointment as a Federal Marshall. That would give me jurisdiction over Sheriff DuFreeze and his men. I could request the help of Colonel Englewood and the troops at Fort Sidney in putting down this hostile takeover."

"This is dangerous business, Jesse. Swan Holmes has a passel of men at his disposal."

"But they'll be no match for the cavalry."

"Someone I know is bound to get killed."

"That's a chance we take everyday living in a nation stumbling over itself to be all grown up and civilized."

"Jesse—," Martha started. "I'm frightened. This situation brings back memories of the uncertain times of the war."

"It does for me, too. But, we can't just sit idle when someone comes in and threatens our way of life. Someone has to stand up to bullies."

"I'm not questioning that. What I am questioning is why it has to be you who does it." Martha began to cry.

"We've had this discussion before and you were in favor of it."

"That was before it grew into such a major undertaking. I

had no idea there would be so many fighting against you." She buried her head in her hands.

Jesse tried to comfort her. "I didn't know it would go this far. But that doesn't change the fact someone has to stand up in situations like this. My question is if not me, then who?"

Martha looked up. "Am I being selfish?"

"No, sweetheart, you are not being selfish. You want our son to grow up with a father. There's nothing selfish about that. And I want that too. What I don't want is for someone to take over the town and drive people like you and me away."

CHAPTER EIGHTEEN

Jesse boarded the east bound Union Pacific train at midnight. Ahead of him was a grueling nineteen hour rail ride to Omaha. Before he boarded he had scanned the depot for watchful eyes belonging to those who might wish him harm. He had found none. Except for those who were getting on the train there were no other creatures about. Jesse had selected this particular train because the locomotive had been in the roundhouse and only recently turned about for the return trip. That insured there were no passengers departing at the station, only those boarding to minimize the chances of someone seeing him leave. In his mind, the fewer who knew the better. That way there was no one to tip his hand before he was ready to play it.

Arriving in Omaha the following evening, Jesse put himself up at a local hotel and turned in.

The next morning he woke early and took his breakfast in the hotel before walking to the courthouse. There was still angry talk among the citizens of Omaha that Lincoln had stolen the capitol city designation from them. The first territorial capitol building had been torn down in 1872 and replaced by Omaha High School, but some citizens still bemoaned the decision to move the capitol. Jesse could see that high school building on a distant hill and learned from townsfolk it over-looked the Missouri River, Lewis and Clark's route to the west.

Jesse found the federal building and learned that the man he needed to speak to, the Honorable Judge Cyril Hashberger, was in his second floor office. Climbing the granite stairs, he found the judge's office.

Judge Hashberger sat behind a huge desk in a room filled from floor to ceiling with row after row of book cases filled with tomes Jesse could only conclude were law books. Hash-berger was a tiny man with thin moustache and tiny grey eyes that seemed to look right through him.

"What can I do for you, son?"

"Are you Judge Hashberger?" Jesse asked.

"I am. And just who might you be?"

"Jesse Jones."

"And what brings you into my office today, Mr. Jones?"

Over the next hour, Jesse poured out the situation in Sidney as best he could. Judge Hashberger sat intently listening and often asked for further clarification as Jesse saw it. To substantiate his answers, Jesse drew from his coat pocket the letters of support he had received from Parson Abel, Doc Hardesty and the retired sheriff, Wade Blanton.

Judge Hashberger pondered each new detail Jesse presented. He read and then reread the letters Jesse brought as evidence for the appointment of a Marshal to rein in the misdeeds occurring 'out west,' as Hashberger labeled it. Once Hashberger walked over to one of the substantial bookcases and removed a volume and leafed through it. His index finger followed a line of type Jesse was unable to read upside down.

"Hmm," Hashberger said. He returned the book to its place

in his bookcase and sat down at his desk. "Yes, Mr. Jones. There is indeed a precedence for what I am about to do."

"Does that mean you are going to appoint a Marshal?"

"I am. There must be law and order for the citizens of Sidney. We cannot have city councils appointing sheriffs willy-nilly. Especially when said sheriff has a history of inappropriate behavior. I am authorizing you to restore order and protect the citizens of the United States."

Judge Hashberger removed a sheet of stationery from his desk and scrawled out his authorization. "This authorization is backed by the Federal Government to the full extent of the law." He folded the paper and handed it to Jesse. "Do you promise to uphold the law to the best of your ability, so help you God?"

"I do," Jesse replied.

Judge Hashberger handed Jesse a five-pointed star engraved with the words *U.S. Marshal*.

CAMP CLARKE SHARED the same sunrise Jesse did although miles apart. Jimbo Livingston rode into the settlement to deliver the news of the takeover of the warehouse in person. He sprang from his empty wagon and knocked at the door belonging to the modest home of Henry T. Clarke.

"Jimbo, what on earth are you doing back so soon?"

"Got something to show you, Mr. Clarke." Jimbo walked the short distance to his wagon with Clarke trailing behind. "Take a look, Mr. Clarke. I brung back an empty wagon on account of the goings on in Sidney."

Jimbo's wagon drew the attention of several of the workers. They had arrived to unload a wagon, but with nothing to empty, they were milling around.

"What's going on?" Clarke asked. "You were supposed to bring supplies in this morning."

"Well, sir. For one thing there's a new sheriff in town and it ain't Blanton no more. The city council stripped him of his badge and appointed Bill Dufreeze, that one-armed man that used to work as foreman at John Coad's ranch."

"That doesn't make any sense."

"No, sir, it don't. It seems that a new council member swayed the vote."

"Who might that be?"

"Swan Holmes."

"The banker?"

"Yes, sir. Now everything in town is changing." Jimbo handed Henry T. Clarke the paper Kodiak gave him two days before. "Some of DuFreeze's men gave me this. Swan wants Jones out of the warehouse. He says for me to tell ya that if you want the supplies already there, it's gonna cost ya double."

"There's no way that I can make that work in my budget. Where's Jesse in all of this? Why doesn't he stand up to these highwaymen?"

"I don't know, Mr. Clarke. I looked for him yesterday and couldn't find him. Potter's around, but he's still recovering from the beatin' he took. Blanton's quit as sheriff. Believe me, there are just too many men agin' us. There's a swarm of men with black bandanas roamin' about like they own the town."

"Speaking of swarming—" Clarke pointed west along the Oregon Trail where a thick cloud of dust was visible and moving in the direction of Camp Clarke. As the dust cloud neared a guidon with pennant became visible.

"Must be the soldiers from Fort Sidney returning from their excursion north," said Clarke.

"Yeah, I remember when they rode through awhile back. Said they was tracking rustled beef," said Jimbo.

Sergeant Major Kelly raised his right hand and the company halted behind him. Dust clung to the troopers turning their blue uniforms grey.

"Dismount," Kelly said. "Grab yerselves somethin' cold ta drink and be ready to remount in an hour." Kelly consulted a small pocket watch. "That means boots and saddles at noon, gentlemen."

The Sergeant Major removed a kerchief from around his neck and attempted to dust himself off with little success.

"Did you find what you were looking for, Sergeant Major?" said Clarke.

"Aye, we did, sir. Someone is a rebrandin' John Coad's cattle and runnin' them north to Red Cloud Agency and sellin' them."

"So what brand are these cattle wearing when they reach the agency?" Clarke asked.

"Sir, they are a-wearin' the double B brand instead of Coad's double F. It's easy enough to put a new brand over the old. Takes a pretty sharp eye to see that the cattle are rebranded."

"So, Sergeant Major, just who is it that owns the double B?" Jimbo chimed in.

"Well, that there double B brand is in honor of a woman who lives in Sidney by the name of Beatrice Holmes, wife of Swan Holmes. Her husband is a banker in town."

Henry T. Clarke removed his hat and ran his hand through his silver hair. "There's that name again, Jimbo. Swan Holmes. That man has his fingers in lots of pies, doesn't he?"

SWAN HOLMES DID HAVE his fingers in a lot of pies. He saw to it that his men had plenty to occupy their time. This same morning he ordered Bill DuFreeze to visit each business in town over the next two days to announce that the new sheriff would protect them. For a fee. The sheer number of businesses made it impossible for Sheriff DuFreeze to accomplish the visits on Holmes' timeline, so he used his Night Riders to lighten his load.

PARSON ABEL GATHERED a few friends around him in the backroom of Swede's Mercantile, in particular Doc and Potter.

"Any word on Jesse?" Potter asked. He flipped an empty wooden crate on edge and sat on it.

The parson removed a telegraph from his shirt pocket. "Just this cryptic message sent early this afternoon. It just has the one word 'Yep' on it. Sounds like Jesse has the authorization he needs."

"That's good news," said Potter.

"So, when's he coming back?" asked Doc.

"He's taking the earliest train possible. That's how we arranged it before he left."

"How come we didn't know about all this?" said Doc.

"He and I decided that the fewer who knew about this the better. With Holmes taking over everything in town we thought he'd take over the telegraph office as well, or at least have DuFreeze use his badge to read all incoming and outgoing telegraph messages," Abel said.

"Jesse plans a brief stop in North Platte to check if Bill Cody is still around. That would give us an extra gun. This whole thing is getting very messy especially with DuFreeze's involvement as sheriff. I knew there was something fishy when Swan Holmes started spouting 'God helps those that help themselves.'"

Without warning Sheriff DuFreeze burst through the door. He was followed close behind by Kodiak and two other men familiar to those meeting in the backroom. Slim and Stetson.

"Well, well, well, whatta we got goin' on back here?" DuFreeze announced. "What do ya'll think yer doin?"

Potter stood. "We're having a private business meeting."

Pressing on his shoulder, Montrose forced Potter back down. "This here meetin' of the backroom club is hereby adjourned."

Kodiak laughed out loud. "That's a tellin' 'em, Slim."

DuFreeze stepped over to Parson Abel and snatched the telegraph he was holding and read it. "What does this mean?"

Potter had stood up again. "If you'd stayed in school past the fourth grade you'd know that 'yep' means yes."

He paid for his sass with a gut punch from Montrose.

"Now, gentlemen, we came here looking for Jones," Kodiak said. "And to be certain, I don't see him. Mind telling me where he is?" Kodiak looked around the room expecting an answer, but didn't get one. "Sheriff, I find these gentlemen in breach of the law. What do you want me to do with them?"

"What law?" asked Parson Abel.

DuFreeze smiled. "Law that we ain't written yet, such as 'illegal assembly.' DuFreeze thought a moment. "Like there ain't ta be more than two people gathered in any one place at a time. How does that sound?"

"That puts my church in jeopardy." Abel snorted.

"Does it? Well now ain't that just too bad," DuFreeze replied. "I don't want no church goers gettin' uppity thinkin' that they're any better than us common folk."

"You can't do that!" Abel shouted.

DuFreeze put a thumb on his badge. "This here badge says that I can do what I—," He paused for effect and looked around at his men. "I'd said something else, but I gots me a preacher present."

That brought a laugh from his men.

"Ya got twenty-four hours to bring Jones to us or there will be hell to pay." DuFreeze removed his hat and took a deep bow. "'Cuse my language, Parson."

Jesse arranged for the engineer to stop his locomotive three miles east of Sidney. He noted the time. Midnight as he de-trained with Bill Cody and Ned Buntline. They mounted horses they'd stowed in an unused cattle car. Jesse anticipated trouble. If DuFreeze had figured out he was not in town he'd likely have some of his men watching at the train station. Sure enough, when the three men dismounted near a of grove of trees south of the train station, they saw a host of men wearing black bandanas swarm over the train like ants swarm a blob of honey.

"Your caution is paying dividends," Buffalo Bill noted.

"We'll wait a couple hours and sneak our way into the fort," said Jesse. "If I'm right, DuFreeze has men waiting for us at our usual places."

"Parson Abel's, your store, your house and the house of your brother-in-law," Buntline noted.

"And I'm bettin' that they don't have the fort covered."

With the trees and underbrush giving them shelter, the three men napped until three o'clock. They led their horses north with the moon providing ample light to guide them into

Sidney. A half hour later they neared the fort with its southern perimeter butting against Lodgepole Creek.

"Halt! Who goes there?" the sentry barked.

"Is that you Stevens?" Jesse asked.

"Who's askin,'?"

"It's Jesse, Stevens. Jesse Jones."

"What are you doing out here, Jonzie?"

"I got Buffalo Bill and Ned Buntline with me and we're rendezvousin' with the Colonel," said Jones.

"Does he know you are coming, sir?"

"I doubt if he has any idea we're coming. Do you have any idea what time it is, Stevens?" Jesse did not allow him to answer. "It's nearly four a.m."

"Pass through," Stevens said.

The three men removed their spurs. The fort was quiet except for an occasional snore from the barracks. They walked gingerly across the parade ground and up to the officer's quarters where they found Lieutenant Colonel Englewood's residence. Jesse knocked. They did not wait long before Englewood open the door a crack.

"Who's out here and what in tar-nation do you want at this time in the morning?"

"Colonel, its Jesse Jones, Buffalo Bill and Ned Buntline. Can we come in?" Jesse said.

Englewood opened the door. "What on earth are you doing here?"

"I figured I'd be welcomed back in only two places. At home and here. I'm betting DuFreeze is watching my house, but didn't figure he'd watch here."

"Things are a little crazy in town with DuFreeze and his mob in charge," Englewood said.

"That's why I've been in Omaha." Jesse opened his vest to reveal his new badge.

"U.S. Marshall. Well, I'll be."

"We've got to get our town back, Colonel," Jesse said.

"And Buntline and I rode along to make sure that happens," Cody interjected.

Jesse pulled out his commission from Judge Hashberger and handed to the colonel. "I'm to use every resource available to me to restore law and order, so I thought I'd come to you first."

"I'm still waiting for my men to return from the Red Cloud Agency, but when they report, I'm guessing you'll have all the help you need."

CHAPTER 19

Jesse settled into a room in the barracks. It was a lonely room with minimum accommodations; bed, dresser with mirror, washbasin and towel. He decided there were two redeeming features. First, he had a roof over his head, protection against the elements. And second, the room was new and so were the furnishings. There was the pleasing smell of newly hewn wood about the place.

Lieutenant Colonel Englewood stationed a security detail outside Jesse's room. Two armed guards would give him around-the-clock protection. "Like you always say, Jesse, desperate men will attempt desperate things," Englewood had stated. "We want to keep you alive to finish the work the government sent you here to do."

It was easy to gather Doc and Parson Abel to Jones' new headquarters. Englewood sent a trooper to fetch them using the ploy that an officer was gravely ill and needed Doc's medical and Abel's spiritual tending. The trooper was questioned by Slim Montrose, but allowed to carry out his orders to bring the two men to the fort.

Buffalo Bill found Adam Potter and Isaiah Blanton in the supply room at Swede's Mercantile. He relayed Jones' message of a meeting at Fort Sidney. They left Adeline in charge of the store and the men exited out the back door and scurried up the alley and through side streets without incident.

A reunion of friends took place in a room off the commanding officer's quarters.

"Boy are we glad to see you," Potter said.

"I'll say," said Parson Abel. "Things are falling apart fast around here. Business owners are being bullied to pay protection or sell out to Swan Holmes."

"We've got Bill DuFreeze's deputies all over the place, threatening people," Blanton added.

"Got a report that J.F. Coad and his son, Ben, are barricaded in their room at the Moore Hotel with DuFreeze holding them both for ransom," Potter said.

"Ya gotta do somethin' Jesse, or we won't have any town left worth livin' in," said Doc.

In their haste to tell Jesse what he missed during his travels the men began to talk over one another. Jones put his hands in the air in an attempt to quiet the group. "Hold on. Hold on. Let's not all talk at once. Everyone quiet down for a minute."

The conversations ended.

"You all know that this is why you sent me to Omaha." Jesse pulled his jacket open so all could see the badge pinned to his chest.

"You got the appointment?" Blanton asked.

"I did. Once Judge Hershberger heard what was going on, he swore me in as Federal Marshall. I called you all here so we can plot a strategy to get our town back with the fewest casualties possible."

"What do you have in mind?" asked Blanton.

"Whatever we do, we are going to need the help of troopers

from Fort Sidney," Jesse said. "Otherwise, we are outmanned and out gunned."

"And we need proof that it's Holmes who's behind the theft of cattle and the attempt to drive your brother-in-law off his farm," Potter chimed in.

"Got the first part of that handled," said Colonel Englewood. "I'm waiting for the return of Company A under Sergeant Major Kelly. I sent them to the Red Cloud Agency. They haven't returned yet." Englewood paused a moment before adding. "There is another complication."

"What's that?" Jesse asked.

"There's a very large shipment of gold on the way here. Should arrive day after tomorrow. It's under armed military guard. Before it ships back east it's spending one night in Swan Holmes' Bank. It's the only bank in the area with enough security."

"Are you thinking what I'm thinking?" asked Jesse. "'Cuz I'm thinking all of these shenanigans is to take our focus off the bank."

"Would Holmes rob his own bank?" said Englewood.

"In a heartbeat," said Jesse.

JIMBO LIVINGSTON WOUND the rope bringing the bucket to the top of the well. He sank his canteen into the bucket and watched as bubbles erupted on the surface of cool, crisp water as it filled.

Behind him he heard what he thought was thunder and turned west to find the source. The sky was cloudless. *What am I hearing?*

In the distance a thick cloud of dust caught Jimbo's attention. Whatever it was, it is heading in his direction.

Is that a stampeding buffalo herd? Jimbo paused the think. *No, that makes no sense. The dust indicates that it's traveling along the Oregon Trail.*

Others must have heard the same sound because they were looking west like Jimbo.

"What do you make of that?" Henry T. Clarke asked.

"Not a clue. Whatever it is, it's headed this way. And fast."

Sergeant Major Kelly joined them. "What do ya make of it, gentlemen? Never seen nothin' like this before."

"Sergeant Major, if you don't mind me saying so, I think you need to have your men at the ready," said Clarke.

"I'm a thinkin' the same thing," Kelly replied. Kelly raced to where his men were bivouacked. "Company A, grab your rifles and follow me!" he shouted.

Kelly arrived at a spot just past the outskirts of Camp Clarke. He positioned his men on either side of the trail, behind fence lines and rocks. "Hold your fire until I give the command."

The distant dust came closer and closer and with it the distinct sound of hoofs.

"Seek shelter everyone!" Clarke commanded.

His command sent men scurrying in every direction. Some chose to scramble down the embankment and into the Platte River. Others sheltered behind the massive timber pylons of the Camp Clarke Bridge. Some ran about the camp unable to decide what to do, like chickens with their heads cut off.

Closer and closer the dust came.

Horses and riders became visible, riding in front of and on either side of what appeared to be a stagecoach. Riders in front of the stagecoach-like object rode on the trail itself. Riders flanking the coach rode off the trail.

Kelly stood and waved his arms frantically. "Don't shoot men! Don't shoot!"

Dust flew everywhere as riders and coach came to a halt in the center of Camp Clarke. When at last the dust settled, all eyes focused on the strange object pulled by a team of horses.

Jimbo identified it as a stagecoach. At least that's what it started out as. But it had been modified and covered from top to bottom with armor. There were gun slits cut into the armor. How many men were inside, Jimbo could not determine. The whole rig was so heavy that it required three pair of horses to pull it. Two horsemen rode ahead of the coach. Three on each flank. And Jimbo saw a pair of horsemen behind. Ten riders in all.

"Dismount!" yelled one of the riders in front. "Stay with your horses."

Jimbo Livingston made his way to the officer in command. Henry T. Clarke joined him.

"The name's Clarke. Henry T. Clarke." He extended his right hand.

"Lieutenant Abercrombie Fitch, sir. Pleased to meet you," he said taking Clarke's hand.

"And this is my right hand man, Jimbo Livingston."

"Pleased to meet you," said Fitch.

Clarke walked to one side of the wagon. The troopers drew their small arms.

"Whoa. I didn't mean to stir up a hornets' nest," Clarke protested.

"I must ask you to stay away from the wagon, sir," Fitch said. He drew Clarke and Livingston away.

"Whatever you've got on board must be very valuable," said Clarke.

"Gold out of the Black Hills. Mind if I have one of my men fill our canteens from your well over there?"

Jesse Jones looked directly at Lieutenant Colonel Englewood. "Do you think we can stop the arrival of the gold from up north?"

The other men in the conference at the fort were all ears.

"What do you have in mind, Jones?" Englewood replied.

"I'm wondering if we could lure Holmes and his men out in the open."

"That shipment is due in two days. That doesn't give us much time," Potter said.

"Get me a map," said Jesse.

Englewood unfolded a large map and laid it out on a table. The men gathered around.

"Alright, Colonel, give me your best guess on where that gold shipment is." Jesse continued.

Englewood bent over the map. He put his finger on Sidney. "Let's see." He thought for a moment. "If the shipment is due here in two days, then my best guess—" He traced his finger along a road leading northwest and stopped at Camp Clarke. "That shipment should be right about here."

"Camp Clarke," Cody announced.

"Yep, they should be at or near Camp Clarke. My guess is that the troopers will stop for a few hours to rest and then start their journey south with a layover about half-way," said Englewood.

"How can we get a message to them?" asked Jesse.

"We could send a telegraph," Buntline interjected.

Doc dismissed the idea. "That won't work. DuFreeze has his men all over the place. They'd prevent us from sendin' out a message like that."

"Doc's right," Parson Abel noted. "We practically had to

walk through fire to get here. We had to lie and say that someone at the fort was dying before we could get through."

"Could we get a rider through in time?" Cody asked.

"Are you the rider?" Buntline said. "That would be just like the old days when you rode the Pony Express. That would make a great story in a dime novel."

"Don't think I could ride like that anymore," Cody said. "Besides I'm several years older and several pounds heavier than I was back then."

That brought a chuckle to the room.

"Not practical from this standpoint either. DuFreeze has all the exits in and out of town covered," said Potter. "There's no way in and out of town."

"Well, that shoots that idea out of the saddle," Doc said.

"What a horrible thing to say," said Abel.

"Sorry, but that was the first thing that popped into my head," Doc replied.

"Maybe it would be better if you kept your first thoughts in your head and didn't let them pop out at all," said Abel.

"We do have an ace in the hole though," Englewood interrupted.

"What's that?" asked Jesse.

"Follow me." Englewood led the men down the hall to a locked door. He knocked.

"Is that you, Colonel Englewood?" came a voice from inside the room.

"It is, private," Englewood replied. "You can unlock the door."

Footsteps were heard from within, followed by the sound of a key turning in the lock.

The door opened a crack and then stopped.

"It's alright, private," said Englewood.

The door opened all the way to reveal a young man in his twenties with dark hair and a pleasant smile.

"I want to show these men our ace in hole." Englewood pushed past the young man and let the others enter. In the center of a table pushed against the far wall was a telegraph.

"Gentlemen, you have never been here and you have not seen this. It is a direct line of communication between Sidney and Camp Clarke. No one knows about this, but I had it put in for the protection of the Camp. We can stop that gold shipment."

"Mr. Livingston! Mr. Livingston!" the frantic telegraph operator burst from his office. He made a bee-line toward the cluster of men near the wagon.

Jimbo Livingston turned. "What is it, Amos? Why all the hubbub?"

Amos unfolded the telegram and read:

Urgent! Halt the gold shipment. Do not proceed to Sidney.
  Lieutenant Colonel Englewood
  Commander
  Fort Sidney, Nebraska

"Mr. Clarke, yer gonna wanna read this." Jimbo handed the telegram to Henry T. Clarke who read the missive, and immediately handed the paper to Lieutenant Fitch.

"Lieutenant."

Fitch read and Jimbo saw a worried expression cross his face. "What's the meaning of this? We have orders to deliver this shipment to Swan Holmes Bank in two days."

"If you are unsure of this order countermanding your original order, you can send a telegraph to Colonel Englewood for clarification," Clarke said.

"I'd like to do that if you don't mind," said Fitch.

"Amos, would you take Lieutenant Fitch with you so he can send a message back to Colonel Englewood?"

"Right this way, sir," Amos said.

Jimbo tagged along to get the gist of what was going on so he could report back to Henry T. Clarke.

Lieutenant Fitch dictated and Amos sent the telegraph wire clacking.

> *Please explain order countermanding my commanding officer.*
> *Lieutenant Abercrombie Fitch*
> *Commanding Gold Expedition*

A half hour passed before the telegraph clacked back Colonel Englewood's response. Amos understood the dots and dashes and hurriedly wrote down the message.

> *Fear robbery imminent*
> *Consulted your commander at Ft. Robinson*
> *He will send new orders*
> *Lt. Colonel Englewood*
> *Commanding Ft. Sidney*

Forty-five minutes passed. The telegraph roared to life and Amos translated.

> *Lieutenant Fitch*
> *Orders revised*
> *Remain at Camp Clarke*
> *Protect the gold at all cost*
> *Colonel Squires*

Commanding Fort Robinson

Jimbo Livingston hurried from the telegraph office with information for Henry T. Clarke. "The gold shipment is staying here until further notice. Not exactly sure what all of this means except that the shipment is in danger."

"We can assure Lieutenant Fitch that everyone here will protect the gold," Clarke announced.

Lieutenant Fitch returned to his men and briefed them on the change of orders.

All the activity heightened Sergeant Major Kelly's curiosity. "Mr. Clarke, would ya mind sharin' what all the commotions about?"

"Lieutenant Fitch has received orders to remain at Camp Clarke and protect the gold. Colonel Englewood suspects a robbery attempt on this shipment once it reaches Sidney," said Clarke.

Again Amos came running this time he sought Sergeant Major Kelly.

Sergeant Major Kelly
> *Support Lieutenant Fitch in manner of his choosing*
> *Remain at Camp Clarke until further notice*
> *Lt. Col. Englewood*
> *Commanding*
> *Ft. Sidney*

Jimbo walked with Henry T. Clarke as the Sergeant Major reported to Lieutenant Fitch.

"Lieutenant Fitch, Sergeant Major Kelly placing my command of Company A under your authority per orders from my commanding officer." He handed the Lieutenant the telegraph Amos had handed him.

"Thank you, Sergeant Major," Fitch said. He turned to Henry T. Clarke. "Sir, is there a good place to secure this wagon? A place where we can defend it if necessary?"

Clarke turned to Jimbo. "What do you think, Jimbo? Is there a place we can secure the wagon?"

"We plan to open Camp Clarke Bridge in a month or so. How about driving the wagon over the bridge and sheltering it on the opposite side of the Platte. That puts the river and the bridge between us and danger if we're attacked."

"That's an excellent idea. I concur. Lieutenant, have your men drive your wagon across the bridge and build trenches. There are trees enough to build some *Chevaux de Frise*," Clarke said.

"And my men'll help ya," said Kelly.

CHAPTER 20

Jones stood near Lieutenant Colonel Englewood. A long silence draped the room. Forty minutes had passed since his last telegraph addressed to Sergeant Major Kelly had been sent.

"Did they receive our message?" Englewood stood over the private manning the telegraph.

"I believe so, sir," private responded. "Can't tell for sure until he gives an acknowledgement though."

"What's taking him so long?" Englewood wondered aloud.

"Don't know, sir."

"It's like a lot of things when it comes to the military," Doc injected. "I believe it's called hurry up and wait."

Englewood smiled at Doc's comment. "You are correct, Doc. Hurry up and wait is a good way to describe it."

When the telegraph receiver clacked to attention once more everyone in the room breathed a sigh of relief.

"Here's your reply, Colonel." The private handed Englewood the response from Camp Clarke.

Message received
   Have placed myself under the command of
   Lieutenant Fitch
   Moving gold to defensive position
   far side of bridge
   Sergeant Major Kelly

"Well, that's a relief," Englewood said. "Gentlemen, let's go back to the planning room."

Englewood led the way.

"What's our next move?" Potter asked upon arrival.

Buntline took notes.

"Here's what I've been thinking," Jesse began. "I think it's time for me to go over to the bank and swat the hornet's nest."

"What do you have in mind?" said Cody.

"Whatever he has in mind, I think it's too dangerous," said Potter.

"Me, too," said Englewood.

"The bank closes in an hour. I figure I'll walk over and have a little talk with Swan Holmes. He needs to know that we're on to him and that the gold isn't heading his direction after all."

"That's only going to make him angry. He might kill you," Potter said.

"Angry men make mistakes," said Jones. "'Sides it's a chance I've got to take. Someone has to stand up to him and his gang."

"Look here," Doc said. "As much as I think Holmes needs putting in his place, I don't relish the idea of patching you up after his gang gets through with you."

"Anybody have any better ideas?" Jesse asked.

"I think I should go with you and give you a little extra authority and a little extra firepower," said Englewood.

"I don't really want to tip our hand that the fort is involved," said Jesse.

"Holmes is no dummy. He's going to wonder how we stopped the gold shipment," Cody said.

"I plan to tell him where the gold is," said Jesse.

"You what?" Englewood was startled by Jesse's reply.

Jones bent over the map Englewood had unrolled over the table. He put his index finger on the spot labeled Camp Clarke Bridge. "The way I figure it is that once Swan Holmes knows where the gold is, he will send his men riding north hell bent fer leather."

He turned to Colonel Englewood. "Colonel, I want you to have your men ready for boots and saddles about fifteen minutes after Holmes' gang rides out of town. Keep yer distance so they don't know they're being followed. If I know Sergeant Major Kelly he'll have his men in a defensive position. When Holmes's men strike Kelly, Colonel, you'll strike them on their rear."

Cody looked at Buntline. "Are you getting all of this down?"
Buntline nodded.

"Cody," Jesse continued, "do you think you can get on the rooftop of a building across the street from the bank?"

"What do you have in mind?" said Cody.

"I'd like Lucretia Borgia—" Jones pointed at Cody's rifle. "To provide a little backup for me in case something goes wrong at the bank."

"You got it. Rest assured if you go wandering into the bank and 'swat the hornet's nest' like you say, Lucretia Borgia is ready to shoot the stingers off a couple of hornets when they fly out."

BUFFALO BILL GRABBED LUCRETIA BORGIA, his trusted rifle, in his right hand and disappeared. Jesse gave him a twenty minute head start before readying himself for the task at hand. First he drew his LeMat, spun the cylinder to count nine cartridges and a shotgun shell in place.

"Jesse," said Parson Abel, "may I have a word with you?"

Abel pulled Jesse aside. "I'm praying for you. Be careful. Any man who thinks God helps those who help themselves, is liable to do anything. Keep your head on a swivel."

"Thanks for your prayers, parson. God only knows how this will all turn out."

Jesse followed Buffalo Bill's lead and wandered the back alleys until he found himself on the opposite side of the bank. Two of Swan Holmes' henchmen stood guard and Jesse assumed there were more inside, more than he'd encountered during earlier visits.

Well, this ain't gettin' it done standing here, he told himself. He stepped into the street. The two men in front of the bank spotted him and drew their pistols.

"We've been lookin' fer you. Where ya been hidin'?" one of the men asked.

"I'm here to talk with yer boss. Is he in?" Jones did not wait for their answer. Instead he walked to the door of the bank and knocked.

"Whatta ya want?" came the words from inside the bank.

"Jesse Jones to see Mr. Holmes and no, I don't have an appointment."

"I'll take yer hog leg," the man on Jesse's left said.

"Ya will over my dead body," Jesse replied. He turned to meet the man's glare. That gave him enough time to look at the rooftop across the street and spy Cody's rifle.

The heavy bank door opened and another of Holmes' minions let him inside. "Follow me," he said.

Swan Holmes was sitting behind his desk. He looked up when Jesse's escort announced his arrival. Holmes smiled a broad smile and showed his teeth under his broad moustache.

"Well, well, well. If it isn't Jesse Jones in the flesh. Remove your hardware while standing in my presence."

Jesse felt the sudden pressure of a revolver shoved into the middle of his back.

"Unbuckle your gun belt and let me hear it hit the floor," Holmes demanded.

Jesse had no choice but to comply. His gun belt thudded against the wood floor.

"I'll insure your safety as long as you are in my bank," Holmes added. "But if we haven't come to an agreement before you leave, you'll be fair game once you leave."

Jesse opened his overcoat to reveal his new badge.

Holmes came from behind his desk and stood toe-to-toe with Jesse. "What's this? Well, I'm in the presence of a U.S. Marshal."

Holmes thumbed the badge with his index finger. "And the badge is real. How about that? Never been part of killing a marshal before."

Jesse looked Holmes directly in the eye. "Not sure what your little scheme is, but I can tell you that the gold shipment you planned to receive in a couple of days is stayin' put at Camp Clarke until further notice."

"Well, that does change things a little, but God helps those who help themselves. And I think my men will swarm all over Camp Clarke. It's too bad, but there might even be a spark that accidentally lights the bridge on fire. Can't say for sure, but it could happen."

"If that happens you'll encounter the full weight of the U.S. Government. I'm here to tell you that I will uphold my appointment to the full extent of the law."

Holmes chuckled and returned to his seat behind his desk. "Good bye, Mr. Jones. We have no more to talk about. May God have mercy on your soul."

TRUE TO HIS WORD, Swam Holmes allowed Jesse to put on his gun without a challenge under the watchful eye of his henchman.

"Once outside you are fair game," Holmes shouted. His words echoed through the bank as Jesse made his way to the front door. "And you might want to check up on that wife of yours. Too bad she's so alone out in the middle of nowhere."

Jesse quickened his pace. *Martha!* his mind screamed.

He burst through the door and onto the street.

"Hold it!" someone shouted behind him.

Jesse stopped dead in his tracks. He wheeled around to face the source of the shout. The two men guarding the door stepped down into the street.

"That's far enough." The voice was the same as before. It came from the man on Jesse's right.

"Holmes gave you safety while inside, but ya ain't inside no more," said the man on Jones' left.

Both men widened their stances and unsnapped the straps over their pistols.

"Too bad you ain't gonna be around when our friends find that wife of yers," said the man on the right.

"Yeah," said the other. "And she's such a pretty little thing, too."

Jesse faced both men. "Am I facin' one of ya or both of ya?"

"Both," the man on the right announced.

"Whether I'm facin' ya one at a time or both together it

don't matter much to me. I may not get both of ya," Jesse said. "But I sure am gonna take one of ya down with me."

Jesse noticed that the man on the left seemed more anxious for action, although he was quieter. The man's hand inched toward his gun. He was close enough to watch the man's eyes. His pupils dilated.

Jesse drew first and shot.

The man crumbled and fell.

Jesse wheeled to face the second man. This man's gun was half-drawn.

Over his right shoulder came the blast of Cody's rifle.

The bullet whizzed by. It thudded into the man's head. He dropped like a limp dishrag.

Jones acknowledged Cody with a wave and shouted, "Gotta get to Martha before Holmes' men do."

At a sprint Jones arrived at the livery, saddled and raced his horse toward home.

Jesse Junior at her side playing in the scrub grass near her feet, Martha worked at hanging her clean laundry.

She heard something in the brush close to the creek. Some second sense told her she and Jesse Junior were in danger. Martha pinned the last article to the clothes line. She reached down, scooped up Jesse Junior and placed him in the clothes basket.

Stay calm, she thought, *don't panic. Everything will be alright if I can make it into the house.*

Martha walked toward the house.

There was that sound again. Like the snapping of twigs underfoot.

She glanced over her right shoulder. Two men emerged from behind the trees.

She quickened her pace.

"What's yer hurry?" one of the men called after her.

She was running now. Jesse Junior bounced in the basket nearly tumbling out.

"Come back," a second voice shouted. "We ain't gonna hurt ya much."

Almost there. She kept running.

The men behind her were running too. And getting closer.

Made it!

Martha dropped the basket sending Jesse Junior tumbling. He cried out.

She slammed the door and wedged a hewn timber in placed to barricade the door. Her pursuers thudded against it. It held.

Fists pounded the door.

"Ah, c'mon," a voice shouted. "We only want to get to know you better. That's all."

The second man laughed a hyenas' laugh.

The pounding continued.

Martha sprang to the shotgun over the fireplace. Cracked it open.

Jesse Junior wailed.

She fumbled through the contents of the bureau. *Where are they?*

Her eyes came upon the box of shells she sought. She clutched a handful. Shoved them into her apron pocket.

Hurried hands had trouble loading the gun.

Somehow two made their way in. Others hit the floor.

Martha snapped the weapon shut.

The pounding continued.

She stood three feet from the door and pulled back both

hammers on the double-barrel shotgun and raised it to her shoulder.

A QUARTER MILE from his home Jesse heard the unmistakable blast of his double-barrel.

Martha! Oh, God, no!

He spurred his horse into action. It leaped forward.

Jesse thundered into his front yard.

What's that at the front door?

He flung himself off his mount and darted toward the house.

Two men lay stone cold outside his door. The door had two fist-sized holes in it.

"Martha!" Jesse yelled.

"I'm here, Jesse," she answered.

"Thank God you're alright."

"But she won't be!" shouted a voice behind him.

Jesse recognized that voice. It belonged to Slim Montrose. Jesse turned to face the intruder.

Montrose had his revolver pointed at Jesse's chest.

"Drop your gun," Montrose commanded.

From inside the house Jesse heard the distinct sound of his shotgun snapping shut. By all indications Montrose never heard it.

"I'm gonna drop ya right where ya stand," said Montrose. He clicked the hammer back on his gun.

"Hit the dirt, Jesse!" Martha yelled.

He dove to the ground and heard the roar of his shotgun from inside the house.

The buckshot tore Montrose apart. He never knew what hit him.

Inside the house, hurried hands freed the timber at the door.

Jesse stepped inside.

Martha lifted Jesse Junior in her arms and they all embraced.

Jesse pulled the door shut. "What did you do?"

"I got a little over anxious with my shooting," she replied.

"I'll say," Jesse replied. "Next time let 'em in before you open fire. Now, I've got to replace the door."

Jesse drove the wagon. Martha and little Jesse rode beside him and his horse trotted along behind, tethered to the wagon.

"That was some real fine shooting back there," Jesse said. "I had no idea you could handle a shotgun like that."

"Brody taught me when I was a little girl," she said. "We were so poor back then that papa handed us a single shell and told us to bring back supper. You get to be a pretty good shot if your next meal depends on it."

"I'd say," he replied. "We're gonna take the back way to the fort. Holmes and his men have the front side covered."

"Did you get the appointment you went to Omaha for?"

Jesse opened his coat to reveal his badge.

"I'd say the answer to my question is yes," she said.

"I can tell ya that Holmes has no respect for the law. He sent a couple of men after me this morning."

"Are they—?"

"Yeah. I got one. Cody got the other."

"What about my brother? Has anyone ridden out there to check up on him? Holmes wants his land."

"Not so far. Brody's smart. He can take care of himself. Especially with that cellar of his."

Martha gave him a look.

"I agree with you though. We need to send someone out there. I have a stinkin' feeling that things are gonna get a whole lot worse before they get better.

"Desperate men do desperate things," she said.

"Yeah, that's definitely something I've heard before," Jesse said.

CHAPTER 21

Brody Belt had ridden north in the late afternoon sun to keep tabs on the spot where he knew the rebranding of Coad's cattle had occurred. To his eye there had been no further use of the place since last time. No obvious evidence anyway. The pit used to heat the branding iron was cold to his touch and there were no new hoof prints in the sand. Turning his horse south, he headed home again. It played in his mind how he'd worked to tame the land. Even the garden patch Cynthia had scratched in had to battle the elements to grow. She'd carry bucket after bucket of fresh water from their well to the garden only to have the sand soak it all away, leaving the tiny plants no hope at all of surviving. It was a hard life, and at times a cruel one.

"The only thing this soil is good for," Cynthia had said, "is for raising cattle."

She was correct.

Each year Brody had added a few more head as he could afford them. Some of his stock came in the normal way through the bull he'd borrowed from a neighbor and the heifer inventory he'd purchased. Other livestock he'd purchased from J.R. Coad. He had a good relationship with J.R.; that's why it bothered him so much that someone was running off J.R.'s livestock. Watching for the return of rustlers to the area was the least he could do.

Brody swung his horse around to the east to inspect his livestock. He'd heard some coyotes howling last night, so it would be good to get a head count to make sure they weren't helping themselves to his calves. He rode to the top of a small ridge and removed his binoculars to take a look around.

What's that? What are those two unsaddled horses doing in with my cattle?

Brody searched a distant grove of trees with his binoculars and found two men obviously camped there. Their bedrolls were on the ground with their two saddles lying across a fallen tree.

DuFreeze hasn't given up. He's sent a couple of men to spy on my family and when the time is right to swoop in and kill us.

Brody took his horse on a wide loop north. He knew the terrain like the back of his hand and hid himself behind the hills just out of sight of his quarry. He had the advantage since he was on horseback and they on foot. When he came to a spot some fifty yards from the two men, he dismounted and drew his Colt.

With great stealth, he crept toward the two and overheard their conversation.

"Tonight," one of the men said. "Tonight, an hour or so after we see the candle in their bedroom go out, we sneak in and kill 'em all."

"I know that's what DuFreeze told us to do, but I don't like the idea of killin' their kid, too," the second man said.

"Yeah, I don't like that either, but orders are orders. Agreed?"

The second man nodded. "I don't like it, but I'll go along with it."

"We ain't gotta like it. We just gotta do as DuFreeze told us."

"On yer feet!" Brody shouted.

One man went for his gun, but Brody's Colt roared to life telling the man just how foolish his move was.

The second man shot his hands into the air. "Don't shoot, mister," he yelled.

Brody Belt marched the man back to his farm and secured him in the cellar. "You can wait out the war in here," Brody said. He closed the cellar door behind him and locked it from the outside.

JESSE PLANNED to arrive at Fort Sidney in time for the evening meal. He, Martha and Jesse Junior picked their way along a route off the main trail leading to their home. His instinct told him that Swan Holmes had dispatched riders as an insurance policy against his return. So, traveling the main route was not an option. About a mile from town Jesse and Martha spotted three men with black bandanas riding west at a gallop.

The horses drawing Jesse's buckboard were skittish. So much so that Jones thought they might give their hiding place away. He pulled back on the reins to stop them and leaped off to reassure the horses everything was alright.

"I can tell you one thing for certain," Jesse said, climbing back on board. "I can tell you that Swan Holmes will have a conniption when he finds out we killed his men."

"Does that scare you, Jesse?" asked Martha.

"It does. Right now Holmes is like a wildcat in a box. You

know that once the box is opened he's gonna strike out at the first thing he sees."

"And I'm scared that it could be my brother."

"Brody can take care of himself."

"Yes, but there's Cynthia and little Will to worry about."

"I'll light out his direction first thing in the morning. Would that make you happy?

Martha gave Jesse a squeeze. That was his answer.

Through the valley 'mess call' was heard.

"We're getting closer," Martha announced.

"And not a moment too soon either," said Jess. "My stomach thinks my throat's been cut."

Colonel Englewood left his place at the table to greet Jesse when he arrived at the mess hall.

"Wow," he said, "if you ain't a sight for sore eyes. C'mon and join me at my table."

"We don't want to be a bother," Martha said.

"You are never a bother," Englewood announced. "Cody's already here. So are Buntline and Potter. We've certainly got room for you, too."

"I didn't hear you mention anything about Doc and Parson Abel." Jesse sat at Englewood's table next to Bill Cody. Martha sat to his right holding Jesse Junior.

"Parson Abel went home this evening. He's preaching in the morning. And Doc wanted to get back to his office," said Cody.

"What happened after you left?" Buntline opened a new line of questioning.

"Two men tried to attack Martha. She made it into the house and let 'em have it with my double-barrel," said Jesse.

Buntline made a note of that.

"She made two holes in the front door you can drive a

wagon through," added Jesse. "When this whole thing blows over I'm gonna need your help straightening up the place."

"I was outside hanging laundry with little Jess playing in the yard, when I saw them coming at me," Martha said. "I couldn't let them do anything to little Jess."

"There's a sayin' that no one should get between a she-bear and her cub," said Potter.

"I've never been so scared in all my life," said Martha.

A private sat the evening meal in front of Jesse and Martha.

Picking up his fork, Jesse asked what had happened in his absence.

"There's been a lot of commotion around the bank, but other than that, nothing new," Englewood announced.

"They've still got J.F. Coad and his son under guard at the Moore Hotel. It's my understanding that they are being held for ransom," said Cody.

"I must be getting old," Jesse said. "In my younger days I'd have said we should set the Coads free and then head on out to Brody Belt's to see what's going out there. Now that I'm older, I think I'd like to postpone those chores until morning."

A TROOPER RACED into the dining hall.

"Colonel Englewood, sir. There's a commotion at the front gate that requires your attention."

"At ease, soldier," Englewood said. The soldier's posture relaxed yet the urgency remained on his face.

"What is this all about?" Englewood asked. "Couldn't your sergeant handle the matter?

"He sent me to you, sir. Said he has no authority in the matter."

"What matter?"

"Authority to free a man Sheriff DuFreeze arrested. The guard on duty said he rode up and asked to be let into the fort. While he was standing there the sheriff walked up and arrested him. The guard told him that the man was seeking asylum and that the fort was obliged to give it to him. That didn't matter to the sheriff. The guard yelled for help and the sheriff for reinforcement. It's a free for all at the gate."

"Did the man identify himself?" asked Englewood.

"I think he said that his name was Brody Belt."

In an instant Jesse sprang to his feet. Cody grabbed him. "Now, hold on just a minute. Let the colonel handle this."

Martha nodded her approval.

Englewood removed his napkin from his lap, crumpled it and tossed it on the table.

"Let's get to the bottom of this," Englewood said. He followed the soldier.

It was an uneasy ten minutes before Englewood returned. He had Brody Belt with him.

"How did you keep that commotion from escalating into a gunfight?" Cody asked.

Englewood seated himself and put his napkin back in place. "I called his bluff, that's all. I told DuFreeze that the moment a man shows up at our gate and asks for admission, I have jurisdiction over that man as if he were already inside the fort. He's in my jurisdiction."

Brody seated himself in the one chair remaining between Martha and Ned. "You mean that ain't true?" he said.

"Nope. But DuFreeze didn't know that. I just told him that if he didn't turn Brody loose he'd bring down the full weight of the U.S. Army on him."

Englewood returned to his dinner.

"Just like that?" said Cody.

"Just like that," Englewood replied. He never looked up from his plate. "Orderly, would you bring Mr. Belt a plate?"

"It's good to see you," Martha said. "How's Cynthia and Will?

"It's good to see you, too," Brody replied. "They're safe and hiding back at the house."

Brody peeked around Martha and directed his conversation to Jesse. "Got something at my place that may interest you, Jesse."

"And what might that be?" Jesse replied.

"Got one of DuFreeze's men locked up in my cellar. Caught him and another fella nosing around my place this afternoon. One made a play for his gun. and—."

"Lived to regret it?" said Jesse.

"No. Right now he's not regretting much of anything. I put the other one in my cellar for safe keeping. Thought maybe you'd like to ride out tomorrow and talk to him. Don't know if he's got anything to say, but it never hurts to ask."

Brody's plate arrived.

"I'll take you up on that. But before we ride out tomorrow morning, we're gonna make a little stop at the Moore Hotel. Understand that J.F. and his son are being held for ransom."

"And how to you intend to free J.F.?" asked Brody.

Jesse held up his hand to plead for time as he chewed his steak. "I don't think we can just waltz in there and say give me J.F. But what we can do is go up the back stairs of the hotel and figure out what room they're holding him."

"Then ask them?" Brody smiled a broad smile.

"Yep. With pistols drawn we'll walk up to 'em and ask 'em politely."

"Do you think they'll oblige?" asked Cody.

Jesse drew his LeMat and laid it on the table. "This here says they will."

IN HIS ANGER DuFreeze kicked at the dirt in front of him. He'd been bested and he hated it. If he had two arms, he'd have choked the first person he saw. As it was the dirt street took the brunt of his anger. Black bandana-ed men in front of Holmes Bank parted in front of him like the Red Sea. They knew better than to do as much as whisper.

He stomped his way to the office of Swan Holmes and went inside, slamming the door behind him.

"What's eating you?" Holmes affixed his signature to a piece of paper in front of him.

"I got out flanked." He plopped himself in front of Holmes and put his feet on his desk.

"I believe, sir, that you are mistaking my office for the back room of some flea-bit saloon. I'll not have the remnants of the horse dung in the street on my desk. So I'll thank you kindly for putting your boots on the floor."

An icy stare greeted DuFreeze. He put his feet under him.

"I want you to take this paper to old man Higgins. I'm foreclosing on his miserable lumber yard. The town is growing, but he acts like it's the early 1860s. His prices are stuck in the basement. No wonder he can't pay me."

Holmes neatly folded the parchment and slid it in front of DuFreeze who dropped it into his shirt pocket.

Holmes waited.

"Now!" Holmes shouted. His fist came down with a mighty crash. "I want this delivered now. Tonight. Not tomorrow! Not next week! Tonight!"

Their eyes met.

"I want you to make sure the place is busy with Saturday traffic. And I want you to waltz right in and demand my money. I want him embarrassed in front of his customers. When he tells you he'll be in on Monday to pay up, I want you to spring the paper on him and tell him he's out. Take a couple of men with you. Clear the place of customers and lock the old man out!"

DuFreeze stood and made it half-way to the door.

"Bill," he heard Holmes say with a soft, almost childish voice. "What was it you wanted to talk to me about? Didn't you say you were 'out flanked'?"

DuFreeze turned. The change in Holmes voice frightened him. *Has he gone loco?* DuFreeze replied aloud, "It ain't nothin', Mr. Holmes. Nothin' at all."

"If something is bothering you, you can share it with me." Again the voice was child-like, haunting.

"It's just that Brody Belt came into town a while ago. I had two men out at his place with orders to wipe him and that misses of his out. You wanted his place and I was getting' it for you."

"That's alright. Bill. That's alright. You'll get another opportunity to kill him."

"So Brody rode into town and went to the fort. I tried to put him in jail, but the Colonel stepped in between him and me. He said he had jurisdiction. Whatever that means. Anyway Belt is inside the fort and I can't touch him."

"Bill," Holmes said. "Don't worry your head over this at all. I want you to get some men ready. Dress them up like Indians. It's going to be the Fourth of July in a couple of days, our nation's centennial. Wouldn't it be something if these Indians started shooting into the fort on the fourth? Most people will think that they're hearing firecrackers, but you and I will know the difference. Won't we, Mr. DuFreeze?"

DuFreeze liked that idea. He liked it a lot.

"It's a shame," Holmes declared with an impish smile, "that General Custer and the Seventh Cavalry is up in Montana and an Indian raid occurs right here in our back yard, and at Fort Sidney of all places."

CHAPTER 22

Parson Abel already regretted the long sleeve shirt he'd selected. Sweat beaded on his forehead as the choir sang the sermon hymn. All about the sanctuary parishioners waved the fans Oldham's Funeral Home had provided. It was the to and fro of these fans that gave forth the only breeze on this sweltering early July morning.

Before Abel had arrived, several Elders had tried in vain to open the windows only to find the heat and humidity stuck them shut like the school marm's rubber cement. They'd handed him a fan the moment he arrived.

The choir began the last verse of *Just as I Am, without One Plea.* Parson Abel unbuttoned the cuffs of his shirt and rolled up the sleeves to his elbows. On they sang.

> *Just as I am: Thy love unknown*
> *Has broken ev'ry barrier down;*
> *Now to be Thine, yea, Thine alone,*
> *O Lamb of God, I come, I come.*

. . .

He waited until the choir had seated themselves, removed his handkerchief and mopped his brow.

"I want to thank Oldham's Funeral Home for providing the fans this morning. Contrary to what Doc may be thinking, the fans were not given to you to bring you relief from all my hot air."

A tittering of laughter sprinkled throughout the congregation, Doc among them.

"As many of you have already figured out, things have changed around town. It's as if a few men have decided that Sidney needs to go beyond some of the wicked monikers already attached to her, that the number of bad things going on in this town are not good enough. We must plunge ourselves deeper into debauchery."

"Wickedness is not a hallmark of any civilized community. Godliness is. We often hear the phrase 'God helps those who help themselves,' and there are those who are indeed 'helping themselves' to things that do not belong to them."

Parson Abel's voice built to a crescendo as he held his Bible aloft. "But, my friends, nowhere are the words 'God helps those who help themselves,' found in the Bible. The Bible does not condone selfishness. Instead the Bible condemns it."

"What should a justified people do in times of injustice? Now, that's a good question. Friends, in two days this nation of ours celebrates its one hundredth birthday. One hundred years ago on July 4th, 1776, our forbearers stood against wickedness and tyranny. One hundred years ago they stood for freedom against a nation that held them captive, that terrorized their businesses and invaded their homes."

"Preach it, Reverend!" someone shouted.

"This is exactly what is happening in our fair city. A group of men has seen fit to foreclose our businesses. Haul innocent men to jail. Steal our cattle and attempt to drive us off the land we have bled and died for. These are not 'just' men whom we have elected to rule over us, but 'unjust' usurpers bent on subjugating us for their own profit.

"Is this any different from that of a nation holding us captive against whom our forbearers fought one hundred years ago? No, my friends, it is not. There comes a time, and I believe that time is now, when citizen's rise and throw off the yoke of tyranny."

Parson Abel continued, "Be watchful. Be alert. There will come a time when free men must stand. Wait for it. And when that time comes be prepared to fight for your freedom. We cannot and we must not condone unjust behavior. There is a time to turn the other cheek as Our Savior did, but this is not that time. Be alert. Be prepared to take up arms on a moment's notice as the Minute Men of old did. You will know when the time is right, the right time to stand up for freedom. Amen."

JESSE FOUND himself awkwardly perched on a rain barrel swinging the business end of a rake at the retractable emergency ladder behind the Moore Hotel. Adam Potter steadied the rain barrel. It took him a couple of noisy swings before Jesse snagged the ladder and pulled it down to ground level. He and Potter spent a few anxious moments hoping their clattering had not raised any suspicions. Satisfied that it had not Jesse began scaling the ladder. Potter followed after staying one floor below.

In the distance the tolling of the bell above Parson Abel's one room church was heard. Church was letting out. People would soon spill into the street returning home. Abel timed his worship services to finish at eleven o'clock, leaving ample time for noon meal preparations. The odor of chicken frying in the Moore Hotel's kitchen already wafted on the breeze, enticing the more affluent members of Abel's congregation to come in.

Jesse wanted to tell Potter how much his mouth was watering for fried chicken but couldn't because of the confining nature of the emergency ladder he scaled. He surmised that J.F. Coad and his son were held on the fourth floor. That was the floor dubbed the 'Presidential suite.' To date no president had slept there. Jesse recalled General Custer and his wife Libby had stayed there once. The community band had attempted to welcome them by playing Garryowen. The results were disastrous.

Adam Potter joined Jesse on the small iron platform on the fourth floor. They drew their weapons, and cracked the door just wide enough to slip inside. At the far end of the hall two men sat in front of a door. The men were oblivious to the goings on of Jones and Potter.

"Playing poker?" Jesse asked in a whisper.

"Probably," Potter whispered back.

A waiter appeared in front of the two sentries, wheezing as he balanced a platter of food. "Got dinner," he breathed out.

"For us or for them?" one of the men asked while pointing a thumb toward the door.

"Them." The waiter looked up and spotted Jesse and Potter at the far end of the hall with pistols drawn.

Jesse put an index finger to his lips not wanting the waiter to give them away. The waiter nodded.

Jesse and Potter could breathe again.

"Wait a minute." The waiter reconsidered. "Why don't I give you boys *this* food and go back down for more."

"That's what I'm talkin' about," one of the men on the floor said.

The second man took hold of one of the plates. "Yeah, them two yahoos can wait awhile longer. They ain't gonna starve to death."

"That's fer sure," said the other as he grabbed a plate. "That Coad fella could live awhile off the fat of the land."

That was the advantage Jesse had sought.

"On yer feet!" Jesse yelled.

Playing cards and food splattered everywhere as the startled men scrambled to their feet.

The waiter bolted toward the stairs and escaped down them two at a time.

The two sentries fumbled for their six-guns.

Potter's Colt and Jones' LeMat erupted in unison.

When the smoke cleared the two men lay in a heap.

Jesse rushed to the door, attempted to open it, but found it locked.

Potter reached the stairway to guard against intruders.

"Mr. Coad?" Jesse shouted toward the door.

"Yes, we're here," said voice from behind the door.

"Step away from the door," Jesse announced. He aimed his gun at the door and fired twice. The door refused to open. Jesse slammed against it and knocked the door off its hinges. Coad and his son squeezed through the opening and followed Jones down the ladder. Potter brought up the rear.

Gunfire had brought the town's attention to the Moore Hotel. Sheriff DuFreeze and his men raced toward the front door as Jesse led his party through back alleys and onto fort property two blocks away.

WORK WAS WELL underway to defend the gold shipment at Camp Clarke Bridge. One of the workmen led a chapel service in the mess hall. It was brief and the moment the 'amen' passed from the Chaplin's lips, the men were back at work.

Henry T. Clarke stopped Jimbo who was loading planking onto a wagon. Jimbo occupied the front end of the bundle himself while two men held up the other end. "How is the planking coming along?" he asked.

"Give me a half hour and we should be ready to cross the wagon over the bridge," Jimbo replied. "Shouldn't we do a trial run?"

Henry T. Clark pulled a telegraph from his pocket. "That's a good idea," he said, "but from what I'm reading between the lines of this telegraph, things are starting to bust loose in Sidney."

Clarke handed the telegraph to Jimbo after he'd secured the load of planking.

"Look, Mr. Clarke," Jimbo said politely, "I'm gonna have to take yer word for it. I can't read."

Jimbo climbed aboard the wagon. It groaned under his weight. He looked down at Henry T. Clarke who was smiling back at him. "Don't say it," Jimbo said. "I know what yer thinkin'. Yer thinkin' that with me on board this wagon the weight is the same as the fully loaded shipment of gold."

"I'm not saying anything," Clarke said with a laugh.

Jimbo coaxed his team of horses onto the bridge. It felt sturdy enough. The horses strained and hesitated yet moved the wagon forward. Jimbo had opted for blinders on the horses. He knew the bridge railings would not give the horses any measure of security. Once on the far side of the bridge workmen unloaded the wagon and Jimbo wielded it around to make the two-thousand foot return trip.

Two more trips followed. From his seat on the wagon Jimbo could see bridge workers stripping tree branches and binding them. This leafy curtain would soon camouflage the gold wagon.

"Give me plenty of gun ports between the branches," Clarke insisted. "Our lives will depend on it. The more I think about it, the less I like the idea of *Chaveux de Frise.*"

Clarke thought the *Chaveux de Frise* would 'make it blatantly obvious,' where they'd hidden the gold.

"I don't want to tip our hand," Clarke had said. "We can let Holmes' men tear Camp Clarke apart. That doesn't matter. We can always rebuild the camp. But once those men start to cross the bridge, we'll be ready for 'em."

Jimbo had instructions to have the men remove the planking from the last third of the bridge once the gold was across and hidden.

"That way it will appear the bridge is unfinished and no one will guess the wagon is on the other side," Clarke had said.

Late that same Sunday afternoon, Jimbo Livingston led Sergeant Major Kelly and Company A into position on the north side of Camp Clarke Bridge.

He returned to lead the soldiers and the Black Hills gold across. The wagon was much heavier than suspected. The weight of the coaches' armor made the timbers creak and groan.

Jimbo held his breath. *Would the planking hold? If it don't, I'm a goner.*

He climbed down from the driver's seat, took the horses' leads and walked the remaining distance. It seemed like an eternity before Jimbo reached the safety of the other side.

Jimbo could breathe again.

He supervised the work as soldiers hid the wagon. When he was convinced the wagon, and the men who defended it, were hidden from view he walked back to the south side of the bridge. Behind him he heard creaking as hammers clawed loose the nails and pried away a third of the bridge planking. Reaching the other side, Jimbo stood to face his handiwork. From where he stood it looked as if workman had stopped for the day leaving the unfinished bridge behind them.

"Nice work," Clarke said. "You and the men just put us two days ahead of schedule. We'll be prepared to meet any onslaught to come our way. I don't know about you, Jimbo, but I'm about ready to sink my teeth into a hot, juicy steak."

Sheriff DuFreeze ran through the front door of the hotel. In the street behind him a horse sped by. By the time DuFreeze turned the rider was stirring up dust in front of Holmes' Bank.

"Who was that?" DuFreeze watched as men took to the street in front of the bank and fired as the rider raced by. From his position three blocks away, DuFreeze could not tell if any of their bullets found their mark.

"Couldn't tell who that was for sure," Kodiak replied.

"Where did those shots come from?" DuFreeze asked the clerk behind the counter.

"Not sure," he responded. "Sounded like they came from upstairs."

"Coad!" DuFreeze yelled. He grabbed Kodiak by the collar. "Get yer butt upstairs and see to it that Coad is where he's supposed to be."

Kodiak sent three men bounding up the stairs.

"Did anyone come down these stairs?" DuFreeze asked the clerk.

"No, sir. Not one person came down those steps." He thought a moment. "There was one."

"Who?"

"Part of our wait staff. He came down after taking the Coads their dinner."

DuFreeze was impatient. "Where'd he go? He never came past me, so he's gotta be inside the hotel. Where is he?"

"In the kitchen," the clerk replied. "I saw him go back into the kitchen."

DuFreeze pushed his way through the crowded dining room, sending platters of food everywhere.

"Hey!" a customer shouted.

DuFreeze pulled his gun and pointed it between the man's eyes. "Ya got any talkin' to do, say it to this."

"I didn't mean anything by it," the man said. His wife's eyes were wide with terror thinking this was the last she would see her husband alive.

"Then you'd better mind yer own business," Kodiak interceded. He pushed the man out of the way and headed toward the only other door in the room. "If he's here chances are good we'll find him in the kitchen."

DuFreeze grabbed the first waiter he saw. "Where'd he go?"

The startled man shook with fear. "Who?" he managed to squeak out.

"The waiter who served the Coads. That's who."

"Umm, that would be the new guy. Ahh. His name is Turnus. He ran into the kitchen."

'One Arm' Bill DuFreeze launched himself toward the kitchen door arriving moments behind Kodiak. "Where is he?" he shouted. He stared into Kodiak's face.

"Gone," Kodiak said.

"Wadda ya mean?"

"The man we're looking for ran in here, shed his apron, and ran out the back door yelling at the top of his lungs 'I quit'. The last anyone saw of him he was sprinting down the alley," said Kodiak.

DuFreeze huffed. "Seems like we're always runnin' one step behind. If that rider hadn't distracted us we'd have been able to get to the bottom of this."

Two of the men DuFreeze had sent upstairs returned. They were out of breath.

"Well?" DuFreeze asked.

"Gone," was all one of the men got out between gasps.

"Coad and that sissified son of his?"

Unable to breathe, the man nodded.

"Whoever it was killed both of our men."

"How is that possible?" DuFreeze asked.

"Best we can figure—" The man put his hands on his hips and bent over to catch his breath. "Is that whoever it was crept up the emergency ladder, shot Gibson and Holly, snatched Coad, and left the same way he came in."

"Who did this? Where did they go? Someone's gotta have seen somethin'. No one just disappears." He turned on Kodiak. "Find me that kid. Turnus or whatever his name is. Find that kid before I lose my temper."

Kodiak and his men scattered like rats.

"All I can say is that Mr. Holmes ain't gonna like this. He ain't gonna like this one little bit."

CHAPTER 23

Brody Belt woke in his own bed. He felt tired today. The constant worrying about what might happen next weighed on him. He had one of the men who worked for Sheriff DuFreeze in his cellar. The second was buried on the hill near the spot where Brody had shot him. Brody's son William must have been tired as well. He could hear his son's deep breathing from the bed near his. He reached his right arm out, but found the side of the bed where Cynthia slept cool to the touch. She'd been up awhile. The clatter of plates in the kitchen let him know she was scurrying about doing her morning chores.

Sliding on his trousers and shirt, he leaned down and grabbed his boots. On the way out of the room, he saw himself in the mirror. Stopping only long enough to see his reflection and shrug. He'd have to deal with his unruly hair later.

"Good morning, sleepy head," Cynthia said. She placed a cast iron skillet on the stove and plopped a dollop of bacon grease into it. "It's about time you got up."

"What time is it anyway?" Brody asked.

"About quarter to seven."

"I can't remember the last time I stayed in bed this long," he said, shoving his stockinged feet into his boots. "Why didn't you wake me?"

"You looked so peaceful sleeping this morning I hadn't it in me to wake you."

"We've certainly been packing a lot into each day, haven't we?"

"One egg or two?" she asked.

"Two."

She cracked the shells. The eggs hit the hot pan sending grease spatters in every direction. "I still can't believe you survived running the gauntlet yesterday."

"That was kinda crazy," Brody said. "I wasn't much fer doin' it neither."

"But you let that brother-in-law of yours talk you into it."

"Yeah, Jesse can be persuasive when he puts his mind to it."

"And you? You're the gullible type."

Brody came up behind her and gave her a hug. She turned her face towards his and they kissed.

"Want me to set the table?" he asked.

"Thank you. Yes." Cynthia went back to her eggs. "So you rode right through town with DuFreeze's men shooting at you?"

"Jesse gave the signal when Coad and his son were safely out of the hotel. I was the diversion." Brody set two plates on the table.

"Go ahead and bring the plates to me," Cynthia said. "The eggs are done. You can set the bacon on the table and grab the silverware if you'd like."

Dishing up the eggs, she continued, "How on earth did you keep from getting hit?"

"That's something I'm wondering about myself," he said.

When Cynthia was seated he offered to pray. "We thank you, O Lord, for these gifts which we are about to receive from Your bounty through Christ our Lord. Amen."

"Amen," Cynthia echoed.

Grabbing a handful of bacon he said, "I tried something yesterday that kept me from getting hit. I saw an Indian do it once and thought I'd give it a try. I slid off the left side of my saddle and put my horse between me and the guns. I didn't slide back into the saddle again until I was out of town."

"No one rode after you?"

"Nope. It all happened so fast I don't think anyone had time to think about following me."

"You told me last night there is something you have to do today to complete your part of the plan. I asked you what that was after we went to bed, but before you could tell me I heard you snoring."

"I'm supposed to ride into town on July fourth and enter the parade with DuFreeze's man tied up and riding in front of me."

THE SEARCH for Turnus was still underway in Sidney. Kodiak and his men scoured the town. Citizens did not make their job any easier. They clogged the streets festooning the city with banners, American flags, and red, white and blue buntings in honor of the glorious centennial celebration planned for the next day.

In the school house the community band rehearsed. Somehow band members had lifted the windows to permit a morning breeze to flow through the building. Every note of the band's rehearsal of the Battle Hymn of the Republic wafted throughout the town on that same breeze. Those with tin ears didn't mind. Those without did.

"We're runnin' out of places to look," Stetson Burnett reported.

"Keep lookin'. Turn the town upside down if you have to, but I want that kid." Kodiak hadn't slept much last night and the dark circles under his eyes showed it. "Now get outta here!"

His men scrambled out the door of the Last Chance, spilling into the street. The saloon's swinging door squeaked to mark their exit.

Early that afternoon Stetson returned and found Kodiak where he had left him. Not standing at the bar as before, but pacing the floor like an expectant father.

"Well?" Kodiak said hoping for better news than he had received this morning.

"Got a line on the kid," Stetson said. "He's old man Higgins' grandson."

"Is that all ya got? You've been gone three hours."

"It's like the whole town has clammed up," said Stetson. "I was lucky to get that."

"Let's go down and have a talk with that old man." Kodiak motioned for a couple men to follow him.

When Kodiak and his men arrived, Higgins' Lumber Yard spewed customers. That left old man Higgins to face him alone.

"Can I help you?" Higgins said.

Kodiak stood in front of the counter that shielded to Higgins, but not much. "Yeah, old man, I want you to tell me where your grandson is."

"Which one? Got three of 'em."

"Don't play games old man, you know the one I'm talking about. Turnus."

"Haven't seen him today."

Kodiak reached across the counter and with both hands on Higgins' lapel pulled him until they were nose-to-nose. "Where does he go when he doesn't want to be found?"

Higgins hesitated, but gave in. "Down by Lodgepole Creek. Got a fishin' hole down there he likes."

"Thanks, old man." Kodiak chased his men out, except for one. When everyone else stepped outside that man sauntered behind the counter and slammed a fisted hand into Higgins' midsection. Higgins' breath left him and he writhed on the floor trying to catch it.

"And if he ain't there old man, we'll be back to finish the job," said Kodiak.

Kodiak found Turnus where his grandfather had said they could find him. In answer to their questions about who he saw at the end of the hallway, Turnus identified Jesse and Potter. Turnus said he didn't remember these men coming through the front door of Moore's, so they must have come up the fire escape.

"Why'd you run away?" Kodiak asked. Two men held Turnus between them.

"I was scared," he answered.

"Well, ya got reason to be. You knew we'd find ya, didn't ya?" Turnus did not answer. "What's the matter? Cat got yer tongue? I want ya to know, boy, who told us where we could find you. It was yer grandpa."

Turnus squirmed to free himself. "You leave my grandpa alone!"

"He's alive, but we did have to teach him a lesson. Didn't we, boys? Just like we're about to teach you."

Kodiak watched his men pummel Turnus. When they were finished, they tossed him into the waters of Lodgepole Creek.

Word reached the fort that old man Higgins had received a beating at the hands of DuFreeze's men. Citizens were up in arms over the maltreatment of such a pillar of the community. Higgins had been transported to Doc's office.

Jesse sneaked through the alleys and arrived at Doc's moments after Higgins. Through his pain Higgins kept mumbling, "Turnus."

"What does he mean, Doc?" Jesse asked.

"He's gotta mean his grandson," Doc replied.

"I don't believe I know him," said Jesse.

"He and his mom just moved back to Sidney last week. They've been gone several years and moved back after Turnus' father died suddenly. Heart attack, I think. Last I heard Turnus had taken a job at the Moore Hotel."

"With the wait staff?" Jesse asked.

"Don't know for sure. That could well be."

"There was a young man involved in our raid to get the Coads. Haven't seen him since then. Last I saw that young man he was running down an alley like he had the Devil himself after him."

Old man Higgins moaned.

"Is he gonna be alright, Doc?" Jesse asked.

"He's gonna be fine. He's gonna be sore for a while though. They beat him up pretty good."

"Any idea who would do such a thing?"

"Kodiak is the name I'm hearing bantered around. Kodiak and his men chased customers out of Higgins' place and after Kodiak left, they found Higgins lying in a heap behind the counter."

From the street below a familiar voice rang out. "Alright, Jones. Come on down. We know you're up there."

"Kodiak," Jesse mumbled under his breath. He stood and made his way to Doc's door. "Gotta go, Doc."

"Hold on a minute." Doc prevented Jesse from opening the door. "That's suicide. You can't go out there. Why don't you go down through the store and out the back?"

"C'mon out Jones or we're comin' up after ya," Kodiak hollered.

"At least go out the back and come around behind 'em," Doc pleaded. "I can hold 'em off for a while. They're at a disadvantage if they try comin' up the stairs."

"You still got that revolver in your desk?"

Doc retrieved it. He spun the cylinder and counted aloud. "One, two, three, four, five, six. Go on now, Jesse. I'll be alright."

Jesse convinced himself that Doc was right. The best way out of this mess was to go through his own store and slip out the back. He'd have to hurry. He didn't want Doc left alone for long. He had no idea when Doc last fired his revolver or what kind of defense Doc could make.

Kodiak and his men were too busy to notice Jesse pass through the store, and into the back room, pushing through a store full of customers as he did. Jesse drew his sidearm and stepped into the alley. He caught one of Kodiak's men by surprise and slammed his gun against the back of his head. He dropped like a bag of sand.

Two of Kodiak's men mounted the stairs. Doc must have heard them coming because his office door suddenly opened and Doc blasted both men to kingdom come. They tumbled down the stairs.

Kodiak fired. His bullet shattered the glass in Doc's opened door.

"Kodiak!" Jesse yelled.

Two men stepped in between Jesse and Kodiak as Jesse's LeMat barked to life. One of the men paid for this interference with his life.

Kodiak fled into Swede's.

The second man drew to return Jesse's fire, but never completed his draw. He dropped dead in the street.

Jesse entered the store. He saw Kodiak enter the back room.

"He's got a hostage!" someone screamed.

Cautiously Jesse entered the back room. The door to the outside was open. He looked down the alley to find Kodiak gone.

Townsfolk gathered at the sound of gunfire. They thought perhaps this was the signal to fight Parson Abel had mentioned in his sermon the day before. Jesse sent men in a frantic search for old man Higgins' grandson along the banks of Lodgepole Creek. They found him just as he had fallen, face first in the muddy water. Dead.

Two men at his arms and two at his feet, they brought the lifeless body back into town. Turnus, a young man who happened to be in the wrong place at the wrong time had paid for the misplacement with his life.

All preparations for the centennial edition of the fourth of July died with Turnus. Even the orneriest boys who delighted in scaring horses with their firecrackers knew better than to disrupt the solemn parade of men carrying the body into town. Men lined the streets and women stood in front of stores, heads down in respect. No one moved until at last the men carrying Turnus stopped in front of Oldham's Funeral Home.

U.S. Marshal Jesse Jones met them there. "Where did you find him?"

"Everyone in town knew where Turnus loved to fish. We found him there. Someone gave this kid one heck of a beating," one of the men said.

"Break it up!" a voice announced.

Jesse recognized the voice of Sheriff DuFreeze as he and Mayor Truax forced their way through the crowd. "Go on home," DuFreeze told the crowd.

No one moved except the four men who carried Turnus. They laid him carefully in the street. "Mister Mayor," announced one of the men, "we ain't going home until we get some satisfaction. We're tired of our town being held hostage by the likes of men like Sheriff DuFreeze."

"You put them up to this," a flustered Claiborne Truax said to Jesse.

"I didn't have to," Jesse responded. "The people of this fair city are sick and tired of being pushed around by the likes of you. The real sheriff of this town was beaten nearly to death and Adam Potter with him. Now old man Higgins has been roughed up and his grandson Turnus killed. When will all of this lawlessness in the name of the law stop?"

"This is old man Higgins' grandson?" Mayor Truax asked.

"See for yourself," Jesse answered.

Mayor Truax knelt beside Turnus' body. "He looks so young." He rose to his feet.

"He's only fifteen." A woman burst through the crowd. "My son is only fifteen. Why?" she wailed. "Will someone tell me why?"

Her fists pounded into Traux's chest. "Why?" she screamed.

Jesse took hold of the woman and pulled her from Truax. Adeline Abel rushed in and took her away.

"This is all your doing, Mr. Mayor. When you sell your soul to the devil, this is the result," Jesse said.

"I didn't mean for it to be like this," Truax replied.

Truax walked toward DuFreeze. "This is all your fault. I'm laying the blame for all of this at your feet. You and Swan Holmes. You're fired! Do you hear me? You're fired!"

DuFreeze stood his ground. He laughed in Truax's face. "You little piss ant. You can't fire me. I don't work for you. I work for Swan Holmes. He pays me a whole lot more than this little hole of a town can pay me."

"You're fired, I tell ya. Fired!"

DuFreeze drew his gun. "Stay away from me, you two-bit mayor. You're a nothin'. A nobody!"

Claiborne Truax kept walking toward him.

"Stop!" DuFreeze shouted. He took several steps backward and took aim at Truax. "Don't make me use this. I'm warning you! Don't come any closer."

A single shot rang out.

Truax fell headlong into the street.

"I warned him. I told him not to come any closer. Now, get back all of you."

Before anyone could react, Sheriff DuFreeze had high tailed it into the Last Chance saloon.

CHAPTER 24

After a humid night in which residents of Sidney, Nebraska slept on sun porches and on their front lawns, July 4, 1876 dawned with bright sunshine and very high relative humidity. No activity whatsoever was needed to bring one to sweat.

Jesse weathered the miserable night inside the barracks of Fort Sidney with his wife and son, not leaving it to chance that one of Swan Holmes men might sneak onto fort property and assassinate him. Windows remained open so mosquitoes were constantly heard outside the mosquito netting that was draped over his bed.

A conversation outside his room roused Jesse from his fitful sleep. He recognized Bill Cody's voice and that of Ned Buntline. A third voice remained a mystery.

"It can't be," he heard Cody say. "That's impossible. There's no way what you're telling me is true.

"I'm sorry, sir, but it is true," Jesse heard someone say. "We got the notification early this morning. Colonel Custer is dead."

Jesse slid on his trousers and made his way to his door, opened it and stepped into the hall. "What's this about Colonel Custer?" he asked.

Buffalo Bill handed Jesse the telegraph the courier had handed him.

Indian Massacre

General George A. Custer and every officer and soldier of his famed 7th Calvary Regiment massacred

"This isn't possible," Jesse said. He returned the telegraph. "No one can kill Colonel Custer."

"We're getting reports of a horrible battle near the Little Bighorn in Montana Territory. Custer and his men were slaughtered," the courier announced.

"Libby," Bill Cody said. "Who's gonna take care of Custer's wife Libby? She's gotta be devastated."

"Two of Custer's brothers, a nephew, and a brother-in-law all rode with him, didn't they?" Ned Buntline said.

"Yeah, all of 'em," Cody moaned.

"This is going to put a damper on the Fourth of July celebration today," said Jesse. "No one's gonna want to celebrate after learning of Custer's massacre."

Jesse was correct. A pall shrouded the day like a thick dark cloud. The humidity seemed even more oppressive as a hot sun scorched the land.

Hatred arose for the accused killers of the glorious Seventh Cavalry, in particular for Sitting Bull and Crazy Horse. Some even imagined that the troopers manning Fort Sidney would be withdrawn and sent north.

Preparations continued for the parade down the streets of Sidney that afternoon. Reports came in to Jesse that a group of DuFreeze's men under Kodiak Crabtree were preparing to drive what remained of the inventory of Coad's cattle.

"There's something on the wind." Jesse's instincts were good. Right now they were on high alert. "Today's the day," he told Colonel Englewood. "If they're driving cattle, that's a perfect cover for a raid on Camp Clarke."

"What are you thinking?" Colonel Englewood stuffed a pinch of tobacco in his pipe and lit it. Smoke wrapped around his head.

"I'm thinkin' that we should have your men saddle their horses. Leave 'em in the stable though so we don't tip our hand. They'll be plenty of time to mount up when Brody rides through town bringing in one of DuFreeze's henchmen."

Gun fire erupted.

Englewood scurried out the door of his residence in time to see the checkpoint in front of the fort overrun.

"Indians," one of the guards yelled. "We're under attack."

Twenty Indians burst through the gate and onto the parade grounds firing at any trooper they saw. Two broke off from the group and headed straight to the Officer's Quarters.

They never made it. Jesse dropped one and Englewood the other.

The fight was over as quickly as it began. Troopers dispatched the invaders without sustaining any losses other than one man who received a flesh wound.

Jones turned over one of the Indians.

"This isn't an Indian," he said. "It's one of DuFreeze's men. He's still wearing a black bandana."

THE RAID on the fort was the first step in Swan Holmes' plan. Kodiak was mounted and ready to ride. His assignment was to round up the remaining cattle in the stockyard and drive them through town. This would block the main routes so DuFreeze and several other Night Riders might be freed up to reconnoiter Camp Clarke and its chief asset, an iron-clad stagecoach loaded with gold. An assault would transpire once Kodiak's forces had united with DuFreeze and begin with a stampede through the camp. Swan Holmes secured himself in his bank. He kept ample gunmen to dissuade an all out attack on the bank itself.

"Mount up!" Kodiak declared. "I'll ride point. Flapjack, nestle your chuck wagon behind the herd. Pack light. We're traveling fast. Spence, take Burnett with you and stoke up the brandin' fires in our usual place. We'll camp there tonight, but I want to be back on the road at first light tomorrow. We're gonna brand all night working in shifts."

The incident at the fort had barely quieted down when cattle poured into the streets. Drovers fired pistols in the air. This wasn't a casual drive through town, it was almost a stampede. Townsfolk hightailed it off the street, their other choice was to get trampled. One of the longhorns snared a ladder leaving the man atop it dangling by a rope as steer after steer raced under him. The bunting he'd been hanging disintegrated under thundering hooves.

Kodiak saw J.F. Coad and his son Ben near the entrance to the fort. Evidently, they thought they could somehow halt the charging livestock.

Kodiak's pistol barked twice as he raced by. Both men dove to safety behind the Officer's Quarters.

Troopers fired back. Kodiak looked over his shoulder and saw one outrider tumble from his horse. The man regained his feet but his spine-chilling scream followed as hundreds of raging longhorns ground him to a pulp.

Kodiak could not see DuFreeze or his men. He knew they were out there kicking up dust in an all out sprint out of town.

PAST BOOTHILL CEMETERY rode Sheriff DuFreeze and ten additional Night Riders. Under his breath DuFreeze thanked Swan Holmes for the brilliant plan. *Panic the people with a stampede. Send me and several others out of town by a different route. It's genius. Pure genius.*

DuFREEZE'S RIDE had not escaped the watchful eye of Adeline Abel. She heard riders gallop by. Scrambling to the window in the parson's study, she watched a rider with only one arm and his ten accomplices spur their horses up the hill toward the cemetery.

Adeline left Turnus' mother behind and when the dust of the stampede ended, made her way to the fort.

"Jesse," she said, "I saw about a dozen men ride north past our house. One of the riders had only one arm."

"DuFreeze," Jesse declared. Colonel Englewood and Bill Cody stood next to him. "Any idea where he's headed?"

"Could be they used the stampede to mask their intentions," Cody replied. "More than likely they're headed out to Camp Clarke. They already know the gold is there."

"A dozen men wouldn't stand a chance if they rode into Camp Clarke. Sergeant Major Kelly and his men are waiting in ambush," Englewood said.

"If the stampede is a diversion, maybe DuFreeze is on a mission to scout out Camp Clarke, find the gold, and then lead the others in a raid to secure it," said Jesse.

"That makes sense," said Englewood. "We'd better get a telegraph off to the Sergeant Major and have him and his men on the lookout for DuFreeze."

Clickity-clack.

Agile fingers of the telegraph operator tapped the keys.

AT CAMP CLARKE a second operator translated the dots and dashes of Morse code into words.

DuFreeze and scouting party headed your way
Put troops on high alert
Colonel Englewood

An orderly folded the message and stuck it in his shirt pocket then brought it to the attention of Sergeant Major Kelly.

"From Colonel Englewood." The orderly removed the telegram from his pocket and presented it to Sergeant Major Kelly.

Kelly soaked in the words. He sent a detachment from Company A into the hills south of Camp Clarke to, as the Sergeant Major said, "Keep a keen eye out for spies".

"What's going on Sergeant Major?" Henry T. Clarke had watched the orderly deliver his message from the opening in his tent, and the detachment of men take off for the hills."

"We're about to be havin' some company, I'm a thinkin'. DuFreeze is headed north. Swan Holmes is takin' the bait, hook, line, and sinker." Kelly handed the telegram to Clarke.

"So are you sending your troops to pick off the spies?"

"No, sir, I gave them no such order. They're to keep their distance and report back to me. I don't want DuFreeze to have any idea, any idea at all, that we're expecting him."

"You're just going to roll out the welcome mat?" Clarke asked.

"I like the expression I heard the other day, 'Welcome to my parlor said the spider to the fly.' When my men spot DuFreeze, they'll pull back into Camp Clarke. When DuFreeze's men catch up with him, we'll let 'em ride on in and spring the trap."

Kelly slapped his hands together with a loud POP!

A flagman stood on the south shore of the Platte and wig-wagged a signal at Kelly's command.

Kelly looked through binoculars and watched the signalman respond.

"What was all that about?" asked Clarke.

"Tellin' the men on the other side to hunker down and keep stock still. If DuFreeze gets up on the hill behind us, he'll be able to look across the valley. Any movement, any move-ment at all, will spell disaster. It'd be like General Bragg a-lookin' down from Lookout Mountain on the city of Chat-tanooga below."

"Were you there at Chattanooga, Sergeant Major?"

"Yes, sir." Curry said. "I was a-watchin' our boys scalin' Lookout Mountain during the 'Battle above the Clouds.' It is somethin' I'll nary forget."

"Darn shame about Custer," Clarke added.

"Knew him and a lot of men in the Seventh," said Kelly. "In my opinion, and that's all this is, is my opinion, the Good Book says somethin' like 'Pride comes before the fall.' Sometimes we underestimate the power of our enemies. And that, Mr. Clarke, is why we're takin' every precaution we can to stay undercover and out of sight until the enemy is well inside our entrapment zone."

"I've got a lot of men here who are innocent civilians and

not military men, Sergeant Major. How can we keep them out of harm's way when DuFreeze rides in?"

"Got any spare clothing?"

"What would that do?"

"I'll have my troopers trade places with your workers. I'll dress my men in civilian clothes and hide 'em in plain sight. They'll have to keep their small arms hidden. Got somethin' they can work on to make it look like construction is going on as if nothin' was happening?"

"Sure."

"Then now is the time to get that done before we have spies lookin' down on us," said Kelly.

It wasn't long before the trade was complete. Troopers dressed as civilians soon were working to complete the work of building the Camp Clarke Bridge. Tucked out of sight were their Army issued handguns. In a time of war what better weapon to have than a Colt Peacemaker.

A HUGE DUST cloud drew Brody Belt's attention. Was the cavalry coming to greet him or was this something else entirely? "Let's get off the main road," he instructed his prisoner. "I ain't taking any chances."

A deep gully cut diagonally into the earth lay not more than a quarter mile away. Brody directed his captive into that gully. He could see the road from there, but because of the angle, whatever was on the road could not see him.

The dust cloud drew ever closer. In an instant, Brody recognized Sheriff DuFreeze at the point of a large herd of longhorns. His heart sank. Were they headed to his ranch? Cynthia could readily defend herself against the attack of one or two men. This would be much more than that.

When DuFreeze reached the spot where Brody had first seen him, he drew up. A rider joined him. The wind blew just right enabling Brody to hear everything from his vantage point.

"What are we stopped fer?" the man asked.

"Ah, it's just that I'm so close to that sod buster's place that I was thinkin' about checking in with the two men I sent to keep an eye on the place."

"Want me to ride on over?"

DuFreeze removed his hat and scratched his head with the only hand he had. "Naw. I'll come back when this whole thing is over." He slipped his hat onto his head and pointed his hand to the northeast. "Let's move out!" he yelled.

Brody sighed. That was closer than he wanted. The thought of the one armed man's return nauseated him. It was not that Brody didn't think he could best DuFreeze in a gunfight, but that DuFreeze would bring a small army with him.

It was a long time before the herd was out of sight. Then Brody felt secure enough to return to the main road and ride into Sidney. By his estimates the parade would be ready to start by the time they got there.

And he was correct. It was parade time. However, today there would be no parade.

Once in town Brody found townsfolk in disarray. The parade was reforming after DuFreeze had driven livestock through the heart of it. Some wagons were tipped over and a few dozen men were working to upright them. The city band had assembled under an oak tree for shade. Not only for the shade it provided, but to assure the director everyone survived. Brody noticed an unidentifiable instrument, flattened in the melee, lying in the street. Buntings were ripped and banners swung loosely in the breeze. What had been meant as an in-your-face gesture to Swan Holmes on Brody's part was now unnecessary and unneeded. He picked his way amid the humanity and debris to the entrance of the fort.

Brody dismounted and turned his attention to his captive. He was grinning ear to ear. "Wipe that smirk off yer face," Brody commanded.

"Been telling you all along that yer no match for DuFreeze. He's out smarted ya at every turn."

The man made the mistake of again showing Brody his broad smile.

Brody drove his right hand into the man's face, entirely covering that broad smile. Blood splattered.

"Next time maybe you'll remember not to smirk when the battle's only half won," Brody chortled.

Brody grabbed the man by the collar and unceremoniously led him to where he saw Jesse Jones and the others assembled.

"Well, what do we have here?" said Jesse.

"This is the slime ball I told you about," came Brody's reply.

Jesse noticed all the bleeding. "What happened to him?" he asked.

"Aw, it ain't nothin'. I didn't like his smile, that's all."

CHAPTER 25

With the 'slime ball,' as Brody called him, locked up in the stockade, Jones was ready for the next step; 'getting in the rear' of DuFreeze and his henchmen. The office of Lieutenant Colonel Englewood served as the impromptu meeting place for those seeking to drive Swan Holmes from his self-appointed position. Ned Buntline took copious notes for another dime novel adventure of *Bill Cody, Western Hero*.

"I sure hope we've got that gold out of DuFreeze's reach," said Jesse.

"I do, too," Potter replied.

"Gentlemen, we're going to have to assume that the Sergeant Major has the situation well in hand at Camp Clarke Bridge," Colonel Englewood said.

"That's the first time I've heard you refer to the place as Camp Clarke Bridge," Cody remarked.

"It just seemed like the right way to refer to it. After all, once the bridge is finished and dedicated, the work site known as Camp Clarke will be torn down," Englewood said.

"Let's just hope and pray that no one decides to strike a

match to the bridge. There are big plans ahead for that structure including a stage line running from Sidney to Deadwood," said Cody.

"It'll be the shortest route to the Black Hills by far," Buntline added.

Jesse thought for a moment. "You know," he said, "All of that ain't gonna benefit us until we get this matter with Swan Holmes settled."

Parson Abel and Doc barged into the meeting room with a sentry lagging behind.

"I tried to stop 'em, sir," the sentry announced.

"That's alright, Private," Englewood said.

"The town's in an uproar," Parson Abel announced. "They've surrounded the bank."

"They're calling for Holmes' hide," said Doc. "If someone doesn't do something, someone's gonna be killed."

Colonel Englewood didn't hesitate. "Private, tell Lieutenant Bailey to form a perimeter around the bank. Tell him to send the citizens home. And under no circumstances let anyone in or out of the bank. Do you understand my orders, Private?"

"Yes, sir."

It was not long before the parade grounds came alive with troopers. Orders were barked. Lines were formed. Troopers from Fort Sidney stepped between citizens and secured Holmes Bank.

"What's your next move, Marshal?" Englewood asked.

"Would you loan me the use of Company B, sir?" Jesse was still forming an idea in his head. "What I have in mind, Colonel, is to get into the rear of those driving the cattle. Unless I misunderstand Kodiak's motives, I'm guessing he's going to rebrand them at his usual spot."

"I can attest to that," Brody added. "About a mile west of

my place, I saw Kodiak lead the cattle drive to the northeast. Likely, they've already got the rebranding underway."

"If I can follow after them at a safe distance with Company B, we'll be in position to attack Kodiak's rear and flank if he charges toward Camp Clarke, or as the Colonel now calls it, Camp Clarke Bridge."

"Where do you want me?" Buffalo Bill asked when there was a lull in the conversation.

"Do you and Ned want to ride with me?"

"I thought you'd never ask," came Cody's reply.

"Potter will supply my eyes and ears here with the colonel?"

"Ah, go on, take Potter with you," said Doc. "The Parson and I are too old to do much fightin', but we can be your eyes and ears."

"What do you say, Doc?" Abel asked.

"Huh?" Doc replied.

"Just as I thought," Abel replied. "Your ears aren't very good. And I've got to question your eyesight, too."

Company B heard 'boots and saddles' and mounted in response. Jesse, Potter, Buffalo Bill and Buntline formed a line behind a brash, newly-minted lieutenant named Nelson. They rode east after Kodiak Crabtree and his men.

Kodiak watched the rebranding from a distance. The smell of burnt hides hung in the air. There was little wind to dissipate it. Flapjack stood near with tin cup in hand.

"Got the beans a-soakin' in the pot," Flapjack said. "I brung ya some coffee to wash the smell down."

"Aw, it ain't that bad. Don't mind the smell. Like my pappy used to say, 'It's the smell of money'." Kodiak took the cup. He blew on it to cool the contents. "Dang," he said. "Did you put this cup in the fire or somethin'?"

Flapjack ignored the comment. "I assume you want the fellas to eat tonight. But, I guess I never did ask ya."

"What?" Kodiak's mind was running ahead thinking about the cattle drive and his role in getting all that gold. Wishin' they didn't have to stop to rebrand the cattle.

"I was just askin' if we was stayin' the night as planned or if we you're gettin' antsy to move?"

"Yeah," Kodiak answered.

"Yeah, what?"

"Yeah, I am getting antsy. I wish we didn't have to wait here like sitting ducks. If Jones is worth his salt, he's out lookin' for us right now."

A wrangler flipped a calf on its side. Four others held it down while a fifth applied the branding iron to its left flank. The larger animals were more difficult to rebrand. A makeshift corral had been constructed with a chute leading into it. Four men stood on either side of the chute and squeezed the cattle between them. With the animal secure, a hot brand was applied over the old one and the critter released into the corral.

"So are we stayin' the night or not?" Flapjack asked. "My beans depend on yer answer."

"Yeah, we're stayin'. At this rate the men will have little sleep tonight." Kodiak took a sip of his still too hot coffee. "Have Spence ride out to get Stetson, will ya?"

"Yes, sir, boss," said Flapjack.

When Flapjack's back was turned Kodiak poured half his coffee onto the ground. He removed a flask from his vest pocket and splashed some whisky in his cup, telling himself that it would cool down the remaining liquid.

Stetson found Kodiak where Flapjack had left him.

"Ya wanted to see me?" Stetson asked.

"I did. I want you to select three or four men and have them put a perimeter around the camp."

"That ain't hardly enough men."

"I know that. I just want to put up a little buffer in the southwest. That's where I figure Jones will come from."

"You're expecting trouble?"

"Yeah. Call it gut instincts or whatever you want. I heard stories about Jones and how he does the unexpected. I don't want him riding in unannounced."

"Maybe we outta start a few head in the direction of Camp Clarke now instead of waiting 'til tomorrow morning. Got a full moon comin' tonight so we could drive 'em 'til daybreak comes," said Stetson."

"I like that idea. Make it happen. But first send out the men I requested to cover our withdrawal," Kodiak advised. "Tell the men branding when they get one hundred head in the corral to release them to join the herd. We're moving out."

When Flapjack saw the herd pulling out and that the intention was for the men to drive cattle through the night, he came running on his spindly legs to Kodiak.

"Did I hear right? Are we drivin' on?" Flapjack barked.

"We are?" Kodiak asked with an impish grin. He smiled and welcomed the tongue-lashing he knew Flapjack had prepared for him.

"Dag nabbit! I told ya I got beans a-soakin'. How in heck to do expect me to feed these men when I have no idea how many are comin' or when?"

A CRIMSON SUNSET brought the day's work to an end at Camp Clarke. Those on the far side of the Platte settled in for another night without campfires. Sergeant Major Kelly had cautioned them that even a wisp of smoke could tip off their whereabouts and hamstring their chances to keep the gold protected.

Kelly had expected some backlash against his command before they crossed over the bridge, and he got it from several of his men. Protests came primarily from the younger men who were not as battle hardened as the veterans of Company A. It was these veterans, many of whom had seen battle after battle during the Civil War, who pulled the younger troopers in line.

"If you want to stay alive," Kelly had overheard one such veteran say, "then you will do as you are told."

The younger man was feeling his oats so he talked back to the veteran. Like a Fourth of July firecracker the veteran exploded and the young man never knew where the first blow came from, but Kelly knew that he'd never forget it. The veteran let loose only one punch. It thudded against the young man's jaw and laid him out cold, face first in the dusty road.

Standing over his fallen comrade the veteran announced, "I don't care if you young guys get yerselves killed, but don't you ever put me in danger of losing my life. 'Cuz when it gets right down to it and it's a question of my hide or yours, I'm protecting mine. Now, do as the Sergeant Major said and get yer butts over to the other side of the bridge. And if the Sergeant Major says there will be no fires until this is over, then they'll be no fires!"

Shortly after the sun began its descent and turned the sky crimson, three Indian scouts arrived back at Camp Clarke. They presented themselves to Kelly.

"Riders come," the taller of the scouts said. He was bare-chested and broad across the shoulders.

"How many would you say Man Without a Pony?" Kelly asked.

"We count twelve. One man has one arm only."

"That's our man alright," Kelly announced. "Did you see where they were headed?"

Man Without a Pony pointed to the south ridge overlooking Camp Clarke.

"Good. That's exactly where we want them," Kelly replied.

"Overheard one armed man say him wait for others. Many men bring much cattle. You want us to kill these men on the hill?"

Kelly took no time to ponder the question. "No. I'm a-thinkin' that we're ready to face all the men they can throw at us. Go get yerselves some grub."

The three scouts disappeared in the sea of humanity making their way to the mess for dinner. Although Camp Clarke was not a military compound, Henry T. Clarke ran it like one. The whole community ate their meals together in a facility set aside for just such a purpose. Staff cooks and orderlies provided a slate of meals not unlike those served in Fort Sidney. Most likely because the kitchen staff at Camp Clarke had their origins in the military.

Sergeant Major Kelly found Henry Clarke's table where he and Jimbo Livingston were discussing the events of the day. "May I join you?" Kelly asked.

"Of course, Sergeant Major," Clarke replied. He politely offered Kelly a place to sit.

"Man Without a Pony, just came back," Kelly said. "He's reporting twelve men are manning the ridge south of camp."

"Are these the men we've been preparing for?" said Livingston.

"They are. He said one of the men had only one arm."

"Are we prepared for what is about to happen?" asked Clarke.

"We're as ready as can be, sir," Kelly delivered with a nod.

WITHIN THE HOUR One-Arm Bill DuFreeze was exactly where Man Without a Pony said he would be. DuFreeze had navigated the rough terrain to the top of the ridge overlooking Camp Clarke and the adjacent Camp Clarke Bridge. His sinewy body permitted him to weave through the underbrush and reach the ridge ahead of the others. He roosted on a fallen tree and waited.

"'Bout time ya made it. What took ya so long?" said DuFreeze when the first of the remaining men emerged.

"That's a steep climb," the man replied.

"Ain't nothing compared to other places I've scaled in my lifetime," DuFreeze announced. "And quit yer lollygagging and put yer eyes on the scenery down there. Tell me if it looks like they're expecting company or not."

The lone Night Rider was soon joined by two others at the top of the ridge. They laid out prone knowing that to remain upright was not an option if they wanted their whereabouts to remain undetected.

"Whatta ya see?" said DuFreeze.

"Nothin' much," one of the men replied. "I don't think anyone expects us. It's really quiet down there."

"See any soldiers?"

"Nope," a second man announced. He sat up and put his binoculars away. "Looks like a sleepy little camp. A few men milling around and the rest are going in and out of the saloon."

DuFreeze removed a flask from his hip pocket and took a swig from it. "Where's that gold wagon sitting? See it anywhere?"

"Nope," came the reply.

DuFreeze scrambled near the others. "Give me one of them spy glasses."

He held out his hand and one of the men filled it. DuFreeze gave the place a thorough scan. "There's the livery. I'll bet ya it's stashed away in there. But, it sure ain't guarded or anything."

"Could be men inside," someone said.

"Ya, but if it's there with as much gold in her as they say there is, I'd expect an armed guard on the outside as well as on the inside," said DuFreeze.

"What do you want us to do, boss?"

"Adams, I want you to wait 'til the sun goes down and sneak your way down and take a looky see if that stage is inside the livery. Someone's gotta find out where that gold is so we can target our attack as soon as Kodiak gets here in the morning."

"What if the stage is on the other side of the river?" Adams asked.

"Give me them binoculars one more time," DuFreeze ordered. He peered through the lens and followed a road to the bridge and traced it to the other side. "Can't make out nothin' on the other side. 'Sides the bridge ain't even completed. Take a look for yerself."

DuFreeze shoved the binoculars into Adams' chest nearly knocking the breath out of him.

Adams traced the same route DuFreeze had with the binoculars. He thought he saw something move on the far side of the river, but wasn't sure. He looked again. Nothing. He came back to the bridge. Sure enough, the last third remained unbuilt. Still there were wagon tracks on the far side.

"There are wagon tracks on the far side of the Platte," Adams announced.

"Gimme that!" DuFreeze grabbed the binoculars and

brought them to his eyes. "Well, I'll be a horny toad." He rubbed his chin. "Still the same, I want you to go down there after dark and check out the livery. Somethin' tells me that this sleepy little camp ain't all that sleepy."

With a generous moon overhead, Adams slipped down the ridge and into Camp Clarke. From the hill DuFreeze watched him ease inside the livery. Moments later he saw a flash followed by the report of a pistol.

CHAPTER 26

S wan Holmes paced back and forth. His office served as headquarters to plots that could bring him a massive fortune. So far the one armed man he'd hand-picked to be his right hand man had come through. Together they'd brought Sidney to her knees. Through the bank he'd loaned money that life-blooded the community. When the bank owned sixty percent of each business, he foreclosed and put his own men in charge. He'd even weaseled his own man into the office of sheriff. His scheme to steal Black Hills gold from his own bank was brilliantly conceived, by his own account.

So why am I on edge? he wondered.

"Jones. That's why," he answered himself. "Every gull-darned time, Jones steps in and everything goes to pieces."

Holmes was feeling insecure and his insecurity was fanned by a torch carrying mob surrounding the bank.

A knock at his door fueled his anger. "What is it?" he barked at the door.

"I thought you'd like to know that the crowd is breaking up. The army has stepped in."

"Thank you," Holmes said. "That is good news."

"But not completely, sir."

"Stop being cryptic. What do you mean 'not completely'?"

"Well, it's just that the army has taken the place of the crowd, sir."

Holmes stormed out of his office and into the lobby. He opened the shutter on a barred window and looked out. The report was accurate enough. No citizens. Just troops. Lots of troops. No torches. Instead stacked arms and campfires.

Swan Holmes opened the front door a sliver. "Who's in charge?" he yelled.

"That'd be Lieutenant Colonel Englewood, sir," a soldier replied.

Sarcasm dripped from Swan Holmes lips. "Tell that *Lieutenant Colonel Englewood* of yours to get over here right now!"

"I'll ask him to do that," the private replied.

"I'm not asking you to do that, I'm telling! I want to know why I'm being held hostage in my own bank," Holmes replied. "I am not at all pleased with your conduct, *sir.*" He spit out the last word then retreated to his office.

What seemed an eternity passed before Holmes heard a knock on the bank door.

"Mr. Holmes, this is Lieutenant Colonel Englewood. One of my men said that you wanted to see me."

Holmes opened the door. "Won't you step inside?" he said with all the sweetness he could muster.

"Sorry, sir, but I'm afraid that I can't do that."

Holmes had opened the door wide enough he could see two armed men, one on either side of the colonel. "I wanted to thank you for driving the crowd away."

"You're welcome. Now, if that's all, I'll return to my men."

"No! That isn't all!" he fired back. "I want to know by what authority your men have surrounded my bank."

"That authority, sir, comes from none other than a new U.S. Marshal appointed to Sidney." Englewood turned to leave. His bodyguards remained focused on Holmes and anything he might do to prevent Englewood's leaving.

"And just who is this new U.S. Marshal and why would he do this to me?" said Holmes.

Englewood kept walking. "Jesse Jones," he said without turning around.

"Jesse Jones?" Holmes bellowed. "Did you say Jesse Jones?"

Swan Holmes' insides were on fire. His head felt like it was about to explode. *Again it's that meddling Jesse Jones.* "I'll kill him!" Holmes fired his words at Englewood's back. He reached into his coat pocket.

Englewood's bodyguards drew their pistols.

Holmes withdrew his handkerchief. He waved it at the troopers in defiance and slammed the door.

"Bolt it!" Holmes yelled at his men. Under his breath he breathed out fire as he walked. "Jones. Jesse Jones. U.S. Marshal, huh? Now if that doesn't take the cake. DuFreeze is gonna have to kill himself a U.S. Marshal."

AT TIMES WISPY clouds slid across the face of the moon diffusing its light. Kodiak was pleased the moon never hid itself, creating sufficient light to drive cattle along the road. His destination was to locate Bill DuFreeze and his cluster of men south of Camp Clarke. He'd decided to take the lead along with Stetson, leaving about a dozen men behind to finish the branding. Kodiak knew the plan was to keep the herd five miles south of Camp Clarke. That way the lowing of the cattle was not carried on the wind to warn the camp of their coming.

Stetson drew his horse alongside Kodiak's. "What are ya thinkin'?" he asked.

"I'm thinkin' about how I'm going to spend all the money I'm about to make," Kodiak replied.

"I've been thinkin' about that, too. Got me a little gal in Sidney. I'm thinkin' about asking her to marry me. Saw some land in Montana once that looks real fine. Think I'll raise some cattle...have a couple kids...settle down. What about you, Kodiak?"

"I'm not the settlin' down kind. I've been thinkin' about playin' the gamblin' circuit. I hear there's money to be made in Abilene now that Bill Hickok's left town. Don't think I want to travel all the way to Tombstone, but I might. Certainly, not gonna show my face again in Sidney. Unless it's to help get rid of Jones."

"What about working for Swan Holmes? Gonna give that up?"

"Yeah. Never really liked the guy. I'm just in this for the money."

A rider thundered toward the pair as they rode.

"Kodiak?" the rider asked.

"I am," Kodiak replied.

"DuFreeze wants you to rest your herd about a mile up the road. Follow me and I'll take you to him."

Kodiak put Stetson in charge and followed the rider. They found DuFreeze on the ridge overlooking Camp Clarke. His men were with him.

"What some jerky?" DuFreeze held out his only hand filled with strips of meat.

Kodiak delighted in the smoky taste. "Did you smoke these yourself?"

"Naw. Found 'em on a shelf after I beat up old man Higgins."

"I know what Swan Holmes would say about this jerky... God helps—"

"—those that helps themselves," they said in unison.

DuFreeze took Kodiak to the top of the ridge and pointed. "Tomorrow morning," he said, "I want you to drive your herd into Camp Clarke. You and I will ride on the right flank." DuFreeze pointed toward a building. "See that building? That's the livery stable. When we get near it, you and I are gonna take a half dozen men and see what's inside. I lost a man in there earlier this evening. My guess is that the stagecoach with all the gold is in there."

"What about those tracks on the other side of the Platte?" one of the men noted.

"*There are* tracks on the other side," said DuFreeze. "What we can't figure out is how they got there. The bridge isn't finished yet there are tracks leading into the trees. I can't explain it."

"Could it be that the bridge was completed, the stagecoach drove across, and the latter part of the bridge taken down?" Kodiak asked.

"That's what I'm suggesting," said the man.

"If that's the case, we're coming out here short-handed," said Kodiak. He realized what he'd just said. "No offense meant."

"None taken," replied DuFreeze. "The bad part is that we don't have time to recruit additional forces. We're gonna have to hope what we're lookin' for is in the livery and not on the other side of the Platte."

Colonel Englewood made his office his command headquarters. From his third floor window Holmes Bank was illuminated by campfire. Englewood felt quite sure that no one would get in or out of the bank without his knowing it.

"You know," said Doc, "we volunteered to be Jesse's eyes and ears at the bank, but for the life of me I cannot figure out exactly what that means."

"To be very truthful with you, neither can I," Parson Abel answered.

Englewood turned his attention away from the scene out his window. "Gentlemen, I'm sure you've heard the expression about the military."

"You mean the one that says the military is nothing but hurry up and wait?" Abel replied.

"That's the one." The colonel returned to the scene out his window.

"It's kinda like doctoring," Abel replied. "You hurry out to a woman in labor and then wait until God says it's time for the baby to be born."

Doc agreed. "Yep. Same as what's out in the street. You set up camp around the bank and then wait until someone inside decides to come out." He paused a moment to collect additional thoughts.

Parson Abel filled the pause. "And in my case I hurry and preach the Gospel and then wait until the Holy Spirit works a change of heart."

"I hadn't thought of this before," Englewood added. "Life is all about hurry up and wait."

"How in the dickens did this conversation become so philosophical?" Abel noted.

"You started it," Doc replied. "You're the one that brought up this whole idea of hurry up and wait."

"*I* never mentioned that," said Abel. "If you recall it was the colonel who asked if you had heard the expression about the military."

"Yes, but you're the one who *specifically* said 'hurry up and wait'."

"The colonel could have meant any of a dozen expressions about the military."

"But, he didn't. He meant hurry up and wait."

"Whoa. Hold on men!" Englewood said. "Something's happening at the bank. Come take a look."

Gunfire erupted. Five shots rang out.

Englewood bolted for the door. "Stay behind me," he said. "I don't want either one of you to get hurt."

In single file they headed toward the bank.

Gun fire continued.

"What's going on, Sergeant?" Englewood said.

"Something's happening at the rear of the bank," he replied.

In a moment the group ran to where the gunfire was coming from.

Troopers had taken up arms and sought shelter. Some hid behind crates in the alley. Others hid behind the corners of adjacent buildings.

Englewood spotted two bodies sprawled out in the alley. Thankfully, they were not his men.

"You! You in the building! Hold your fire!" Englewood yelled.

Gunfire ceased.

"Throw down your weapons! We've got you completely surrounded!"

"Is that you, Colonel Englewood?" Englewood recognized the voice. It was Swan Holmes.

"It is."

The back door opened a crack.

"Do you know who you're talking to, colonel? This is Swan

Holmes. I own this bank and I own this town. You have no right to hold me here!"

"Mr. Holmes, I want you and your men to lay down their arms before somebody else gets killed tonight."

"Come in and get me!" Holmes yelled back.

Englewood signaled to his men on the other side of the open door.

Pressed against the wall, several troopers eased their way down the alley.

When they were in position one soldier pulled open the door and the others entered.

Gunfire followed.

Then silence.

After what seemed forever to Colonel Englewood, all his men came out with Swan Holmes hog-tied between them.

"The others are dead," a trooper reported.

"Well," said Doc, "it looks like good things do come to those who wait."

Lieutenant Nelson raised his right hand and the men of Company B halted behind him. Jesse Jones could see where wagon tracks and hoof prints veered off the road and headed northeast into the sandhills.

"Marshal, may I have a word with you, sir?" said the lieutenant.

Jesse nudged his horse forward until he and Lieutenant Nelson sat side by side.

"I believe this is the spot we talked about, is it not?" Nelson said. "Glad we have a full moon or I'd never have seen it."

Jesse nodded. "That's where they left the main road alright. The branding spot we talked about is about five miles in that direction. I'm going to take these three men with me and we're going on ahead of you to find out if the branding is all finished."

"Do you still want me to do what we talked about?"

"I do. Stay here with your men. Give me a half-hour head start and then follow at a walk. If you hear shooting come a runnin' because it means we've been discovered. Otherwise, if you come to the branding sight and no one is around, angle your troops to the northwest and ride until you intersect with the main road. You should find yourself about eight miles south of Camp Clarke. Stay there until I send someone for you."

Jesse led Adam Potter, Buffalo Bill, and Ned Buntline into the night. Overhead, the moon gave them all the light they needed. Kodiak and his Night Riders were nearby. Jones could feel it. Were they still rebranding or had they finished? That he didn't know.

Jesse scanned the horizon looking for signs of a fire. So far, there were none.

Deeper into the night a coyote howled. Jesse recalled how, as a young boy, this howling used to raise gooseflesh on him. The years had changed that. Through the years he'd grown accustomed to the sound. His wife Martha had not. She would always awaken at the first banshee-like howl, frightened by this normal night sound of the prairie. Lying in bed together, Jesse would pull her close and speak soft words, tender words that calmed Martha's soul. The closeness of their bodies, the tender words and a gentle rocking back and forth relaxed her until sleep returned.

Now he heard hooves. Thousands of them. In the distance like a thunderclap that carried the promise of rain.

"We're behind them alright." Jesse guessed at the distance. "Maybe a mile or two behind."

"I think that's plenty close enough for now," Cody interjected.

Buntline had pad in hand but was finding it hard to write with the frequent passing of clouds in front of the moon.

"Will you be able to read yer chicken' scratches?" Potter asked Buntline.

"I don't know. Sometimes what I write seems clear when I write it and then makes no sense at all when I read it the next morning," he said. "I may have to trust my memory."

"Or just make somethin' up like you usually do," said Cody.

"I never do that," Buntline replied, giving Cody a quick wink.

"Let's start angling back to the main road," said Jesse. "I think we've accomplished everything we set out to do. We're in the rear of the cattle drive and close enough we can strike with the full force of Company B when Lieutenant Nelson catches up with us."

"Kodiak's in for one heck of a surprise," Cody added.

CHAPTER 27

Kodiak was ready long before daybreak. He hadn't slept well. Anticipation of the day's events wore on him. They didn't used to. That all changed when he reached forty-five. Now he saw his own mortality. He could easily remember names and faces of younger men who found early graves. And that bothered him. There were times he wanted to cut and run, but he knew men like Bill DuFreeze, would hunt him down. He was in too deep.

Kodiak had allowed only a small fire this morning. In fact, he'd started it himself. There would be no breakfast cooked over this fire, only the large coffee pot Flapjack had somehow managed to make fit over the flame. Like Kodiak, Flapjack hadn't slept well. The two men sipped their coffee in silence.

Men slept on the ground around them. Some moaned. Others snored. Some stirred at the smell of Flapjack's fresh coffee. One or two had already flung off their blankets and rolled them up. Kodiak watched one hightail into the trees obviously feeling the cumulative effects of Flapjacks beans. Kodiak looked at Flapjack who shrugged in reply.

"Alright, Flapjack," Kodiak said. "Time to wake 'em up."

His timing was perfect. Just as these words left his lips DuFreeze came down the hill with the remainder of the men.

"Grab some coffee, men," DuFreeze ordered. "Camp Clarke ain't awake yet, but it's time you are."

DuFreeze walked about kicking the boots of anyone who had attempted to sleep past his ordered wake up call. "Ya got ten minutes ta drink yer coffee and get mounted. We're stampedin' this herd right through Camp Clarke. They'll never know what hit 'em."

Kodiak made sure DuFreeze's order was followed. Two were not saddled and ready to ride. These two had evidently not learned a trick the other riders had. They had somehow missed that their companions first added cool canteen water to their hot coffee before chugging it.

Within fifteen minutes of DuFreeze's command everyone was mounted and riding in the direction of their places around the herd.

Kodiak mounted and awaited any last minute instructions. He looked down at DuFreeze.

"Aren't you riding with us?" Kodiak asked.

"Not in a stampede," DuFreeze said. "Can't ride and shoot at the same time." He held up his one arm. "Gonna stay up here 'til the herd moves through. Find that gold. I want that gold. God helps those who help themselves."

With those words Kodiak realized how much like Swan Holmes DuFreeze had become. He heard the words "Will do" come from his own mouth in reply.

Kodiak rode to his spot on the right flack of the herd. This time there would be no point man. Swing riders, flank riders and drag riders would drive the herd forward. The plan was to contain the stampede as best they could until it hit Camp Clarke. Then all riders would get out of the way and let allow the longhorns to destroy the camp. Ten men would trail the herd and gather it together. All the others would take over Camp Clarke and claim the gold shipment hidden there.

A single shot from Kodiak's revolver put everything in motion. Other shots followed.

First one longhorn bolted.

Then a second.

Then a third.

Then the plains erupted with the sounds of thousands of hoofs.

Cattle raced past Kodiak.

Everything became a blur.

Horse. Rider. Cattle.

Swing rider and flank riders somehow kept the herd contained.

Everything hit the junction with the Oregon Trail.

Somehow outriders turned the herd west.

More gunfire.

More speed.

The herd separated from the outriders and spread out.

A tornado of hoofs and horns crashed headlong into Camp Clarke.

THIS TORNADO WAS MET at once with rifle fire. What DuFreeze could not see through his binoculars were men hidden behind the façades of camp buildings. Winchesters rained fire on what? The herd? The riders? Wounded riders tumbled from horses. Some were able to stand only to be impaled or trampled to death.

Within minutes the herd was gone.

Passing clean through Camp Clarke.

Smashing anything in its path.

Ten men followed after the herd to bunch it back together.

Nearly one hundred nightriders remained. These sought shelter anywhere they could from the rifles above and the small arms fire below.

Sergeant Major Kelly hunkered behind a carriage in the livery stable. Two others hid themselves in the hay loft above him. Kelly had planned this ruse. He'd counted on DuFreeze ordering men to attack here, especially after killing a spy the night before.

Flapjack was assigned the task of leading men in a frontal assault. He and most of his men safely ran the gauntlet of rifle fire. They pushed open the heavy livery door and stepped inside. Kelly saw the surprised look on Flapjacks' face when he discovered only a single carriage and not the longed for stage coach. That look didn't stay long. A hail of bullets cut his surprise short.

"Stay put men!" Kelly yelled. "We haven't seen the last attempt."

Outside he heard the sounds of death.

Horrible sounds.

The thud of bullets pounding into flesh.

Screams of agony made by dying men.

Pleas for water. Pleas that someone would end the pain.

Kelly recognized the voice of Kodiak Crabtree issuing commands.

"Spence, get around to the back of the livery. Take a couple men with you."

Spence argued. "I ain't gonna do that. It would be like committing suicide."

Kodiak swore a blue streak. Still Spence refused.

A gun went off.

Spence screamed out in pain. "Why did ya have to go and do that for?"

"Now get around back with some men before I finish ya off!" Kodiak bellowed.

"I'm going! I'm going!"

Sergeant Major Kelly turned to face the back door of the livery.

Moments later Spence burst through that door. Four others followed.

Guns drawn.

Kelly saw Spence's blood stained shirt.The spot where Kodiak had winged him.

"Drop 'em!" Kelly shouted.

Hoping to randomly hit their hidden quarry, the five men fired.

They didn't.

Sergeant Major Kelly and his men did.

KODIAK STILL HAD plenty of men. That wasn't his problem. The problem was he was no closer in obtaining the gold DuFreeze had sent him to retrieve. He considered an all out rush against the livery as one of his options. This, too, was a problem. His men were too spread out and in many instances too pinned down to do much of anything. What was obvious was that his surprise visit had not surprised anyone. In fact, it had been anticipated.

"Fall back!" Kodiak yelled. "Regroup in there!" Kodiak pointed to the mess hall.

Kodiak took off at a sprint. He sought shelter where he could find it. Behind rain barrels, water troughs, and in doorways. Bullets shattered windows in front of him and behind him as he dove through the door to safety.

He ventured to sneak a look outside. Men were fighting their way in his direction. He provided cover by shooting a trooper off a nearby roof top. The trooper fell lifeless through a store awning and onto the ground, landing with a heavy thud.

A handful of men followed Kodiak's lead and made it to the mess hall. Others were delayed by withering gunfire. Some died in the street. Some arrived with horrible gunshot wounds.

"There are soldiers out there," one of the men managed to breathe out. "Did anyone else see soldiers out there?"

"Of course there are soldiers out there," Kodiak announced. "They wouldn't send a stage coach loaded with gold without soldiers. All of you here knew they'd be risks, didn't ya?"

AT THE FIRST discharge of gunfire, Jesse had Lieutenant Nelson order 'boots and saddles'. Jesse was quite sure the sound of Company B's bugler would not be heard over the ruckus of distant gunfire. By columns of two abreast, they rode behind Lieutenant Nelson at a gallop.

Jesse recalled last evening's discussion.

"Once we turn toward Camp Clarke, Lieutenant, how do you want to play this?" Jesse had asked.

"I was thinking of putting the left flank under your lead and taking the right flank for myself," Nelson answered.

"Mind if I take Potter with me? We've ridden together a long time. Besides, I gotta watch his back. He's getting married when we get home."

"Not a problem, Marshal. I'd hate to have to take responsibility for a man about to be married."

Potter had taken the good natured ribbing in style.

The troopers halted when they reached the outskirts of Camp Clarke. Ahead of them was sporadic gunfire from a mixture of small arms and rifles. It appeared to Jesse that the majority of the shooting centered on the mess hall.

A flash of sunlight caught Jesse's attention. The flash came from a hill south of town.

"Did you see that?" Jesse pointed in that direction. "I just saw a flash at the top of the hill. Like sunlight reflected off of something."

"Didn't see it." Potter removed his field glasses and aimed his gaze in the direction Jesse was pointing. "Oh, there it is," he said. "Yeah, there's someone up there alright. Couldn't make him out for sure, but I think that's Jim DuFreeze."

Jimbo Livingston lumbered down the street. "We got a bunch of men cornered in the mess hall. We're trying to work a few men around back to box 'em in."

Lieutenant Nelson weighed in. "Marshal, why don't you take your men and put a block perimeter around the mess hall. I'll dismount my men and go door to door rounding up anyone with a black bandana."

"They're getting away!" someone yelled. "They're headed for the bridge."

About thirty men wearing black bandanas raced out the back door of their mess hall entrapment.

Jesse whipped his horse about and sent it charging down an alley with Potter close behind. Four blocks ahead, men clamored onto Camp Clarke Bridge. Jesse identified one of them as Kodiak. Some of the men turned and fired at their pursuers. Two troopers fell to the ground.

Camp Clarke Bridge had little protection to offer the men standing on it. Some knelt to fire. Others stood.

It looked to Jesse like Kodiak was more interested in

surviving than fighting. Once Kodiak reached the bridge he never turned. He just kept walking with urgent resolve.

Troopers soon secured the southern end of the bridge.

"Give yerselves up!" Henry T. Clarke yelled. "You can't get across, the bridge isn't finished."

There were some who tried to fight their way through the troopers. They were met by a hail of bullets and died trying. The other surrendered their arms.

Jesse drove his horse through these surrendering men and galloped across the bridge after Kodiak.

Kodiak stopped and turned around. "That's far enough, Marshal," Kodiak shouted.

"Kodiak," Jesse began, "I've come to put you in jail."

"That ain't happening, Marshal." Kodiak widened his stance. He drew his coat back at the waist exposing his Navy Colt.

Jesse dismounted. "Look, I rode all the way out here to bring you to justice. I'd prefer to bring you in upright, but if I have to, I'll bring you in draped over your saddle. You choose."

"I ain't riding in upright just to hang. I seen men hang and I want no part of dangling from the end of a rope."

"Suit yerself." Jesse slid his coat back. "I hate to draw my LeMat, its awful gall-darned heavy and I ain't as fast."

"Deal with it," Kodiak said.

He went for his Colt.

Despite the weight, Jones was faster. A crimson stain spread in the middle of Kodiak's chest. He took a few halting steps and tumbled from the bridge into the muddy Platte River.

J IM D U F REEZE TOOK in the scene from his perch south of Camp Clarke. He watched as his dream of wealth was blasted to smithereens like a Fourth of July firecracker. His binoculars took him from one defeat after to another. The raids on the livery stable and the arrival of Jesse Jones, Bill Cody and Company B. His eyes followed when his men took sanctuary in the mess hall, and then bolted onto the bridge. He witnessed their surrender and the shootout between Jones and Kodiak.

In disbelief he stood with binoculars in hand, paralyzed in place by the events that had unfolded before his eyes. When at last he raised in binoculars for one final look, he found someone near the bridge looking up at him. Like him, this man held his binoculars to his eyes. DuFreeze adjusted his view.

Bill Cody. The man looking back at him was Bill Cody.

DuFreeze watched Cody talk with Jesse. Cody pointed up the hill to the spot where DuFreeze stood. He saw Jones nod. Cody jumped into his saddle. He was riding hard and DuFreeze knew exactly where he was heading. Toward him. DuFreeze mounted, turned his horse south, and spurred it into action.

Cody was a mile and a half away. But that mile and a half would disappear very quickly. DuFreeze's horse had to navigate the hillside before linking up with the main road heading back into Sidney. At that juncture the road flattened out. DuFreeze could only hope his horse could manage the downhill portion without breaking a leg. From that point on, it would be a sprint between two horses.

DuFreeze hit the intersection first. He took a glance over his shoulder and saw Cody's horse kicking up dust less than a half mile away.

Made it, he thought to himself.

He dug his spurs into his horse's flank. The horse responded with more speed. The distance between DuFreeze and Cody widened.

About three miles north of town a curve in the road hid DuFreeze from Cody. There DuFreeze turned off the road and headed into the sandhills. His horse needed a rest.

DuFreeze found a spot where he could watch the road without being seen. Cody rode past and was soon out of sight.

After dark, DuFreeze wandered into town. There were no signs of life at the bank. He heard sketchy conversations about Swan Holmes' arrest as he rode by a group of men standing in the street. He felt lucky no one noticed him.

He dismounted in front of the Moore Hotel. Hunger had driven him there. DuFreeze shed his black bandana and stuffed it deeply into his saddlebag before going inside.

At the far end of the restaurant sat J.F. Coad and his son, Benjamin.

DuFreeze's drew his revolver and walked to where they sat.

"Well, well." DuFreeze pointed his revolver at J.F. "I haven't really had an opportunity to *thank you* for firing me."

J.F. Coad looked up from his plate and into the barrel of a gun.

"Surprised to see me?" DuFreeze asked. "Take a good look. It's the last thing you and your kid will ever see."

The hammer on his revolver clicked into place.

A single gunshot rang out.

DuFreeze staggered. He looked down at the hole in his chest, then at the hole in the table.

Benjamin Coad placed a Colt .45 on the table. It was the last thing one arm Bill DuFreeze ever saw.

CHAPTER 28

Parson Abel stood on his portico. The first few drops of a rare July rain splashed about him. Some of the cool drops splattered on his shirt. He drew in a deep breath. There was freshness in the air, the freshness that comes on the heels of a welcomed summer shower. He looked heavenward and offered a silent 'thank you.'

As if in response, lightning lit the sky and a clap of thunder followed. Rain pelted him with increased frequency. Parson Abel stood unaffected by the rain.

Jesse Jones joined him.

"I would call this a *cathartic* rain," Abel said.

"Never heard of that word." Jesse placed his cowboy hat on his head to keep the rain off his face.

"Cathartic is a Greek word meaning 'therapeutic cleansing'."

"There ya go again with another fifty dollar word."

Parson Abel looked straight ahead. "I do that sometimes. Let me see if I can put it in a better way." He was silent for a minute or two. The rain intensified. "This whole town has been on edge lately. Our emotions wound tighter than fiddle strings. Now with Swan Holmes behind bars along with the rest of his gang, our emotions are getting back to normal. To me this rain is like God cleansing that entire stench out of the air. Cleaning things up. Returning things to the way He wants them to be."

Not minding the rain, the two men stood together looking over the city.

"What on earth are you two doing standing out here?" Doc interrupted. "Yer both gonna catch yer death of cold."

"It's *cathartic*," Jesse declared.

Doc stood staring at Jesse in disbelief. "What are you talking about?"

"Parson Abel says that this rain is *cathartic*," Jones replied. "That's what he thinks."

"And *I* think," Doc said, "that the two of you don't have enough sense between ya to come in out of the rain. Well, if you want to stand outside in the rain, go ahead. As for me, if I want to get wet I'll take a bath. Which I will do Saturday night, thank you very much."

The front door slammed.

"Crazy old fool," Abel said. "He's got himself so wrapped up in things that he can't enjoy the simple things in life, like an unexpected shower."

"I have to admit I am feeling pretty silly standing out here getting soaking wet," Jesse said.

"Yes, I do see your point," said Abel. "Doc could be right, you know. Maybe there is a thin line between cathartic and a good soaking."

Martha and Adeline met the two men as they stepped inside.

"You know, Martha," Adeline began. "At times I think these two don't have the sense to come in out of the rain."

Parson Abel defended himself. "I was just telling Jesse that I find the rain rather cathartic after Swan Holmes' reign of terror."

"I wouldn't call it cathartic," Adeline said.

"Then what else would you call it?" Abel asked, following Adeline and Martha down the hall and into the dining room.

"A reprieve perhaps," she responded. "Better still the calm before the storm."

"Why do you think that?" said Abel.

"Have a seat everyone," Adeline said. "Help yourselves before breakfast gets cold."

Doc didn't wait for a second invitation to eat. He sat down at once. Jesse and Abel waited until their wives were seated before joining them.

"You haven't answered my question," said Abel. "Why do you say that this is the calm before the storm?"

"Do you want to pray?" she asked her husband.

"Is this your way of distracting me?" he said. The expression on Adeline's face told him not to press his luck. "Let's pray. Bless us, O Lord, for these Thy gifts which we are about to receive from Thy bounty through Christ our Lord. Amen."

Abel watched as his wife took a large spoonful of scrambled eggs. He cleared his throat as a reminder of her failure to answer his question.

Adeline looked his direction. "Until a jury has convicted Swan Holmes, this little reprieve is nothing other than the calm before the storm."

Jesse remembered Adeline's words when the trial of Swan Holmes began the last week in July 1876. This was the first trial of its kind since the construction of Sidney's first courthouse in 1871.

Doc commented on what he called 'them high-priced attorneys from back east.' Five of them sat around Holmes at any time. Doing 'lots of whispering and conniving' as Doc put it.

The first defense tactic tried was that Swan Holmes had been 'swayed' to follow the scheming of One Arm Bill DuFreeze and DuFreeze's associate Kodiak Crabtree. That scheme was blown out of the water when Spence, one of the lone survivors of the gang, testified that DuFreeze and Kodiak both got their marching orders from Swan Holmes.

From his seat about halfway back and to the right of where Swan Holmes sat, Jesse could see a growing uneasiness about the man. At times he yelled at his defense team at the top of his lungs.

"Order in the court!" the judge bellowed. "Gentlemen, if you cannot control your client I'm going to ask that he be removed from this courtroom."

"Don't you understand your honor?" Holmes announced. "The Good Book says that God helps those who help themselves."

"Bailiff, remove the defendant," the judge ordered. "And the jury will disregard what they have just heard."

With Holmes out of the courtroom, his defense team tried a second tactic to save his life. They pled him guilty by reason of insanity. They cited as precedent the murder trial of Dan Sickle in 1859.

"Our client is obviously insane, your honor. His actions in this courtroom prove it," his lead attorney said.

THAT EVENING over dinner in the Abel's home, Jesse noticed how the conversation gravitated to the trial.

"Holmes keeps coming back to what the Good Book says," said Doc.

"The sad thing is that the Good Book never says that." Parson Abel helped himself to the mashed potatoes as they made their way around the table.

"Didn't you do a sermon about that awhile back?" Martha Jones asked.

"He did," said Adeline.

"Holmes' expression is like expressions we hear where the Bible is taken out of context," Abel continued. "It's like the expression money is the root of all evil, when what the Bible really says is that the love of money is the root of all kinds of evil."

Adam Potter put a bite of steak in his mouth and said, "So, Parson, do you have any predictions about how this trial will turn out?"

"Yeah, any guesses?" Elizabeth Archer asked.

"I'm not in the predicting business," Abel announced. "I'm rather fond of putting everything into God's hands and letting him take care of things. He's a lot better at things like that than I am."

Someone knocked twice at the front door and then opened it.

"Can I come in?" Everyone recognized the voice. It belonged to Bill Cody.

"We're in the dining room," Abel replied.

Cody stood in the doorway. "Hate to barge in like this, but

Ned and I are leavin.' Bill Hickok is dead. Murdered in Deadwood."

Buffalo Bill tossed a telegram onto the table.

Abel stood. "That's two friends dead in two months for you. Custer and now Wild Bill. I'm so sorry."

"You know as well as I do these are troublin' times," Cody replied.

Abel gave a nod to his wife. "Adeline likes to say that these times are the calm before the storm. And she's right to some extent. But I believe that after the storm. . .after the storm there comes a time of peace. We have to believe that God has His hand in all of this. Otherwise, there is no hope. And without hope people wither and die."

THE TRIAL of Swan Holmes ended abruptly. The judge declared Holmes could not use insanity as his defense. To save their own skins, other Night Riders testified against Holmes. His defense team quickly found themselves overwhelmed by the evidence against their client. In the end the best legal team money could buy could not save Swan Holmes from hanging by his neck until he was dead.

On August 4, 1876 Parson Abel stood on the scaffolding next to Swan Holmes. The hangman put a noose around Holmes' neck. He was a forlorn shell of himself. Earlier in the week his wife had packed her bags and headed back east.

"Swan," Abel said. "This is your last opportunity to confess your sins before God. To seek His forgiveness and receive His full pardon for what you have done. Jesus Christ and His death on the cross make this all possible."

Swan Holmes looked at the hangman standing nearby.

"Let's get this over with," Holmes said.

Parson Abel closed his Bible and descended the thirteen steps to ground level. Holmes never flinched. He defiantly looked ahead.

A mighty thud gave notice the trapdoor had opened. Holmes fell through that opening, suspended between heaven and earth by the rope around his neck.

EPILOGUE

August 4, 1876 was notable for another reason. As Swan Holmes was falling through the trapdoor and into his eternity, the armored stagecoach bearing the gold he so desired to possess arrived. The gold was confined to the safe in Swan Holmes' bank overnight and the next day loaded aboard a train for Omaha. Troopers from Fort Sidney provided the military escort a shipment of gold this size required.

Later that year J.F. Coad appointed his son Benjamin to manage his ranch and he returned to Bellevue. Benjamin set one time Night Rider Spence Duggan as ranch foremen. Cattle sales with the Red Cloud Agency proved very lucrative. Spence made good use of Camp Clarke Bridge to drive Coad's cattle to market quickly and efficiently.

Dignitaries from across the United States dedicated the Camp Clarke Bridge. This sturdy bridge gave rise to the shortest route into the Black Hills and gave impetus for a pony express route to carry mail from Sidney to the mining companies in Dakota Territory. Stage service followed. Camp Clarke Bridge became a vital link for military forces along the Sidney-

Black Hills Trail. At one point during the fall of 1876 an estimated fifty to seventy-five freight wagons loaded down with four tons of supplies each left Sidney and drove north each day. Swede's Mercantile sold its fair share of this merchandise as Jesse told it.

In October the much anticipated wedding of Adam Potter and Elizabeth Archer took place. The day started out hot and humid and Parson Abel's little church building was crammed full of people. Funeral homes fans waved back and forth while providing the only air movement possible. The suit Adam Potter had ordered for himself arrived the day before his wedding. Wedding pictures taken of this occasion show a man stuffed into a two sizes too small suit.

Edith Archer, the bride's mother, gave her daughter away. Parson Abel said that since Elizabeth's father was deceased it was altogether proper for her brother to walk her down the aisle and her mother to join in when he asks 'who gives this woman to be married.' Parson Abel's sermon that day preached of God's desire that man should not be alone and to that end God had created woman. He wove in the importance of Jesus Christ as the third strand in marriage.

Adeline Abel sat near the front as she always did. Sitting beside her were those members of society some considered outcasts and unwanted. These she felt close to, wanting them to experience the love of Jesus so that they might spend an eternity in His presence. Her ministry led to multiple baptisms in Lodgepole Creek.

Brody Belt and his wife Cynthia returned to their farm east of town where they raised cattle and children, adding two sons and two daughters in addition to their first born son, William.

And through all of these changes Doc always remained his cantankerous self.

Jesse Jones resigned his commission as U.S. Marshal. He

desired to fulfill his roles as husband to Martha and father to his son Jesse Junior. His interest in Swede's Mercantile made him a very wealthy man. As a younger man he had longed to own a home with a portico like the home occupied by Parson Abel and Adeline. Now, however, nothing satisfied him as much as waking up early to step outside, coffee in hand. He found it very satisfying to sit on a stump and write down his memoirs outside his home along the bank of Lodgepole Creek.

Jesse Jones IV

DEAR READER

Thank you for reading **Gunfight at Camp Clarke Bridge,** the final book in the Man With The LeMat series. Jesse Jones' story begins with **Death Rode to Lodgepole Creek**, continues with **At The Point of A Gun** and concludes with **Gunfight at Camp Clarke Bridge.**

Reviews are lifeblood to authors. Please consider leaving a review of this book at your retailer's website or at places like Goodreads and BookBub.

ALSO BY ZACHARY LANE

Death Rode To Lodgepole Creek

Man With The LeMat book 1

There are many reasons settlers came west after the Civil War. Jesse Jones came to escape his past but the haunting memory of revenge for a friend's murder stays with him. He now wields the man's LeMat pistol. Stationed with the army at Sidney Barracks, Jesse uses his skill with the unusual pistol to guard the railroad from attack by the native Cheyenne.

After a vicious attack by Union soldiers, Sarah Fitzpatrick plans to become a singer but ends up working as one of Madam Roger's girls. With each encounter she despairs of ever being free of the memories. After a chance meeting with Jesse, her life takes a turn for the better.

Custus Leverette controls Sidney, 'the wickedest town in the west', and no one dares cross him. When he decides he wants Sarah, he'll destroy anyone or anything standing in his way.

Who will survive the battle between Custus' knife and Jesse Jones-The Man with the LeMat?

At The Point Of A Gun

Man With The LeMat book 2

It's been a year since Custus and Jesse fought over Sarah, and Sidney, Nebraska, the wickedest town in the west, is returning to normal. Except for Cincinnati Culver, owner of the Last Chance Saloon. Using his gang of thugs and misfits, the small man with a big ego is hell-bent on controlling every business in town. Including Swede's Mercantile.

Jesse Jones now owns the mercantile and isn't about to sell out. No matter the price. No matter the threats. A young woman searching for her brother, and a shootist following his sister's trail arrive in town, complicating Cincinnati's plans and Jesse's life.

Gunfire occasionally lights Sidney's dark streets. Far too often the horseplay turns to gunplay where blood is spilled and men die.

Gunfight at Camp Clarke Bridge

Man With The LeMat book 3

The promise of Black Hills gold is drawing prospectors and greedy men to Sidney. Plans are made for a bridge to span the Platte River, cutting days off travel time to the Dakota Territory. Jesse Jones and Swede's Mercantile are chosen to supply the materials needed to build the Camp Clarke Bridge.

Jesse leases a warehouse from banker Swan Holmes, a cheerful man who often claims, "God helps those that help themselves." When the phrase is repeated by the one armed man, Bill DuFreeze, and the town is overrun with shady men all wearing black bandanas, Jesse takes on the job of acting sheriff. In his search for answers he faces rustlers, accusations, destruction, and fear. What price will he have to pay to finally bring peace to Sidney, Nebraska?

ABOUT THE AUTHOR

Zachary Lane is a native Nebraskan; a small town kid who has always had a big imagination. A family vacation to a battlefield sparked his interest in the Civil War. The 'old shed' in his back yard soon became an officer's quarters or a fort. Lane fueled his imagination by reading books about this epic war that pitted brother against brother. His personal library is filled with books. Lots and lots of books. So many books that an ultimatum has been issued in the Lane household—if a new book comes in, an older one must be boxed up and put on a shelf in the garage.

Zachary began writing seriously after visiting a rest stop near Sidney, Nebraska. Observing and reading a historical marker overlooking the railroad and town in valley below set his imagination free to tell the story of life there in the 1860's and 1870's.

He still lives in Nebraska where he enjoys walks with his wife, playing with grandchildren, grilling on summer's evenings, smoking ribs and pork butts and stretching his imagination by writing new stories about early Nebraska.